NO STRINGS ATTACHED

"You can't do commitment, Eric. But that's okay. I know this relationship is strictly short term and we're both in it just for the sex."

That stung. "Hey, that's sort of jaded, isn't it? There's more to this than just sex, Tess," he said, slipping his hand down her back.

"Oh yeah? What, exactly?"

He couldn't answer because she was kissing him, and now she was in his lap, and his other hand had somehow accidentally slipped under the leg of her shorts.

It only took one smooth, practiced movement and she was under him. The shorts came off easily and the satin panties were hot pink and maybe he wasn't going to respect himself in the morning, but that was then and this was now . . .

BOOK YOUR PLACE ON OUR WEBSITE AND MAKE THE READING CONNECTION!

We've created a customized website just for our very special readers, where you can get the inside scoop on everything that's going on with Zebra, Pinnacle and Kensington books.

When you come online, you'll have the exciting opportunity to:

- View covers of upcoming books
- Read sample chapters
- Learn about our future publishing schedule (listed by publication month *and author*)
- Find out when your favorite authors will be visiting a city near you
- Search for and order backlist books from our online catalog
- Check out author bios and background information
- Send e-mail to your favorite authors
- Meet the Kensington staff online
- Join us in weekly chats with authors, readers and other guests
- Get writing guidelines
- AND MUCH MORE!

**Visit our website at
http://www.kensingtonbooks.com**

STRAIGHT TO THE HEART

Bobby Hutchinson

ZEBRA BOOKS
KENSINGTON PUBLISHING CORP.
http://www.kensingtonbooks.com

For Stan Sauerwein,
who understands from experience the loneliness of the long
distance writer. Thank you, my talented friend for always
being within e-mail reach.

ZEBRA BOOKS are published by

Kensington Publishing Corp.
850 Third Avenue
New York, NY 10022

All Kensington titles, imprints and distributed lines are available at special quantity discounts for bulk purchases for sales promotions, premiums, fund-raising, and educational or institutional use.

Special book excerpts or customized printings can also be created to fit specific needs. For details, write or phone the office of the Kensington Special Sales Manager: Kensington Publishing Corp., 850 Third Avenue, New York, NY 10022, Attn. Special Sales Department, Phone: 1-800-221-2647.

Zebra and the Z logo Reg. U.S. Pat. & TM Off.

First Printing: September 2003
10 9 8 7 6 5 4 3 2 1

Printed in the United States of America

1.

Alice doesn't live here anymore

The Saturday morning of his fortieth birthday, Eric Stewart began to wonder if maybe his crazy sister Anna was right about the stormy effects Uranus was having his astrological chart. Eric didn't personally know Uranus from a hole in the ground, apart from hearing Anna blather on, but there was no doubt turbulence was in the air.

"I don't want a relationship; all I want is sex," Nema screamed, letting fly with a piece of pipe he'd been saving to use as a tail for the dog he was welding out of iron rebar. Garbage was how he made his living, but dodging it wasn't his favorite pastime.

She was panning the area for more ammunition. "We discussed it in the beginning. Why can't you stick to the plan?"

Judo and great reflexes helped at times like this. Eric was able to dodge again, even though Nema's aim was deadly. At six-one, she was not just tall but well muscled, and he was grateful she didn't have a gun; she'd taken marksmanship, hoping to get a part on a television cop show currently being filmed in downtown Vancouver.

He'd met her at a party where a lot of the guests were actors. He'd figured he'd been invited for comic relief; the cretin giving the party kept introducing him as the garbageman. It backfired, though, because Nema dumped the guy and came home with Eric.

On the way she'd said, "So, are you really a garbageman?" She ran her fingers through his hair. "Clean-cut, blond curls, baby blue's, you don't *look* like a garbageman."

"I'm undercover, and I bathed before the party," he'd joked. "Actually, I own a garbage disposal business, Junk Busters Inc.," he'd explained. "Garbage has been good to me."

"Ohhh, a real, live blue-collar hunk who's taller and stronger than me, that's such a turn-on," she'd said, and then she'd gone down on him right there in the car. But that was eight weeks ago, and other things had gone down since then, like his enthusiasm for Nema.

"I don't want to come to your birthday party," she was shrieking, "and I don't want to meet your sisters. I don't want to talk about acting or welding or movies or books. I don't want to look at the junk you make out of junk. I just want to get naked and *come*. What part of that don't you get?"

She looked around the room for something else to throw, but fortunately everything else within her reach was way too heavy. Thankfully, he'd salvaged only big pieces of iron this week.

"Easy, honey." He knew from years of experience raising three sisters that when a woman was this mad, reason didn't work. Soft and soothing usually didn't either, but it was worth a try. "Calm down, let's talk about this."

To his amazement, this time he got lucky. Nema's pretty face crumbled and she collapsed on the chair he'd made out of discarded plumbing supplies. She shook back her flaming hair and swiped at her wet eyes.

"It was so good in the beginning, Eric," she wailed. "Why do you have to mess it up like this with birthday parties and family and conversation?"

He let out a breath and wondered if he dared sit down. She could go off again without warning, he reminded himself. Better stay on his feet, keep a few yards away.

He tried to figure out strategy. It wouldn't be smart to tell her the truth, that he was bored crosseyed with being a sex object, that he didn't always want to drop his pants and his blowtorch just to get it on with her.

That even for a guy in his prime, six times in a twelve-hour period was pushing it. He'd read that book about Tantric sex; he knew there was a school of thought that figured it was dangerous to deplete your store of vital essence. Besides that, his balls were sore from overuse.

And there was his pride to consider as well as her temper. What guy in his right mind wanted to admit that welding pieces of discarded iron into useful shapes could get to be way more interesting than sex?

"You're a gorgeous woman, Nema." That seemed safe enough, and it might buy him time to figure out what else to say.

"But? I definitely hear a 'but' coming." Her sultry dark eyes narrowed and her full mouth tightened.

He eyed her warily. "No 'buts,' honest, honey. Truth is, I think I'm having some sort of mid-life crisis." That wasn't technically true, at least he hoped not, but he'd watched a television program about male menopause a couple days ago, and it might just get him off the hook here.

"It has nothing to do with you, and everything to do with me. I'm questioning a lot of things about myself lately."

Most of which had to do with whether he'd get the financing for two more trucks and forty more bins, which meant he could expand into Vancouver's bedroom communities. That would mean Junk Busters Inc. was in the big league when it came to removal services.

He had four trucks and as many regular drivers. He had ninety bins to drop off wherever people needed them. He was making more money than he'd ever thought possible back when he was sixteen, which was when he'd quit school and bought a beat-up half-ton for seven hundred bucks. He'd started carting junk away from building sites to pay for it.

He hadn't realized then that there was no ceiling to the garbage business. As long as people kept throwing stuff away, somebody had to pick it up and take it away. So much of modern society was disposable.

So now he was worth a million and a half on paper, and the ironic part was that he still sweated bullets sometimes at month's end when the bills were due. Equipment rich, cash flow poor. That would level off when he got the two latest trucks paid for, but it made it touchy when it came to expansion. His brother-in-law, Bruno Lifkin, who was also his accountant, assured him the business was doing fine financially.

Garbage had also given Eric a hobby he loved. A lady he'd dated once or twice—Ainsley? Amy?—he couldn't remember. Anyhow, she'd dragged him to an art exhibit, and he'd seen what some guy made out of old car parts, a weird and otherworldly sculpture that was only good for looking at, and inspiration had struck.

Eric was practical. The things he scrounged from the trucks and then welded together now furnished his apartment—tables, chairs, lamps, his sofa. The dog was the first thing he'd done that wasn't strictly functional. Welding unlikely bits of scrap energized and thrilled him. It also gave him the feeling he was making something out of nothing, which in turn gave him hope for his future.

It was really too bad Nema didn't thrill him any longer.

"I'm actually considering talking to somebody, Nema."

His bank manager, with Bruno in tow, first thing Monday morning.

"Like a shrink?" He saw the horrified look on her face and realized he was on the right road here. He shrugged and tried to look depressed.

"Analysis. That's it; that's the straw." She shot to her feet and grabbed the oversize quilted handbag she used as an overnight case. "I'm outta here. I already went through this with a guy once; we ended up sitting in this geek's office talking about our *mothers.* I'm just not into that head stuff. What is it with guys these days, anyway? Call me when you're over it."

A moment later, the outside door slammed behind her. He blew out a breath and let himself flop onto the sofa. He looked out the tall, uncurtained windows at the busy street and the wild and windy June morning and tried to figure out how he felt about her walking out on him instead of the other way around, whether he was making a huge mistake here, whether his pride ought to be hurt, when the door banged open again. His heart gave a thump and he leaped up, ready to duck.

"I forgot, here's your keys." Nema lobbed them into one of the hubcaps he'd fashioned into a bowl. "Have a nice life. If you happen to come to your senses, you've got my number."

The door slammed again. He heard the lock engage, and now he had the spare set of keys. It felt final this time. He tried to remember if she had any stuff in the bedroom or the bathroom. He didn't think so; he was pretty careful about letting women leave anything at his place. Generally, he preferred their bed to his, that way he could get up and come home, but Nema had four roommates, so they'd spent more time here than he was comfortable with. He didn't care if women stayed over Friday and Saturday, but Sunday night he'd always made it a rule that they went home and took everything they owned with them. The weekend rule, he called it.

He didn't want them to get any ideas about moving in, and it was easier to maintain the status quo if there were rules. He was vigilant about making sure they didn't leave makeup bags and wisps of underwear behind, and in turn he never left so much as a razor at their places either.

He'd kicked himself for allowing Nema to have keys to the place. She'd cajoled them out of him early on, in a particularly vulnerable moment. Before he got so disillusioned with being a stud.

It wasn't noon yet, but he figured he deserved a brew after what just happened. Besides, it was his birthday; how often did a guy turn forty? He got up and retrieved a Bud from the fridge, screwed off the cap and flopped down again, considering things.

He took a long swig and choked when the door buzzer sounded. She was back. He thought of hiding, but he'd never been a coward. He walked to the door and opened it cautiously, wishing he was wearing a cup. He'd seen her practice kick-boxing; it was a scary sight.

"You got muscle strain?" Rocky Hutton gestured at Eric's hand, which was hovering over a vital part of his anatomy.

"I thought you were Nema." Eric glanced up and down the hall and sighed with relief when there was no sign of her. "C'mon in."

"You guys having a fight or something?" Rocky picked up the box of plumbing parts he'd brought and carried them inside. "Happy birthday, I thought you could use these old fittings to make more hat racks." Rocky was a plumber. He often brought Eric valuable secondary material. "I won't stay. You and Nema will wanna make up when she gets back."

"She's gone for good. With any luck she isn't ever coming back." Eric got another beer from the fridge and handed it to Rocky. "Sit down, I'm celebrating."

"Jeeze. You really okay with her walking out on you?" Rocky took off his baseball cap and scratched his head. Eric figured the Rock had no idea that his thick black hair had molded itself to the shape of the cap. As usual, it was mashed flat on top and sticking up over his ears and around the back of his head.

"I might not be in a couple weeks when I get horny again." He hadn't had a single chance to feel horny for the past two months, not since he'd met Nema. "Right now it feels pretty good to have her gone. That sex thing all the time was starting to wear me down."

"Yeah, that could be a real problem, all right." Rocky gave Eric a doleful look. "I struggle with it myself. So how many is that you've gone through since January?"

Six months? Eric shrugged and tried to add it up.

"Six, maybe. Seven, if you count that mail carrier, but that only lasted two weeks." Her legs had attracted him. She had first-class legs; it was all the walking, but talking about postal zones and the weight of flyers proved to be a real turnoff.

"It must have to do with being blond and having curly hair." Rocky took a gulp of his beer. "I'm thinking of getting a bleach job and a perm. Y'know, I hate to say it, but Sophie's right about you and that catch-and-release thing."

"Yeah, well, Sophie's a smart ass." His sister was also an ER physician, and she'd heard the phrase after chatting with a patient in the ER, a fisherman who was getting a hook extracted from his ear. You fished for the sport of it, the guy told her, and when you hooked one, you took the hook out and put the fish back into the water. The mouth was somewhat damaged, but it healed.

Catch and release. Eric thought it had a nice generous ring to it, but his sisters had an entirely different opinion. They'd started keeping score of the women he went through, which had tended to make him secretive in the past few months.

"Does Sophie know about Nema?"

"Nope, none of the girls do. I was going to introduce her tonight at the party, but now there's no real reason to mention her. They look at one another with that expression on their faces, like here we go again, and then when it's over, they get on my case about being fickle and how the poor girl must feel and life passing me by. What they don't know won't hurt me."

"Gotcha." Rocky knew all about the self-help books on commitment phobia Eric's sisters had been buying him. "They worry about you, Eric. I wish I had some sisters to worry over me, Dad and I are turning into old guys with hair in our ears and nose and not enough on our head."

"Your head still looks pretty well covered to me. And you and Fletcher have it made, single, no women breathing down your neck and giving you a hard time about commitment."

"Yeah, no hot chicks like Nema hanging around, either."

"What about Chloe?"

"That's history." Rocky had hired Chloe to do some paperwork for his plumbing company, and they'd been going out for months. "She joined the Hare Krishnas, says she's decided to be celibate. She's in that temple down on Marine Drive."

Eric whistled. "Wearing those robes and all that, dancing at the airport?" Chloe had always been a little left of normal, but this was extreme.

"The robes, yeah. I don't know about the airport."

"She's a good-looking lady. Smart, too. Go figure."

"Yeah. The celibate thing sorta smarts. I thought that part was going okay, unless she was faking."

"They all do that sometimes. Nobody else on the

horizon?" Apart from being tall and well-muscled, Rocky wasn't what anybody would call handsome, but his broad face and chocolate brown eyes shone with goodness. Eric had known him since high school and would have trusted him with his life— and several times, he'd come pretty close. He'd certainly trust him with his sister Sophie, if Rocky would only wake up and smell the antiseptic, which on Sophie took the place of perfume. For years now, they'd been out of step. When Sophie wasn't in a relationship, Rocky was, and vice versa.

"Not at the moment."

"Give it time." Which maybe wasn't the best advice in this case. Rocky married his high school sweetheart, Melanie, right after graduation. Mel died in a car wreck two years later, and a month to the day after that, Rocky's mother dropped dead of a heart attack. So Rocky moved in with his dad, Fletcher. The two of them had grieved together and stayed together. Fifteen years later, they were still the odd couple.

"Your sisters feel bad about giving you such a hard time when they were growing up." As usual, Rocky didn't want to talk about his foibles when Eric's were available for dissection. And with no brothers or sisters of his own, Rocky loved hearing about Eric's.

"Yeah, well, they have good reason to feel guilty. I learned too much about the worst of the female gender from them. It's a wonder I'm not alcoholic and bald after what they put me through." Hell, it was a wonder he wasn't *gay;* raising them was enough to put anybody off women. He shuddered even now, remembering that with three of them, somebody always had PMS, which meant that three weeks out of every month were unbearable, and the one left over was no picnic either. It was no wonder a lot of his relationships hadn't lasted twenty-eight days.

"I really wish they'd stay the hell out of my love life. I wouldn't exactly say any of them are experts on relationships. I don't see Sophie galloping to the altar." *Although she might if you asked her, Dumbo.* But then again, maybe Rocky just didn't find Sophie appealing.

"She still with that surgeon?"

He did keep up with the men in Sophie's life, though.

"Nope. That ended a couple weeks ago. She said he had no sense of humor."

Rocky nodded enthusiastic agreement. "What about Anna and Bruno? They've been married what—a year now?"

"Fourteen months. They're doing okay."

"She getting any clients yet?"

"Not that I know of." Anna had just given up a pensionable job teaching high school to do private consultations in astrology. Eric figured she could benefit from private consultations with a shrink, but at least that was now Bruno's problem and not his. He'd spent enough time watching Anna take classes in everything from tarot card reading to past life regression. He'd thought marrying a steady guy like Bruno might straighten her out, but obviously it hadn't happened.

"How's Karen doing?"

"Pretty good." His baby sister was a single mom with two rambunctious little boys. She was the one Eric worried over the most. "You coming over there for dinner tonight?"

"Nope. Karen called and invited Dad and me, but we figured it's best if we meet you guys afterward at the pub. Birthday dinners oughta be just family."

"Too bad. With the three of my sisters in one room, there's way too much estrogen for Bruno and me to handle."

"You'll manage, you've got a Ph.D. in estrogen." Rocky finished his beer and got to his feet. "Gotta go, I'm putting in a hot water tank this afternoon. See you later."

After he left, Eric swilled the rest of the beer, tossed the bottle in the trash, and reached for his welding mask. With Nema gone and a fresh supply of plumbing parts, thanks to Rocky, he had the whole afternoon to finish the dog. The party wasn't until six.

His spirits rose. He put on his protective glasses and sparks flew from the welding torch, and after a few minutes he started to whistle.

What was Anna's latest litany? *Whatever is happening now is right for you*—that was it. Maybe she was onto something there.

By seven that evening, Eric knew for certain Anna was, as usual, dead wrong. Family tradition dictated that gifts were opened when the birthday cake was served, and along with the double-chocolate layer cake Sophie handed Eric a plain white envelope. He looked down at it, and then up at his sisters.

Three sets of nearly identical wide blue eyes were fixed on him. The girls—all over thirty, but always the girls to him—were all back to their natural blonde at the moment, and there was no denying the fact that they were pretty, even though Karen was way too skinny and Anna had gained a few pounds.

More than a few, and although she claimed it was a side effect of rapid spiritual growth, Eric knew it had more to do with her passion for pecan caramel ice cream.

"Open it, big brother," Karen said.

They were all smiling at him with the straight, white teeth that had cost a fortune, and his heart sank, because he saw through those smiles right away. They'd used them way too often when they were trying to put something over on him.

Even Bruno had a nasty smirk on his face.

"What'd you get, Uncle Eric?" Five-year-old Simon bounced up and down in his chair. "Mommy wouldn't tell us. She said it was a surprise."

"A *'prise*," mumbled three-year-old Ian around a mouthful of cake, sending chocolate crumbs spraying in all directions.

"Don't talk with your mouth full, idiot," Simon admonished, punching his brother on the arm.

"Simon hit me," wailed Ian, spraying even more and letting half-chewed brown lumps slide out of his mouth and down his chin to plop onto the white tablecloth. "He called me *idiot*. Idiot your own self." He doubled up a fist and returned the punch.

"Don't fight. Simon, don't call your brother names." As usual, the boys paid no attention to Karen, and punches flew. They'd figured out long ago who ran the household, and it wasn't their mother.

Over their screams, Karen hollered, "Eric, speak to them, okay?"

"You guys want to leave the table now and go to your rooms?" Eric gave his nephews each a withering look, and in turn they shook their curly redheads and pretended to look scared. Eric didn't appreciate being cast as the boogeyman, but Karen was out of her depth with these two.

"Sorry, Ian," Simon offered without prompting.

"Sorry your own self," Ian responded, sticking his tongue out.

Peace finally reigned, and Eric turned his attention to the envelope, ripping it open and extracting the single sheet of paper inside.

He had to read it twice before it sank in. The typed message was on heavy bond with a stylish letterhead that read *Synchronicity,* and it said that Eric Stewart was the recipient of a gift membership. He was asked to come in for a personal assessment, after which he would be matched with suitable companions. The letter was signed, in a flowery scrawl, Clara Beckford.

Underneath, in capital letters, was printed,

PROFESSIONAL MATCHMAKER

2.

The sound of one hand clapping

"A *matchmaker?*" Eric knew he sounded horrified, but he couldn't help it. "You guys enrolled me in a *dating service?*" He could feel his blood pressure rising. He looked at his sisters. "This is a joke, right?"

He could tell by their expressions that it wasn't.

"Don't hyperventilate," Sophie advised in her take-charge ER voice. "Take some deep breaths and we'll explain exactly what's involved here. It's actually very current; more and more people these days are using matchmakers. Everyone's busy and it beats picking up strangers in bars or coming on to someone at the supermarket."

"It works for me." Eric couldn't see what was wrong with that.

Sophie raised her eyebrows. "Need I say more? You could definitely benefit from some professional advice."

"I agree," Anna chimed in, "but I think the matchmaker ought to use astrology. For instance, if I took a look at someone's chart, I'd know whether the person he was dating was compatible. It would cut out a lot of guesswork; it's a more scientific approach. Astrology is the roadmap for our lives, after all." She shoved her long straight curtain of hair back and got that know-it-all look on her heart-shaped face. "As soon as you get lined up with someone suitable, Eric, I'll do your combined charts and then we'll know for sure if you're meant for each other."

Eric swallowed his outrage and tried for a rational tone because anyone sane knew Anna was heading toward certifiable nutsville. "Nobody seems to have noticed, but I don't exactly have a problem meeting women."

"Yeah, but you have a problem keeping them. You go through them like tissue paper," Bruno commented with a grin.

Eric had known Bruno since high school, and he was a lot less fun since he'd married Anna. The bastard was enjoying this. Eric scowled at his brother-in-law, resplendent tonight in a navy satin shirt with silver snaps. Bruno wanted to be a cowboy in his next incarnation. He was the only accountant Eric knew who wore cowboy boots to the office.

"He's right, Eric," Sophie declared. *Sophie*, the only one of his sisters he could usually rely on for common sense. Total betrayal, go figure.

"We're all getting to the point where we don't even bother remembering their names," she went on. "It's not quantity, bro; it's quality you're lacking. You're not meeting the type of women you could get serious about and settle down with, and you're not getting any younger either, which is where this matchmaking thing comes in."

Eric started to say something about the serious and settling down part, but Sophie was on a roll.

"Synchronicity guarantees that you'll meet women of a better caliber. What the heck, you date anyway, why not try this?" Her cobalt blue eyes, the exact shade of his, challenged him.

"I sort of like the caliber of women I meet now," he said, but nobody listened.

Simon and Ian were chanting *"Ice cream, ice cream,"* and Bruno was getting it from the freezer. Anna was telling Sophie something about Pluto going retrograde.

"We thought it would be a different birthday gift, Eric." Karen was sitting beside him, and she was blinking in that nervous way she had lately. Her hands, stained with purple hair dye from the salon, restlessly rearranged cutlery. "I guess we should have asked you first, huh?"

For sure they should have asked him, but one look at Karen's face told him this was no time to say so. He wouldn't hurt her for the world, so he tried to summon up a facsimile of a smile. Besides, the damned certificate was a gift, and his nephews were human sponges. They parroted whatever he and Bruno said and did, so he needed to be careful here. *Polite, remember polite.* Simon and Ian had heard enough lectures from him about manners, he had to walk the walk.

"Hey, I'm just—well, I'm sort of stunned, sweet pea. I know you girls put a lot of thought into this, and I appreciate it, really I do. Thanks, thanks very much," he managed, even though it nearly choked him.

"Lotsa moola too," Bruno was finished spooning out ice cream for the boys. He winked at Eric and rubbed thumb and finger together. *"Ouch."* He grimaced and rubbed his leg when Anna kicked him under the table.

Jesus. Eric hadn't gotten around to thinking yet about what the gift had cost. This was getting worse and worse. Sophie earned good money as a doctor, but Soph had a mortgage the size of Canada on the fancy waterfront town house she'd bought last fall; Eric knew because he'd cosigned for her.

Karen had barely enough money to pay rent and food and babysitting; he knew because he regularly slipped her extra. Jimmy Nicols, the no-good deadbeat asshole she'd married, sent her money when it suited him.

And then there was Anna, using Bruno's income to try and set up her goofy astrology business, so it was technically Bruno who'd paid her share of this fiasco, and he and Anna had just bought a house. Eric knew because he'd commandeered one of his trucks and two of his huskiest drivers to help move them.

The thought of his family spending more than they could afford on an idiotic, unnecessary, dumbass stupid thing like this matchmaking really got to him. The only consolation was that there had to be a simple way to get their money back. He'd just go in and tell this Beckford woman he didn't need or want the membership. Tuesday, he'd go; he had the financial thing Monday.

After dinner, Karen's sitter arrived and with help from Bruno herded Simon and Ian into the bathtub, and then Eric and his family headed for their neighborhood pub for the second half of the celebration.

They walked into Riley's and Eric cringed when he thought of the ribbing he was going to endure when Rocky and Fletcher got wind of the matchmaker thing. The place was in the midst of Saturday night rush hour. The crowd looked a little rowdier than usual, there were lots of tattoos and leather around. Rock and his father had secured a large round table, and they hollered and waved when the others arrived.

"Sit here, Sophie." Rocky held a chair, and Sophie slid into it.

Eric watched Sophie turn up the voltage. "How's business, Rocky?"

Rocky's ears turned vermilion. "Ahhh, you know, same old, same old, blocked pipes, leaky pumps, flooded basements."

"Not so different from my job," Sophie purred close to his ear. "Blocked arteries, hemorrhaging wounds, people with psych problems. Glorified plumbing, we should compare notes some night."

"Yeah," Rocky said, hitting his foot with the ball as usual.

"Happy Birthday, Eric." Rocky's father, Fletcher Hutton, extended a hand and Eric shook it. "Forty's a milestone," Fletcher commented, smoothing his fingers across his handlebar moustache. He added with a wink, "Now sixty-five, there's a roadblock. It's taken me a whole year to get over turning sixty-five." With rusty hair curling past his thin shoulders and hazel eyes reflecting his gentle smile, Fletcher looked more like an aging hippie than a semiretired, cutthroat divorce lawyer.

"Yeah, but you don't look a day over sixty-four, Pop," Rocky jibed his father, and everyone laughed.

Eric wasn't paying a lot of attention to their good-natured bantering. He was still stuck on the damned gift, and he downed a glass of beer in one long swallow. He wasn't a booze hound; he'd learned when he was half the age he was now that hangovers were too hefty a price to pay for the buzz liquor provided. But tonight he needed a little buzz.

He also needed a little enlightening. Karen was sitting beside him, and while the others were laughing and talking, he said under cover of their voices, "How did this Serendipity thing happen to come up, Karo?"

"Synchronicity. Well, we were talking, and I mentioned that I had a friend who worked for a matchmaker, and we were trying to figure out what to get you, and Sophie said it was a great idea."

"*Sophie* said that? I'd have guessed Anna, but not Soph."

"I thought it was a good idea, too." Karen gave him a lopsided grin.

He grunted and took Karen's fingers in his, running a thumb down the stains on her hand. "Purple isn't your color, sweet pea. You forget to wear gloves again? This stuff can't be good for you."

Sometimes he thought plain old living wasn't good for his baby sister. She'd lost weight again; she was so skinny now it scared him, but he didn't want to nag her about it. "You get around to telling that witch you work for you want a raise?"

"Not yet." Karen didn't look at him as she picked up her beer. "Junella's been in a bad mood lately. I'll do it, I just need to choose the right moment."

"You're great at doing hair, Karo. You could get a job tomorrow at any of the big salons, you know that. You don't have to stick with that joint, take abuse from dried-up old Junella. You won all those awards when you were in beauty school; that has to mean something."

Karen's shoulder-length silver blond mane swirled

as she shook her head. "There's a lot of new stylists out there, Eric. Scissor Happy is close. I can ride my bike to work and get home in decent time to see the kids. Junella's not that bad. Besides, it's a competitive business; things changed a lot while I was away having babies and being a housewife."

And getting your nose broken by your asshole husband.

He should have realized her marriage was heading downhill. Nicols hadn't been working regularly, and he was a sullen, bad-tempered son of a bitch at the best of times. But Eric had been preoccupied with Junk Busters, one of the drivers was ripping him off and it had taken him time and detective work to figure out just how the nerd was doing it, which was how come Karen called Sophie the night Nicols punched her. By the time Eric got there, Nicols had taken off. He'd stayed away from her, but that was two and a half years ago, and Karen still wasn't divorced. Eric and Sophie and even Anna had tried to make her see reason, insisting that she needed to go for child support and custody, that she needed to be free of Nicols once and for all. Finally, two weeks ago, she'd had Fletcher draw up the necessary documents.

"Did you get a birthday card from Mom and Dad, Eric?"

"Nope." Their parents, hippie musicians, spent most of their time in Mexico. They'd long ago bought a house in some village called Malachi. Eric's attitude was out of sight, out of mind, back at ya. "You know they never get the dates right on any of us, if they remember at all," he reminded Karen.

She nodded and wound a hank of her hair around one finger, a sad and wistful look on her angular face. Eric knew that look. It made his heart feel like a fist was squeezing on it, and he wanted to wrap his arms around his sister and pull her onto his knee, the way he had thirty years ago when she was four.

"I sent them those pictures of Simon and Ian, the ones you took at the Christmas party at Simon's kindergarten?" Karen was the only one of them who wrote to Sonny and Georgia regularly, hoping in spite of everything that they might still grow up and become if not caring parents—it was way too late for that, even Karen should see it—then at least grandparents who remembered they had two little grandsons. "I haven't heard back from them yet."

Eric sighed and thought, as he had so many times before, *It just ain't gonna happen, kid.* They'd all told Karen that, he and Anna and Sophie, numerous times over the years. But against all reason, she went on hoping.

There was a desperate little girl inside Karen who'd never grown up, never gotten used to having one idiot parent who still believed he was about to become the next Bruce Springsteen, and another who devoted herself to some Mexican orphanage instead of remembering she'd popped out four kids of her own.

He looped an arm around his sister's shoulders and gave her a hug, remembering the scathing letters he'd written, the pictures of the girls he'd mailed off that would have torn the hearts out of Bonnie and Clyde, the bills he'd paid over the years that Sonny ought to have been responsible for.

"The parental units live in some fantasy world of their own, Karo. I have nightmares about the day

I'll have to bring them back to Vancouver and find a care facility that'll put up with Sonny's guitar and Georgia's singing."

He'd hoped that might bring a smile, but instead, he felt her suddenly jerk as if she'd been stuck with a needle. She made a sound in her throat and her whole body stiffened.

Eric turned to see what she was looking at.

Karen's husband, Jimmy Nicols, had just walked in the door.

3.

I love pain 'cause it feels so good when it stops

Nicols, a large man himself, was with someone bigger and bulkier whose forehead was so low his hairline met his eyebrows. Jimmy scanned the room, saw Karen, and moved toward them. He had a sheaf of papers in his hand, and his pretty-boy features were screwed into a mask of rage.

"You want a divorce, you could ask me straight out, never mind putting the law on me, Karen."

She was trembling, and afterward, Eric didn't remember getting to his feet. He did remember getting into Nicols's personal space and saying in a low voice, "You broke her nose, asshole. And then you ran away like the fucking coward you are." He was aware of the utter satisfaction he felt when he grabbed Jimmy's shirt with his left hand, drew back his right arm as far as it would go, and felt bone shatter when his fist connected with Jimmy's nose.

"That's for hitting her," he growled. Blood squirted as if a tap had been turned on, spraying all over Eric's shirt.

Jimmy was a stevedore, and he had the muscles to prove it. He drew back a fist and aimed for Eric's jaw. Fortunately, he missed. The blow hit Eric's shoulder instead, and he staggered, at which point Lowbrow wrapped a massive arm around Eric's throat from behind, and Bruno and Rocky let out a simultaneous roar of outrage and grabbed Jimmy.

For Eric, throwing the guy hanging on his throat was automatic; one of the defensive moves in the judo class he'd once taken was learning how to flip someone over your shoulder. Lowbrow went flying and crashed into a waiter carrying a tray of drinks. They both went down in a rain of beer and broken glass, unfortunately falling on someone's table, which collapsed. More glass shattered; women screamed; guys shot to their feet, hollering.

Peripherally conscious that Jimmy had shaken free of Rocky and Bruno and was heading his way, Eric missed the bouncer the approximate size of a Brahma bull also closing in.

Rocky made a grab for the bouncer, and Eric saw the guy land a good one on Bruno's chin. Over the din the bartender was hollering into the phone, which wasn't a good sign, but it was a little late now to vacate the premises.

Eric figured later that with his friend's help, he could have taken the bouncer, but just then someone else tackled him from behind and he went down hard, slicing his hand open on broken glass. Something hit him over the head, hard enough to make him dizzy. He bit his tongue, and there must have been a patrol car nearby, because he was still trying to get up when the officer arrived, one small uniformed woman blowing a whistle for all she was worth.

Nobody paid any attention. The fight had become a free-for-all, and the officer methodically and without prejudice pepper-sprayed the people who looked as if they were most involved.

Suddenly Eric couldn't breathe or see. He could hear, though.

"Out, all of you," the lady cop ordered in a deep voice. "Anyone still here in two minutes goes to jail."

Half-blinded by the spray, gasping and choking, Eric couldn't see the door, but someone helpfully shoved him in the right direction. He staggered, felt fresh night air on his skin, and then Karen grabbed him by the arm.

"What did you think you were *doing*, Eric?" She was furious and scared, her nails digging into the skin on his arm. He could feel her shaking, and now that it was too late he was sorry he'd reacted the way he had. "I don't need you to go punching Jimmy for me. He's got a bad temper, and he never liked you anyway. Now he'll go to a lawyer and have you charged with assault. Or else he'll get you alone somewhere and beat you up."

Eric tried to say *Let him try*, but his tongue was swollen and what came out was indecipherable. The entire birthday gathering was now out in the parking lot, grouped around Sophie's sports car. She had her medical bag in the trunk, and she got it out and went into doctor mode.

"My eyes are burning like a son of a bitch," Rocky moaned.

Bruno was making choking, gagging noises.

"Where's Fletcher?" Eric couldn't see, and he knew he was lisping. He thought he was probably losing his eyesight as well as his lungs. His eyes were on fire, streaming tears; his throat burned with every labored breath. His tongue felt way too big for his mouth, and he figured it was probably hanging down like a dog's did in hot weather.

"Right here." Fletcher sounded upbeat. "Nice to know the papers got served; that's what Nicols was waving around. I'm gonna have to send him another set, though, because I think he left those on the table."

Eric coughed and then gagged before he could manage to say, "You girls all okay?"

Sophie said. "Fletch got us outside just before the cop arrived so none of us got sprayed. Don't any of you rub your eyes; it'll make it worse," she warned in a stern tone. "Anna, run to that grocery on the corner and get me a gallon of milk. It's alkaline; it's the best thing for pepper spray."

"I can't run, I'm wearing platforms," Anna said. "And my chart for today indicates the possibility of minor accidents."

"So walk then," Sophie expelled her breath in a sigh.

"Skim, two percent, or whole?"

"Whole, I guess."

"I don't have much money on me," Anna announced next. "Bruno, do you have ten dollars on you, honey?"

Eric, prevented from hollering by his tongue and using every ounce of willpower he possessed to stop from burying his fists in his burning eyes, yarded out his wallet with his good hand and threw it hard in the direction of Anna's voice. He hoped it hit her a good one. He knew Bruno would totally understand.

He must have missed. "Thanks, Eric," she purred. "You mind if I get some polish remover while I'm there? My nails are all chipped."

"Just *go*, Anna, would you?" Bruno sounded as

frantic and desperate as Eric felt. "We're dying here, and you're worrying over your damned nails?"

"Well, you don't have to be *that* way about it." Anna was huffy. "I'm not the one who got us kicked out of the pub. And I did warn you about the disruptive effect Saturn could have, didn't I?"

Finally, Eric heard what he fervently hoped was gravel crunching as Anna strolled off. He also heard Fletcher laughing.

Sophie took what seemed an awfully long time tending to Rocky before she got around to Eric. She dabbed his cut palm with something that burned almost as bad as his eyes. "You really ought to have stitches in here. I'll do it for you when we get back to Karen's place." She wrapped a gauze pad around his hand, and then he heard her telling Bruno to open his mouth so she could have a look at his teeth.

"Couple loose ones, it'll make chewing hard for a week or so, but they'll tighten up again by themselves," she said in a cheery tone. "And just rinse that cut inside your cheek with saltwater." She sounded as if she was starting to have as good a time as Fletcher.

"Lucky the cops aren't fond of paperwork," he was saying. "I'd rather not spend tomorrow in front of a magistrate trying to get you all off on drunk and disorderly."

Finally, after what seemed like most of the night, Anna came puffing back carrying the milk. "There were two guys in there and they needed money for food, Eric, so I gave them twenty dollars each," she announced, tucking his wallet back in his shirt pocket. "Giving and getting are exactly the same, you know."

Eric couldn't muster up a response. He pressed

the milky pads Sophie handed him against his eyes, and slowly, the pain receded a little and he could squint around. His pals were a sorry sight. Bruno's Western shirt was torn, and his mouth was puffed and bloody. Rocky's cheek was bruised and swollen. Their eyes looked as though they were bleeding, running tears as if they'd been peeling onions for the last week.

"That bouncer must have been wearing a suit of armor," Bruno complained through gritted teeth, cradling his right hand. "I think maybe two of my fingers are broken."

Sophie grabbed his hand and manipulated the fingers.

"Owwww. Go easy," Bruno yelped, bending double.

"They're just sprained," Sophie concluded. "What all of you need is ice and Tylenol, lots of each."

"What all of you need is a brain transplant," Karen declared, her voice high and trembling. "How am I supposed to teach Simon and Ian not to hit people when their uncles act like Rambo? I didn't care about the divorce, I told you that. I didn't want to have to see Jimmy again."

"What happened to him? Where'd he and his friend disappear to?" Eric had to maneuver his sore tongue around the words.

"I saw them getting in a cab. Jimmy's probably at St. Joe's ER right now getting a deviated septum splinted," Sophie said. "Too bad I'm not on shift tonight," she added in a low tone to Eric. "Sometimes that procedure can be really painful." She raised her voice and said, "Okay, everybody, let's take this party to Karen's place so I can finish the repairs. Leave your car here, Eric, you can get it tomorrow. You can't drive one-handed, and you can't see properly. I'll give you a ride home afterward."

Eric thanked Fletcher and Rocky for their backup. Anna had already loaded Bruno in their car and driven away.

At Karen's house, Sophie froze his palm and sewed it up.

"Sorry for causing you grief, Karo," Eric mumbled. "How the hell did Nicols know where to find you?"

"The sitter said a man phoned here and asked where I was, so she told him."

"I'll stay here tonight in case he comes back." The thought of crashing on Karen's lumpy sofa in the shape he was in wasn't exactly inviting, but he didn't want her left alone.

Sophie said, "I can stay."

Karen shook her head. "Nobody's staying. Jimmy won't come here. Anyway, I've got those new locks you put on."

Eric wasn't convinced. "I think one of us ought to be here."

"Well, I don't." Karen sounded desperate. *"Please,* both of you, go home. I really don't need a babysitter. I need to be by myself for a while."

Eric was about to argue, but Sophie gave him a look and shook her head. As they were leaving, Eric forced his tongue to cooperate one more time.

"Karo, thanks for my birthday dinner, it was great."

"Everybody brought stuff. I only made the cake. I'm glad you enjoyed that part of it, anyhow," Karen said. She gave him a strained smile and a kiss. "Don't forget this." She handed him the envelope with the gift certificate inside. He'd forgotten all about the gift, which almost made the pepper spray worthwhile.

When Sophie reached his building, he lisped, "You're sure Karen's okay on her own?"

"I'm sure she just needs time alone to settle down." She reached across and patted his arm. "Don't tell Karen, but I think punching Nicols was a great way to celebrate your birthday, big brother. I've always longed to hit that big turd hard with something heavy."

"I've never figured out why Karen married him in the first place."

"Well, she was pregnant. And he was there, that's sometimes all it takes." She reached over and planted a kiss on his cheek as he was getting out of the car. "If he does press charges, I've got the X rays from when he hit Karen. We'll see how far he gets when the judge sees that. Ice and milk and Tylenol," she reminded him. "You'll feel lots worse in the morning." She gunned the motor and gave him a cheery wave as she sped off.

As usual when it came to medical matters, Sophie was right. Getting out of bed Sunday morning was a preview of what Eric figured ninety-seven was going to feel like if arthritis, eye infection and a brain tumor set in simultaneously. His tongue was still too big for his mouth when he called Karen.

"I'm fixing breakfast for the boys. We're all fine." She added in a low tone, "Jimmy won't come here, so quit worrying, okay?"

"Okay." He didn't know what made her so certain, but he decided to take her word for it. He'd drooled all over the pillow, and the hand Sophie had stitched burned like battery acid when he finally made it to the shower. His knuckles were sore and scraped raw, his head ached, and when he caught sight of himself in the mirror, he had to grin. Bloodshot eyes with black and purple bogs underneath, drooping mouth, unshaven—he looked as if he'd had what Sophie delicately called a cerebral accident.

There was an upside to this, though. He was going to make sure he didn't look much better by Tuesday, which was when he planned to go in and get his sisters' money back. That old matchmaker would take one look and beg him to take a refund.

His birthday had been a disaster, but there were better days ahead.

In a second-story office where the only concessions to modern technology were two telephones, a shoebox-size microwave and an antiquated answering machine, Tessa McBride was having one hell of a time keeping her solemn vow to never smoke again. There had to be better days ahead, because this was one was heading for the cesspool at high speed.

Clara Beckford, her boss and the owner and founder of Synchronicity, Vancouver's Most Personal Matchmaking Service, usually kept Tessa on the straight and narrow. Clara made a habit of reminding Tessa that kissing a smoker was like licking old ashtrays, and the smell of smoke was not an aphrodisiac, and if she wanted a meaningful, long-time, committed relationship like she said, she should plan on having lungs that went the distance. And that if she ever caught Tessa smoking in the office, it would result in instant dismissal. But Clara hadn't been at work for six days now, and the steady stream of complaints from the matches Tessa had lined up was enough to make the Dalai Llama light up.

"I honestly had no idea Louie had dentures," she said to Rebecca Hyacinth, who, thank god, had phoned instead of barging in to complain the way others had done. "He didn't mention them on the information sheet. I have it right here." She rustled a blank piece of paper—the relevant bloody files were lost somewhere in the bulging file cabinet—and listened as the forty-three-year-old woman went on and on about eating dinner and having the chompers suddenly fall half out, which put Rebecca off her food, because they apparently were well laced with globs of spinach. What in blue blazes were they doing eating spinach on a first date? Honestly, people were unbelievable.

"He wore a green suit and blue socks with brown shoes? No, he didn't mention being colorblind, either." Rebecca did have a point there, but Rebecca herself had a shoe polish–black beehive hairdo and a high, round belly that could have held an eighth month pregnancy, which made her just that *teensy* bit hard to match up. Tessa didn't say so, of course, which should have earned her at least one good lungful of nicotine as a reward. Instead, all it got her was another set of teeth marks on the pencil she was chewing. She had excellent teeth at the moment, but pencils could change that.

"No," she explained for the seventh time that morning, "Clara isn't in. She's recovering from a bad case of the flu." She wondered whether to give

Rebecca Clara's home number, and decided against it.

"It's personal, my business," Clara was fond of saying. "People don't want to leave messages on some machine when they're feeling excited or discouraged about romance. They want to talk to *me*. I don't mind having them call me at home." No doubt about it, Clara was a bit of a megalomaniac. But things weren't normal with Clara right now, so Tessa wasn't sure what to do.

"Yes, Rebecca," Tessa cooed, "I'll be happy to put your membership on hold until Clara gets back and personally arranges a match for you, and in the meantime I'll pass along your concerns to her." She hung up the phone and blew a raspberry. "Eat glass and die, Becky, baby."

In the ten months she'd worked for Synchronicity, there'd been other occasions when Clara left things in Tessa's less-than-capable hands, but there was a frightening difference this time. Tessa figured her boss was having an emotional meltdown. In the last month, it seemed as if a light had been switched off in Clara's gypsy dark eyes. Gone was her vivacious attitude, her bouncy walk, her optimism, her decided opinions. She didn't come in, and she didn't seem to give much of a damn when Tessa called to update her on what was going on.

What was going on was a filing disaster. Clara had her own peculiar system when it came to keeping track of clients, and as long as she was on deck, it worked. In the past week, Tessa had spent untold frantic hours trying to figure out who had been matched with whom and when. She'd finally figured out that a good portion of the information must be floating free-form in Clara's head.

The truth was, Tessa was beyond exasperated with Clara's point-blank refusal to use computers or even let Tessa have one in the office, insisting that computerizing the business would make it the same as every other slick commercial dating service. Tessa figured it would simply yank Synchronicity into the twenty-first century where it belonged. The business had upward of a hundred-fifty members; it begged for an efficient cross referencing system, which at the very least would prevent matching another poor unfortunate guy, wearing dentures and blue socks, with Rebecca.

And it would allow her to make faces at photos on the screen while being bitched deaf, dumb, and cross-eyed on the phone.

At first, Tessa had been totally disillusioned to find out that matchmaking involved more complaining than it did hearts and happy endings. Clara had explained the Zen attitude, where the matchmaker simply did the best possible and didn't dwell on the fact that only one or two percent of the people who joined actually found someone to ride off with into the sunset. The fact was, Synchronicity *made a living* on those who sought without finding. They were the ones who renewed their membership regularly. Not that she and Clara ever stopped genuinely trying to find mates for people, goodness gracious, no. But it was impossible to succeed for everyone, even God didn't do that, Clara had been known to declare.

But Tessa didn't think God spent the major part of Her day listening to endless grumbling while She tried to figure out who to slap together next in a relationship sandwich, either.

She poured a cup of coffee, picked up a fresh pencil to chew, and dialed Clara's number. She needed to know where the missing files were, when Clara might be planning on coming in, and how many members had called to tattle on the miserable matches Tessa had made for them.

When the phone was picked up on the fourth ring, however, the voice on the other end wasn't Clara's. It was Clara's husband, Bernard Beckford, and Tessa felt her hackles rise. Clara's husband was the exception to the rule that everyone had some good in them. Bernard Beckford, excuse the language, was a prize asshole.

"Is Clara there, Bernard? It's Tessa." She knew she sounded snippy, but every time she heard Bernard's smarmy tenor she flashed back to the Christmas party last December when she'd stepped out of the upstairs bathroom at the Beckford house and straight into Bernard's muscular arms. A chef had no business being that strong. He'd imprisoned her, and before she could even struggle his mouth came down on hers, open and wet and guppy cold.

Tessa shuddered at the memory and rubbed a hand across her mouth.

His hands had cupped her bum and pulled her in against his crotch, banging against her rhythmically like a dog in heat. This was no easy feat considering the roundness of his gut, but the size of his erection exceeded even his girth.

By the time a plump, reasonably attractive woman reaches her thirty-fourth year, she's had some experience with being groped. Tessa certainly had, but being groped by the husband of a woman she adored, a woman who also happened to be her boss, made the situation tricky.

Normally she'd have resorted to the old knee to the groin and hard smack on the face routine, but

Bernard had ambushed her when she was least expecting it, and she was off balance. She tried to be moderately polite, which proved a mistake. She closed her mouth, turned her head and shoved at him, but he was tenacious as a magnet with iron filings. His tongue, overly long and thick, probed her lips, and she gagged.

She pushed with all her strength against his chest, and at the same time brought up her knee, narrowly missing her target but at least getting his attention. What made him pull away wasn't Tessa's guerrilla maneuvers, though. It was Clara's voice, dangerously close.

"Bernard, sweetie, are there any more of those luscious cream cheese things?"

"Sorry, sugar, duty calls," he'd whispered wetly in Tessa's ear, for all the world as if she were the one who'd started things. That same oily voice now said, "Clara's still in bed, honey, why don't you call back later?"

Tessa put the phone down hard without saying another word.

"*Honey,*" she muttered with indignation. "You fat prick, where do you get off calling *me* honey?"

The door buzzer sounded from downstairs, no doubt signaling yet another disgruntled client. The new pencil she'd been chewing in lieu of a cigarette now had tooth marks all down it. "Come right up," she said into the intercom, using a mock cheery voice, pasting a smile on her face. A few moments later the door swung open.

"*Good* morn—" the rest was lost in a horrified gasp.

Tessa stared up at Eric Stewart, and she felt her eyes bug out as her brain went blank. Her heart began to hammer, and she had to swallow several times before she could get any of her faculties working again.

Suddenly, Bernard Beckford wasn't first on her list of losers. If you were talking despicable, this guy beat Bernard, no competition.

4.

Time wounds all heels

Tessa hadn't seen Eric Stewart since she'd left Vancouver at the age of eighteen, and Clara had promised she wouldn't have to deal with him at Synchronicity. When his sisters bought him the membership, Clara had *promised* Tessa she'd personally and forever after deal with Eric Stewart, and now here he was and where was Clara? At home with loser number two.

"Holy shit." His appalled and involuntary exclamation told her he was as shocked as she, but he recovered faster. His voice took on a phony heartiness. "Hey, it's Tessa McBride."

"Good memory, Eric." Unless he'd studied at the Actor's Guild while running a garbage company, he hadn't known till this minute that she worked at Synchronicity. "Karen didn't mention I was working here?"

He shook his head. "I guess she thought it would be a surprise."

Some surprise. Why the hell hadn't Karen told him?

"So how are you, Tessa?"

She cleared her throat, looked straight at him, and tried for grown-up and civilized. "I'm very well, thank you, Eric."

No thanks to you.

"Won't you sit down?"

He did, and she took a closer look at him. In the years since she'd last seen him, surely the rat should have acquired the face and body he deserved. Instead he was still tall, broad shouldered, height and weight proportionate. And his body wasn't just adequate—the years hadn't budged him from the upper percentile of male hunkiness. Although they were seriously bloodshot, he still had those lazy cobalt blue peepers that looked at you as if he knew way more than you wanted him to know. Which, when it came to her, he did. Tessa swallowed hard.

He said, "So I guess you and Karen have been in touch? Since you moved back here?"

"Not really. We met by chance at Oakridge Mall one day, a couple of months ago." Before that, they hadn't talked in years. They'd lived in different cities, married, had kids, not had kids, divorced. Over coffee, they'd tried to recapture something and failed. Karen was different. Tessa was different. During their conversation, though, Karen had talked about Eric. After all, he *was* her brother. She'd said he'd stayed single. And if she hadn't told Tessa that his garbage company was thriving, the way he looked today Tessa would have guessed that Eric had fallen on hard times. He wore jeans that were way beyond worn and well into ragged; his tee had once been navy, but it had lost a battle with bleach. His eyes had purple bags underneath them, and he'd given up shaving recently, maybe because his jaw was swollen on one side. He sounded as if his tongue was in the way of his teeth. One big work-roughened hand had a strip of gauze across the palm.

"You have an accident, Eric?"

He grimaced. "Nope, an altercation."

He didn't say she should see the other guy. Well, well. Maybe karma was a reality.

"So, Tess, have you seen a lot of Karen since you got back? When you were kids, you two used to be like Siamese twins."

"Just that once." It hurt a little that Karen apparently hadn't mentioned meeting Tessa.

"I thought you were living in Calgary. Didn't I hear you got married? So your name's probably not McBride anymore?"

He still had that bloody smile, that sardonic half grin that suggested he was thinking about sex when the truth was he was probably thinking about—sex. Eric was nothing if not single-minded, she had good reason to know that.

"I kept my own name, which saved a lot of paperwork when the marriage ended. I moved back to Vancouver thirteen months ago."

She'd lost a husband and he hadn't even lost his hair, for pity's sake, which would seem only fair if bad guys got what they deserved. It wasn't long and tied back with a leather shoelace anymore, but there was plenty of it. It was conservatively cut, curly and thick and sun-streaked and golden. Messy. Sexy. There was no justice.

"Sorry to hear that your marriage didn't work."

"It was a learning experience." *Like you were, Stewart.* She remembered being eighteen, at a party where she'd just broken up with her steady. She'd just graduated high school; she was just barely not a virgin. Ripe pickings.

Eric had breezed in with some of his friends, black leather jacket, Elvis lip curl, skin-tight Levi's, cowboy boots. She knew the rumors; her mother had warned her. Eric Stewart might be a good brother to his sisters, but at heart he was a hooligan. He was dangerous, and far too old for Tessa to date. Why didn't mothers realize that guys like Eric were the drug of choice when you were eighteen?

"No kids?"

"Nope." So it took her seven years to figure out that *Not just now, honey* really meant "Not ever, sucker," at which point she'd found that ball breaker of a divorce lawyer. "No kids." It always stung to admit it, but she'd be nuts to show him any weak spots. "How about you, Eric?"

"Kids? God, no. Footloose and free, that's my style."

Ahh, yes, how well she remembered his style. He'd asked her to go for a ride that night, and she said yes. He parked and kissed her, and when he slid his hand under her new pink sweater and undid her bra, she still said yes. She moaned it, actually. She practically yarded up her sweater and begged him to suck. He had style, all right. It was spelled S-E-X.

And right now, a hot, traitorous tingle went sliding from her right nipple to her groin at the memory. She felt herself getting damp, and it infuriated her. She felt like cursing at the injustice of life. Why should she still be able to remember how his lips felt on her nipples? How his hand had slid inside her panties and found the exact right place, first try?

She couldn't remember things like that about Gordon, her ex, and she'd been married to him for seven goddamn years while she was learning firsthand the meaning of *Marry in haste, repent at leisure.* Gordon hadn't found the right place even when she pointed it out with the light on. She couldn't for the life of her remember at this particular moment what it felt like to have Gordon inside her—and he must have been there a few times, even taking into account his weenie little sex drive.

But her groin, traitor that it was, remembered all these years later exactly how Eric had felt. Thick and hot and throbbing, like her head at the moment. She needed to get on with the job and get this man *out of here.*

"So, Tess, how come *you're* working *here?*"

Trust him to make it sound like she was running the local whorehouse. He was still an expert at the art of mortification, but now she was immune.

At eighteen, she hadn't been. He'd lectured her about being easy after sex that made her scream for the first and only time in her deprived life. This, after him throwing back his own head and making a sound like a cement grinder that went on and on—the turncoat. The smug, pious, self-righteous bastard.

The client, who, Clara insisted, was always right. She tilted her chin up and put extra starch in her tone. "Ms. Beckford needed an assistant. I needed a job."

Idiot. Why did people usually work? Mind you, she'd also thought working for a matchmaker would make it easier to find the rich, attractive, intelligent, sexy, funny man who was her destiny. Ha bloody ha to that fantasy. There were men, sure, but so far, even with Clara's advice and assistance plus free access to the files, Tessa hadn't come across one man of any age with even two of her basic qualifications.

"You enjoy working here?"

"I love it." *It was losing appeal by the instant.*

He obviously didn't know what else to say, and she couldn't speak because she was experiencing a moment of pure, out-of-control rage at Clara, who had faithfully promised Tessa she'd never have to have a thing to do with Eric Stewart, and here she was, being interviewed by him.

"Now, Eric, I'll just have you fill in this form." Aspartame was the name of the game, so deceptively sweet on the tongue it masked the bitterness underneath. With one finger—thank heaven she'd had a manicure on the weekend—she slid a personal profile form across the desk along with a pen, careful not to touch a single one of his skin cells.

He shoved it back without so much as a glance.

"This was all a misunderstanding, Tessa." He shook his head, and for one insane instant she thought he meant their personal history. But of course he didn't.

"My sisters made a big mistake, buying that gift certificate," he said. "See, I don't need the services of a matchmaker; it's a big waste of everyone's time to continue with this. The best thing is just to drop it. So could I get their money refunded? Or at the very least, transfer the membership to Sophie or Karen? They're both single; they'd probably benefit from it way more than I would."

He hadn't lost that little boy charm, dipping his

cleft chin and looking at her from under those obscenely long lashes, softening his voice until it was husky and endearing. He was using testosterone full strength, and it would have worked on any other poor unsuspecting female. Tessa was proud of being impervious to it. Maybe they could draw her blood and create a vaccine to protect her gender from the likes of him.

"Oh, no. I'm afraid that isn't possible." It felt so good to thwart him. "I'm sure you read the fine print. It specifically states that we don't give refunds or allow the membership to be transferred once the contract is signed. I know Clara went over every detail with your sisters, and she would have insisted they take at least forty-eight hours to really think it over before any money changed hands; she always does. And there's the three-month clause as well; I'm sure you saw that if you read the fine print."

"Yeah, I did, but let's just review it here. If you can't find a suitable match in three months, you refund the money, right?"

"Not quite. Synchronicity has three months to find *possible* companions for you before the contract is voided. If we can't come up with *anyone* for you to date in three months, then we refund your money."

"And how many times has that happened?"

It isn't always true that the truth will make you free, dearie.

"In the two years I've been here, never." She gave him a wide-eyed crocodile smile. "Clara is the best in the business; we have lots of members. We don't guarantee you'll meet your *ideal* companion in three months; that's not realistic. But we'll certainly put you in touch with people we think would be compatible." And for you, Stewart, that will be a challenge. "If the candidates we send you are totally in-appropriate, of course we don't expect you to go on seeing them—but we do ask that you give each new contact at least three opportunities to get to know you. Meeting strangers is nerve-racking, and we've found that the three-date rule prevents a lot of impetuous mistakes."

"What if the lady refuses to see me again?"

"That's her privilege, of course. And yours as well, but we do assume that applicants are willing and eager to make a connection; that's why they come to Synchronicity."

He leaned toward her and looked earnest. "Look, Tessa, I'm gonna be up-front with you here. The last thing I need is a matchmaker. I do *really* well all on my own." A modest and rueful shake of the head. "A little too well, truth be told."

Arrogant asshole alpha male. "Your sisters seem to think differently."

"Yeah, well, they don't exactly follow me around. So Tess, just tell me straight up how to get their money back."

"Well, Eric, you'd have to discuss that with Clara. But I'd give some thought to how that's going to make your sisters feel. They did give you the membership as a gift."

Good one. His eyes narrowed and his jaw tightened. "I could have my attorney contest the conditions of this contract. I don't believe it would stand up in court."

Probably not. Tessa wondered about the legalities of the contract herself. Clara definitely ran by her own set of rules, but Tessa wasn't about to admit to Eric Stewart that she had misgivings about anything.

"Of course, you're free to do whatever you

choose," she said in a haughty tone, tilting her chin high and forcing herself to meet his gaze head-on. "Go ahead and treat your sisters' gift with disrespect and contempt. Personally, I believe you have a moral obligation to them to give this a fair shot, but if you want to hurt them by"—she almost said being a jerk, but caught herself in time—"by rejecting a generous, thoughtful gift, well, it's entirely up to you."

She gave him a look that she hoped would imply that she expected nothing more than crass behavior and utmost rudeness from him anyway, and it must have been effective, because he blew out a breath and nodded.

"You're right, it was a gift." *Good. He had the faintest vestige of a conscience; mankind was progressing.* She shoved the form back across the desk.

He pulled his own gold pen out of somewhere and flipped through the form, muttering, "Guilt, guilt, how come all you women come hot-wired with the guilt gene?"

Survival 101, dear heart. She watched as he read for a moment, scowled, and then went back to the first page.

"What the hell *is* this hogwash, anyway? *'Describe the qualities of the person you now consider to be your best friend?'* What has my best friend got to do with dating somebody? He's a guy; I'm a guy."

Yup, and we both know for sure you're not gay, Eric. She kept her voice soft and conciliatory, even though it nearly choked her. "Haven't you ever considered that a long-term companion should also be your best friend? Knowing the qualities you value in a friend gives us great insight into the kind of woman you'd be attracted to."

He blew a raspberry, and Tessa's hand ached to

smack him a good one. He pretended to concentrate. "Let's see, now what is it about Rocky I like? He's good-natured, kind to old people and babies. He works hard, plays hard, does a minimum of complaining. He never uses guilt to get me moving."

He was making fun of her. Oh, how she wanted to tell him to take his smart mouth and shove it and his entire arm up his—*Nose. Up your nose, Stewart.* She glanced at her watch, making sure he noticed. "I'd appreciate you finishing that sometime this century. I do have another client arriving soon."

She might have; she couldn't remember. She did know she needed to get him out of here so she could break her one-day, four-hour, twenty-five minute, all-time non-smoking record. There was a convenience store across the street and down half a block; she'd lock the door and sprint for it the moment he was gone.

He snapped upright in his chair and pretended to salute. Then he scribbled rapidly in each category, and she could tell he wasn't treating the questions seriously at all. In a few moments he stood up and handed her the completed form. He put a hand on his midsection and gave an exaggerated formal bow.

"All finished, Teacher. Now can I go out and play?"

Oh, how his ego begged to be reduced. She visualized flayed testicles and breathed deeply before she answered. "Clara and I will go over this carefully, and from it we'll assess your personality type"—BOZO—"and the women who are most likely to be compatible"—BIMBOS. "You'll be contacted with their names and phone numbers, and they'll also be given your name and number. We ask that you arrange a meeting and a date as soon as possible after that first contact."

He nodded. "Got it. Nice seeing you again, Tess." His eyes did a quick flick up and down, which she might have missed if she wasn't making determined eye contact. She could do this; she was a professional. In another minute, he'd be gone.

"You're looking really fine, by the way."

He was out the door before she could begin to figure out a suitably nasty, polite reply to that one.

Outside, Eric felt like beating his sore, aching head against the brick wall of the building. Why in everything that was holy or fair hadn't Karen told him that the friend who worked for the matchmaker was Tessa McBride? And, if she was any kind of a sister, she'd have added that her childhood pal had grown up to be a babe.

You're looking really fine, Tessa? Brilliant, Stewart, just bloody brilliant. What happened to adjectives like *stunning* or *gorgeous* or even plain old *wow?* And what was with *Nice seeing you again?* She probably figured he was mocking her. They hadn't exactly parted friends. He shuddered at the memory. Under the circumstances, it was idiotic of him to say anything of a personal nature to her. Damn his big mouth, anyway.

He needed a coffee. He needed to forget about Tessa McBride and focus on his original intention, which was to get the girls' money back, but he just hadn't expected to find the one woman he didn't want to see again in this lifetime sitting behind the desk in that jazzy little office with the plants and the billboard covered with wedding invitations. If he had, he'd never have deliberately gone for the heavy grunge look, old jeans, stained shirt, three-day beard, while she was in that silky blue suit thing with the slippery neckline that made it hard to keep his eyes on her face. She'd always been sexy, but god, she was *really* sexy now that she wasn't a kid anymore.

He ducked into a Starbucks.

"Morning, sir, what'll it be?"

"French roast, black." The fleshy woman behind the counter gave him more of a smile than one plain mug warranted. Tessa had been her size back then. She wasn't exactly skinny now, but there was definitely less of her. Lush, ripe, great boobs. Mind you, she'd had boobs back then, too. He remembered them vividly. His palms got hot just thinking about the weight of them, the taste—

"Here you go, enjoy, anything else I can get for you?"

One time machine and a lobotomy. Why had he been such an idiot?

She had those puffy lips that women paid big money for these days, he'd forgotten that. Her hair was the same, but lots longer, a crazy halo of thick inky curls going halfway down her back. Hair like that looked the same after sex as before.

Wake up, Stewart. Smell the smoke. Tessa's trouble. She has that vicious, sadistic streak, you remember that. And that bloody stubborn jaw. And she still has the girls' money.

Tessa had been right, much as it galled him to admit it: The membership was a gift; he didn't want to hurt his sisters. Getting Fletcher involved wasn't a good idea, because he'd laugh his head off to start with. There had to be a way to make Synchronicity give up and practically beg to hand him a refund. Damn, things weren't ever as straight-forward as they could be.

His cell rang; it was Bruno.

"We got turned down on the financing for the new equipment, Eric. Keller said try again in a few months. You want to go somewhere else? He's new, the old manager would have given it to us."

"Shit. Maybe it had something to do with you and me looking like we got the short end in a long fistfight. He seemed the kind of dude who put a lot of emphasis on appearance."

"We can go somewhere else. We're not married to him."

Eric thought it over. "Nope, let's wait until the red and the black are a little less evenly matched on the month-end statements." Maybe it wasn't such bad news. He knew about using the bank's money, but he hated not being in complete control of his affairs.

"So how'd it go with the matchmaker?"

He'd told Bruno what he was planning. He wasn't about to tell him how it had actually gone. "About the same as the bank."

"No go with a refund?"

"It's complicated. There's an outside chance, but I think I'll have to resort to sabotage, make certain the women I get lined up with go scream-ing back saying they don't want to see me again. When enough of them do, it'll be game over. But I've gotta make it seem like I'm really trying."

"Whatever works." Bruno sounded distracted.

"Everything okay with you?"

"Just an argument with Anna, she wants me to sign up for yoga classes. It's not my thing."

"Hang tough. She'll cave." Maybe. Anna had a

one-track mind. But Eric couldn't imagine Bruno in cowboy boots and a leotard, either.

"Yeah, well, good luck with the dating game. Getting out of it, I mean."

After he hung up, Eric gave it more thought. It seemed as if it should be possible to discourage women, but after practically raising his sisters, the only thing he knew for sure about the species was that just when you figured you had them figured, they did the opposite of what you expected. It wasn't going to be a walk in the park.

For the first time, he felt a little excited about the whole project. It was a challenge, and he was up for it, although the fact that Tessa McBride was involved was a stroke of rotten luck. She'd do everything she could to make things rough on him. What could he do about that?

He had a second coffee and thought about it. It wasn't good to have her as an enemy; she held too many cards here. He could give her a call later and suggest they find a way to bury the hatchet. He could say that what happened between them was a long time ago. He could quote Anna, that crap about how unhealthy it was, carrying around old emotional baggage.

Maybe there was something to that, after all. He'd had heartburn in his chest the whole time he was around her today. Probably an aftereffect of pepper spray.

He'd also had a major hard-on, what the hell was that about?

5.

If you leave me, can I come, too?

It was all about computers, Tessa fumed. If Clara wasn't such a mastodon about computers, this whole thing with Eric Stewart couldn't have happened, because everything would be organized, people would make appointments, she'd have checked the screen and known he was on his way in and bolted out the back door. Except there was no back door.

With an unlit cigarette clutched between the first two fingers of her right hand and Eric's questionnaire on the desk in front of her, Tessa forcefully dialed Clara's number with her left forefinger, and this time her boss answered.

"Clara, it's me." Outraged or not, Tessa didn't want to dump this whole problem straight into her sick boss's lap with no warning. She did her best to ease into it slowly. "I called earlier. I spoke to Bernard."

"He didn't say," Clara said in a monotone, as if it didn't matter to her one way or the other that Bernard the Beast was withholding messages. And she actually sounded impatient when she added, "What is it, Tessa? Why are you calling me?"

Maybe because you're the Boss Lady who always insists on knowing everything that's going on down here? Tessa looked at the phone as if it were possessed and took a long, dry, hungry drag on the cigarette she'd managed so far not to light.

Clara always called her *dollink*. She'd never used this snappy tone before. She'd always treated Tessa as a cherished friend as well as a valued employee. This new attitude was hurtful and confusing and crazy making, as if Tessa really needed one more stressful encounter today.

It was tough, but she kept her own voice level and sweet. "I called earlier because of some files I can't locate, I wonder if you accidentally took them home with you?" *Like in your head?* "And I need to talk to you about that new client, Eric Stewart? The one whose sisters bought him a membership for his birthday, remember we had a discussion about it?" She let the cigarette dangle from the corner of her mouth. Clara had told her nothing looked as rude and sluttish, and that was exactly how she was feeling.

The discussion, Clara, when I told you I'd rather not have anything to do with him, that I had old, serious, emotional issues with Eric Stewart, and you asked if he had a criminal record or was a rapist or had AIDS, and when I said no, you said he was your client, I wouldn't ever have to—

There was a long pause. "Oh, that gift membership. His sisters came in, didn't they?"

"Yes, Karen and Sophie and Anna." What the heck was going on? Clara never forgot names; she was a walking directory. Tessa was getting really scared here. She searched through her bag and the desk drawers for a match, knowing she'd deliberately thrown them all away. Maybe she could light a tissue in the microwave?

"Anyway, he came in for his preliminary interview this morning, and I really don't think you should keep him as a client, Clara. He's—" she tried to think of an adjective negative enough to describe Eric apart from asshole.

Finally, she managed to blurt, "He's belligerent and negative and sarcastic; he doesn't want to meet anyone. He says he does fine all on his own, probably with barmaids, and he treated the questionnaire like a joke—where it says occupation, he put garbageman when I happen to know he actually *owns* a profitable disposal company. Where it says what three things about myself do I really like, he put *penis, sex drive* and *testosterone*. Describe the person you think you'd be most successful with in a relationship? His answer was my best friend, Rocky— but the sex wouldn't work. And he kept asking how he could get the money his sisters paid refunded. He even tried to threaten me, saying that he'd ask a lawyer about our contract; he doesn't think it's entirely legal."

"Legal?" At last, Clara's voice took on some strength. "Of course it's not legal; it's more like a handshake. I intended it to be that way. It's an honorable contract." Now Clara sounded pissed off, not with Stewart, but with Tessa, which was just grossly unfair. Whatever was going on, Tessa was getting really tired of it.

"And as far as refunding any money, Tessa, I expect you to do whatever you can to avoid that situation."

"I did. I explained that he'd have to talk to you—"

Clara wasn't even listening. "We are absolutely

not refunding anything, no matter what. The business can't afford it."

Tessa knew her face must look like a cartoon version of someone in shock. As far as she knew, Synchronicity was doing well financially. They were busy, the odd client was actually pleased, once in a while two people they matched up staggered to the altar, and the rest signed up for another twelve months of trial-and-error.

Tessa had had enough. "Okay, Clara, what's going on? You're mad at me, I know there've been some complaints, but I'm doing my best, and this file situation is driving me nuts, and we really need to have a talk—"

A low, anguished wail came over the phone, and Tessa's mouth fell open. Clara was sobbing, gulping hard, struggling to say something. Clara, who only cried at clients' weddings, dainty little mock tears that she blotted before they hit her lavender silk blouse. But these tears were coming straight from her gut. Tessa was gripping the phone so hard her hand ached, and she bit the end off the cigarette in her mouth.

"It's—it's Bernard." Clara blew her nose, loud and wet. "He's leaving me, after twenty-five years, for—for that *Lolita, that child,* that assistant *chef* he hired six months ago, that—that Ruby person. That—little *slut,* that *whore.*"

Hearing Clara use such words was proof of how far she'd gone over the edge. She was an absolute stickler for ladylike language. She blew her nose again, hard. "Bernard says she's everything he's ever wanted in a woman. He says that I'm not interesting anymore, that I don't pay enough attention to him, that I'm—I'm not interesting or fun in b—" Clara was wailing, but she caught herself.

"In—in any way," she temporized, but Tessa easily filled in the bed blank.

That Bastard Bernard, Tessa fumed.

Clara sniffed. "That's where the money problem comes in, because when he wanted all that new equipment for the catering business last fall I loaned him money from Synchronicity, and he hasn't paid a cent back. I didn't get a proper loan agreement—after all, he's my husband—and now he says I owed it to him because he helped me in the beginning, years back when I was starting the dating service. He did, but it was much less money, and I paid back every cent." She took an overdue breath and wailed, "But I don't have any records."

Tessa didn't know the details, but she didn't have to. She figured she knew enough about Bloody Bernard to know that he was perfectly capable of embezzlement, or theft, or grand larceny, whatever this amounted to. He certainly was capable of screwing outside the marriage bed; she knew that for sure.

Clara wasn't finished, either. "And now he's saying he wants his half of what the house is worth, and I don't know how I'll come up with the money to buy him out." Clara was wearing down, at least she was sounding depressed instead of suicidal. "The amount I'll owe him means that I'll need to take out a mortgage. The business is doing fine, but there's lots of competition, all this ridiculous Internet dating and singles clubs."

Tessa shook her head and rolled her eyes. This obviously wasn't the time to say it wouldn't hurt to install a computer, get with the program.

Sniffles. "I shouldn't be unloading all this on you, Tess. But I can't help it; I'm distraught. At this point I'm just not *capable* of making decisions. Don't promise any refunds. I'll look around for any files I have here and send them over by courier. And I promise I'll get this sorted out as soon as I can." Her voice squeaked up on the last word, and Tessa knew Clara was crying again as she hung up.

Shaking her head at the perfidy of the male species and admitting that chewing a cigarette didn't quite provide the same effect as smoking it, Tessa put the phone down and went into the bathroom to spit and brush her teeth.

How much did it cost these days to have some-one castrated? Ballsy Bernard just didn't deserve to live the rest of his life as anything but a eunuch. Maybe she could get a cut rate on two for one and have Eric done at the same time, although a treacherous little voice reminded her what a sinful waste that would be.

Righteous indignation on Clara's behalf gave way to despondency when Tessa realized she had the whole Eric Stewart thing back in her own ample lap. It was all very well for Clara to tell her to do her best, but what good would her best do when he was bent on doing *his* nasty best to screw things up?

She knew he was; he'd had a devilish, cunning expression on his face as he whipped through the answers on the form. She'd read them the instant he left, and they'd made smoke come out of her ears. A couple might actually have been funny under other circumstances, but she hadn't been tempted to laugh, anymore than she was laughing about Bernard.

Her eyes narrowed and her lips curled. She'd made Eric pay before; she could do it again. It just took strategy. In a battle of will and cunning, she could beat his tight narrow butt any old day. All she had to do was find his weak spots and keep her heart and her body safely out of his reach.

Maybe the best way to find out all about Eric would be to renew her friendship with Karen. It wouldn't be sneaky or deceitful, Tessa assured herself, because she really wanted to get to know Karen again. Karen had two little boys; she'd love to meet them. Karen had given her the phone numbers for her work and her house. Tessa dug them out of her handbag.

She'd love to grow some boys or girls of her own while there was still time. She was only thirty-four. Women were having babies at fifty these days, but she wasn't a patient woman. Neither did she want to be a single mother. She needed to find her perfect match, and soon.

The buzzer sounded.

God damn it to hell. She also had to find a match that lit rather than one that dovetailed with the client's profiles stacked in front of her, because she was going to die childless unless she had a jolt of nicotine sometime in the near future.

6.

What you see is not always what you get

At Scissor Happy, smoking in the salon was strictly forbidden, but Karen's customer, Myrna Bisaglio, could have been deaf and blind for all the attention she paid to Karen's quietly repeated reminders and the cutesy signs Junella had everywhere.

Myrna lit up a Camel for the third time, and Karen told her for the third time that this was a no-smoking salon, that it was downright dangerous with all the hairspray and chemicals around. Just as she had the other times, Myrna took two hefty drags and blew smoke in Karen's face before she butted the thing, using the pretty china saucer Karen kept for hairpins.

"This still isn't right, dear. I wanted champagne blonde, the color Junella showed me in that book," Myrna whined in her loud, squeaky voice, squinting at the hair Karen had just carefully dried and combed out. For the second time.

"Can't you do it again?"

The answer was no. Karen said it softly, respectfully.

"No, I'm sorry, Myrna, your hair is just too fragile, stripping it and recoloring again could make it break off."

But in her mind she screamed it. NO. NO. *NO*. Her hands were shaking. To disguise that, she fussed with the green cape around Myrna's shoulders. She'd colored and dried and styled and then recolored, redried and restyled Myrna's hair. She'd been at it for over five hours, and she absolutely, positively wasn't going to do it again. No matter what color her hair was, or what style Karen came up with, Myrna looked like a gerbil anyway, nothing was going to change that.

Had anyone ever pointed that out to her? Karen bit her tongue.

She had other customers waiting. She had an appointment with Simon's kindergarten teacher at three forty-five. She figured Simon had probably been using bad language again; the teacher hadn't told her what it was about. And now she had Junella breathing down her neck and giving her significant looks because it was a rule at Scissor Happy that the customer was always right. "I can't possibly color it again today, Myrna, because the chemicals will seriously damage your hair," Karen explained for the third time.

"Well, I suppose I could come back tomorrow."

Karen's stomach was cramping again. "That's way too soon, Myrna. I'm going to give you some products to revitalize and strengthen it. I'd wait at least a month."

"A month? A *month?* Oh, no, I can't live with this for a month. When I called for an appointment, Junella told me you were wonderful at coloring, and now just look at this, and I have a cocktail party to go to tonight."

Myrna's retrograde chin disappeared entirely into her skinny neck and her eyes became mean little slits. "I don't want to be unreasonable, dear, but I'm not paying until I get what I want."

Which meant that Junella would deduct the entire amount the salon charged from Karen's paycheck, and she had that whopping bill from the boys' dentist to pay, and she'd have to ask Eric for money again.

Bargain. Stay calm; try to placate. "I'll only charge for a wash and set today, how's that?"

Myrna's voice rose another octave. "I don't see why I should pay anything, dear. This is *not* what I requested. I'll just have to speak to Junella about it."

"You do that." Karen tried to remember the hints Soph had given her about managing anger, but it was all she could do to stop herself from screaming at Myrna. "Junella? Myrna would like to talk to you."

Junella materialized behind Karen's station, her marble hard eyes at odds with her maple sugar smile. "Is there a problem?"

She knew darned well there was. Everybody in the shop knew there was. Karen could feel the other operators' sidelong, pitying glances. They knew, just as she did, that Junella had deliberately given her this impossible customer, because Karen needed her job too much to refuse. Everyone knew one of the other girls had quit two months before because of Myrna Bisaglio.

"I don't like to complain," Myrna lied, "but just look at this color, does this look like Champagne Blonde to you, Junella?"

Junella had never in living memory defended any of her employees and Karen figured she wouldn't start now, so she squirted hairspray on

Myrna's do and left the two of them agreeing that the color was definitely wrong.

She tried to stop her hands from shaking as she combed out Emily, a sweet little lady with a walker and not enough hair to do much with. Karen dropped a can of mousse twice, and still Emily tipped her. When Emily was done, Karen changed her shoes—Junella insisted that everyone wear heels in the shop—grabbed her handbag and headed for the back door where she kept her bicycle.

Junella called, "Karen? Karen, I'd like to speak to you, please."

Karen figured it was the better part of valor to pretend she didn't hear. She hurried out the door. If she had to deal with Junella now, she was liable to blow the job.

Her heart was hammering. On the street, she took time to look around carefully before she got on her bike. Ever since the fight in the bar, she'd wondered if Jimmy might be waiting for her after work, waving those divorce papers and ranting over them and the broken nose Eric had given him.

"An ordinary guy doesn't have a chance with you, not with Saint Eric around," Jimmy used to sneer. He'd been a foster child, moved from one home to the next, never knowing what it was to have family. She'd thought in the beginning that she could love him enough to fill that emptiness, that having the boys would make Jimmy whole, but instead it had made him even more insecure. He drank, and they fought, and yeah, she ended up comparing him with Eric. And when that final fight went spiraling out of control and he hit her, she'd admitted it was over.

So why had she dragged her feet about the divorce? Somewhere, deep down, had she gone on hoping that Jimmy might grow up, that he might become the man she'd thought he was in the beginning? Maybe. But as months passed, and then years, and he never made an effort to see her or the boys or support them on a regular basis, she'd realized that Eric and her sisters were right. Jimmy might not have it in him to be a husband or a father, but he did have a monetary obligation to his sons. She'd had Fletcher draw up the papers, and she'd signed them, and now she'd have to take the consequences. She was pretty sure Jimmy wouldn't come to the house, but she'd warned the boys not to open the door until she looked through the peephole. They'd dissolved into giggles, because they thought she was saying pee hole.

Pedaling hard toward Simon's school, the fresh air and the freedom of movement eased the ache in her stomach and the tightness in her chest. Tessa was coming over tonight, and Karen couldn't wait to introduce her old friend to Simon and Ian.Eric was coming too, to take the boys out for soccer boots, so she and Tess would have time to catch up on old times.

What would she tell Tess about her marriage? Sure, it had been bad. Maybe Jimmy was a psycho like Sophie claimed, but she'd tell Tess she'd never regretted marrying him, because of her boys. Tess would understand.

She'd told her sisters that once, and Soph looked at her as if she were nuts.

"You could have chosen someone sane and had them anyway," Sophie reasoned.

"But then they wouldn't be Simon and Ian."

"No, they wouldn't," Anna agreed. "Every soul has one particular astrological pattern; no two are exactly alike." Then she spoke to Sophie as if Karen wasn't sitting right there. "She chose this particular path as a drastic lesson in self-esteem. The universe does that sometimes; she had to marry Jimmy so she'd really begin to understand her own worth."

Sophie blew a raspberry. "Isn't that sort of like hitting your head on the wall because it feels good when you stop?"

"The universe has no respect whatsoever for our personal comfort," Anna proclaimed in a prim voice.

Anna, and her answers for everything. She had a husband who adored her, yet for all her so-called insights about other people, she didn't see that since she'd gotten on this astrology kick Bruno wasn't as lighthearted as he'd always been. Karen knew by the way he was with the boys that Bruno wanted a family. Anna always said she wanted kids, but not right now. As the oldest of the girls, thirty-six, she didn't exactly have eternity to make a move.

Which was exactly what Sophie said about Rocky. No doubt about it, the Stewart family wasn't doing so hot in the relationship sweepstakes.

"Getting Eric to settle down with one woman is a lost cause," Sophie had said six weeks ago, when they found out he'd dumped someone they'd all half-liked. "We've left him to his own devices where women are concerned, obviously it's time for us to step in."

So they'd methodically screened all the eligible women each of them knew. Anna's friends either taught school or did past life regression, and although they'd had lunch with the two most likely, they'd had to eliminate them. The teacher was hung up on unions, which wasn't Eric's favorite subject, and the regressionist kept talking about somewhere called Lemuria.

Next they tried a doctor friend of Sophie's without realizing she was a lesbian. Anna even did her chart without cluing in to that little detail, which showed how far off astrology could be.

Karen couldn't think of any possibilities. There were two single stylists at work, nice women, but definitely not the brightest bulbs in the lamp.

And then Karen had met Tessa at the Body Shop in the mall and had what Anna called an epiphany, because all at once Karen remembered that Tessa had been in love with Eric the whole time they were growing up.

Tessa was single again, sexy, smart, sassy and heterosexual. Not only that, but she was a Taurus, which Anna had said was a perfect match for a Gemini as far as marriage was concerned. There was the little matter of getting them together without making Eric suspicious.

It was Sophie who came up with the brilliant idea of getting him a membership at Synchronicity for his birthday. Sophie was devious in a way Anna and Karen weren't. "If he has any idea we're manipulating him into dating Tessa, he'll go to any lengths to avoid her," Soph explained. "But if we give him a membership, he'll have to at least talk to her. Oh, this is *sooo* perfect." Sophie rubbed her hands together with glee. "He's gonna absolutely hate getting a membership for his birthday, and he'll be worried about the money and try and get a refund—we'll make sure he can't—and then he'll find some way to piss off all the women they line him up with. And all the while, Tessa will be

there right under his nose. Don't even mention
her name to him if you can help it."

Karen hadn't. She hadn't even told either of
them that both of them were coming to her place
tonight. Knowing Eric's track record, Karen was
worried about Tessa. "Should we maybe give her
some idea what we're doing, see how she feels
about it?"

"No can do," Sophie insisted. "They both have to
figure this is their own idea if it's going to work."

"But Tessa could get her heart broken, you
know what he's like with women," Karen argued.

Anna had been tapping frantically on her laptop as her sisters talked. "Listen to this," she com-
manded. "I don't have Tessa's exact moment of
birth, but even without it, she and Eric are compatible. Their relationship is in the ninth house; it
has a fated feeling about it."

"There you go," Sophie said. "Who are we to
argue with fate?"

Tessa wasn't arguing, but Shelby Goodlight must
have thought she was, because she kept going over
and over the fact that the dentist Clara had lined
Shelby up with had turned up for their second
date wearing black dress socks with sandals, which
Shelby considered ugly, ugly, ugly, no matter what
Tessa might think.

Tessa thought that after twenty-three minutes
on the same subject, it was past time to move on,
and that matching Shelby, who had an overbite,
with a dentist could have been a bracing experience all round. Wrong again.

"He also suggested I have my teeth bonded,
whatever that involves," Shelby was saying. "Then

when I asked what the chances were of him giving my mother a discount on a root canal, he went ballistic."

Shelby raised her eyebrows and held her palms out in a go-figure gesture. "Dentists just aren't sexy, Tessa. I know they make good money, but obviously they're cheap, and besides you'd have to floss before and after, maybe even during, so don't line me up with anymore, okay?"

Tessa made ridiculous promises and sympathetic noises and Shelby finally left. Tessa ate a Zone bar to keep up her strength and to counteract the cigarette she'd smoked just before Shelby arrived. When the phone rang, she almost let the machine take it, but she told herself she did have a responsibility here. She sighed and picked up.

It was her mother. Why hadn't she followed her instincts?

"Tessa, you busy?"

Tessa sighed and steeled herself. "No, Mom, not at the moment."

Maria was a good mother, in the sense that she loved her daughter, cared what happened to her, wanted the best for her. The trouble was, she'd somehow gotten it in her head that since they were both single—she and Tessa's father, Walter, had divorced when Tessa was twelve—and since Tessa lived in Vancouver again, they should be girlfriends.

Maria had decided that every Friday night was their "date night." Tessa was trying to break her of it, but it wasn't proving to be easy. She loved Maria. You had to love your mother, but she didn't see how this best friend thing could ever work, and she was right.

The last time they'd been out together on one of these Friday night disasters, Maria must have read an article in *Cosmo* on what girlfriends talked about. Leaning across the vegetarian pizza they were sharing, she'd said, "Tessa, which vibrator do you think is worth buying?"

What did you say when your mother asked a question like that?

"It's a matter of personal taste, Mom," she'd managed to gulp. "And also on how much money you plan on spending."

It wasn't natural to discuss vibrators with your mother. Next thing, her father, also single, would be asking her advice on Viagra.

"I'm calling about tomorrow night," Maria said, and Tessa was pathetically grateful for an iron-clad alibi.

"Sorry, Mom, can't make it, I've got a date tomorrow night."

Three weeks ago, Clara had matched her with Alistair Farnsworth, a dot-com millionaire. Tessa had been out with him twice and she figured he was a dot-com dud, but she was duty bound to play by Clara's rule—three strikes before you dumped him.

"That's why I'm calling. So have I."

Tessa waited a beat. "So have you what?"

"Got a date." There was smugness in Maria's tone, but there was also apprehension.

Tessa sat bolt upright. This was new, this was interesting. She'd been on the verge of trying to line her mother up with her favorite older male client, Kenneth Zebroff, just to get out of any more discussions about vibrators. "You *have*? Way to go, Mom! God, this is wonderful. I'm thrilled for you. Is it anybody I know?"

Maria drew in an audible breath and let it out

again. She spoke so softly Tessa had trouble hearing her. "Actually, it's Walter."

"Walter who?" Tessa didn't know a Walter, except for—

"Walter as in *Walter McBride?* My *Dad?* You're going out with my *dad?"* She couldn't keep the horror out of her tone. These were two people who'd fought their way through Tessa's childhood, battled ferociously over the divorce settlement for five years after the fact, and couldn't be in the same room without having an explosive argument that left Tessa sick to her stomach and anyone else present running for cover.

"What happened to—" *Don't go there, Tess.* The last time she'd visited her father, maybe three weeks ago, there'd been a blonde named Buffy at his apartment at ten on Sunday morning, and she'd seemed very much at home. She had bigger breasts and smaller hips than Tessa.

She rearranged the question. "What happened that made you think this was a good idea?" *Besides brain seizures that erased every scrap of cogent memory in both your graying heads.*

"It was your grandmother Belinda."

"Ma, Grandma Blin died sixteen months and"— Tessa glanced at the desk calendar—"four days ago." Maybe her mother had actually had a stroke or something, because she wasn't making much sense.

"I know that, Tessa. Of course I know when my own mother-in-law died, for goodness' sake. But I think losing her has changed your father, for the better. We've talked quite a lot and we both feel we're older and wiser now, and maybe for the good of the family we should try to at least be friends."

The family? What family? The last she'd heard,
Tessa had been an only child, and she and Maria
and Walter were family by merit of blood alone.
Maybe she had a sister somewhere in an institution,
and they'd never told her?

"*Please* don't tell me you're doing this for me,
Ma. Because I'm really okay with you guys being
divorced, honest. I mean, I wasn't when I was a
teenager. I pretty much despised both of you and
longed to be an orphan, but most teens hate their
parents whether they have reasons or not."

She was babbling, but she had provocation. "It
wasn't as if I had no one to talk to about it either;
there was always Grandma Blin."

*Who used to agree that the pair of you were prize ass-
holes.* Tears filled Tessa's eyes as a nostalgic grin
came and went. Tiny, optimistic, fiery Grandma
Blin had been Tessa's mainstay all during her
childhood, and it was her death that had allowed
Tessa to quit her boring job and move back to
Vancouver, because Grandma Blin had left Tessa
her house, an adorable pink two-bedroom cottage
on a quiet street just off of Cambie, stuffed with
furniture and layered with the crocheted doilies
Gram churned out.

"So where are you guys going?"

The thought of her mom and dad out on a date
made her desperate for a smoke. There was the
faint possibility that she and her own date could
walk in some restaurant and meet, God help her,
her mother and father.

Tessa didn't think she could handle that.

"To Bellingham."

"*Bellingham?*" It was a town just over the U.S.
border. "Why are you going to Bellingham?"

"There used to be a pub that your dad and I went to. We want to see if it's still there."

At least it got them out of the city. Tessa was tempted to tell her mother to take mad money with her for transportation home, just in case things went as usual, but she held her tongue.

"I want you to know where my will is, Tessa. It's in that cubbyhole in the sideboard. It's really straightforward; it leaves everything to you. You know who my lawyer is, Trudy Hopman at Maxwell and Hopman."

"Your *will?*" This was getting too weird. "What are you worried about your will for, Ma?" Surely she didn't think Tessa's father might murder her? Through years of her yapping, Walter had never laid a hand on Maria.

"Because we're going on your father's motor-cycle."

7.

Will you let me get lucky with you?

Tessa felt her eyes widen and her chest contract. "Mom, please tell me you're joking. You know Dad's had a couple of tickets for speeding on that thing, and if you're going to a *pub*—Mom, this is not a good idea."

"As long as you know where my will is, Tessa, I'm fine with it. Walter always rode a motorcycle; it was one of the things I liked about him."

It was the first positive thing Tessa had ever heard her mother say about her dad, and it wasn't reassuring in the slightest.

"Do you even have a helmet?" Tessa's brain was having serious difficulty with the mental image of her chubby mother holding on to her overweight father's middle, balancing on the back of a candy apple red Harley. "What are you going to wear?" Leather did protect somewhat, but Tessa's leather pants wouldn't begin to go around Maria's hips. They barely went around Tessa's, since she'd almost stopped smoking.

"I'm buying new jeans. My old ones don't fit.

I've gained a few pounds. And Walter has a spare helmet."

Tessa just bet he did. He'd undoubtedly been tearing around with Buffy wearing it.

"Walter's promised me that if he has anything to drink, we'll just stay down there and come home the next day. There's a motel there that's decent; we used to stay there when we were dating."

Tessa felt like gagging. The motel might be decent, but the thought of her parents having sex in it was far worse than the motorcycle thing. She couldn't do this anymore.

"Mom, I've gotta go. I have clients."

She did. She just didn't have any at this exact moment. She hung up the phone and did some deep abdominal breathing before she lit a cigarette, but just as she was reaching for one the phone rang again.

Tessa snatched it up. Maria had probably come to her senses.

"Mom?"

"Nope, it's Eric."

Thursday had gone so far south the Gulf of Mexico was only a memory. "If you're phoning to find out if I've matched you up for the weekend, I have to confess I haven't found *quite* the perfect match for you just yet." Buffy the Vampire Slayer was otherwise occupied. "But I'll line something up by the weekend, I promise." Which gave her exactly one day to do it.

"That's not why I'm calling. I've been thinking things over, Tessa, and I think we need to talk."

If it had been anyone but Eric, she would have believed she was hallucinating. In living memory, she couldn't ever remember a single guy using that line. Wasn't it copyrighted for use by females only? There had to be a catch.

"Talk? Talk about what? Actually, I'm pretty busy right now. Could it wait?" Guys used *that* line all the time, why shouldn't she?

"I want to clear the air. About what happened between us. Those two nights we dated. Back when we were kids." His voice was low and intense.

"When *I* was a kid." She felt like saying that at the time, she was still shitting yellow. That had been one of Gram Blin's best lines, but she held her tongue. "You were over twenty-one, if I remember correctly."

"Now that's the sort of remark that makes it hard to apologize to you, Tessa."

"You want to *apologize?*" She'd waited a long time for this. "So go ahead; I'm all ears." But she had butterflies in her stomach.

"I'd rather do it in person. Can you meet me after work?"

She could. She wasn't due at Karen's until six, but did she want to?

"Please, Tessa?"

"Oh, all right. Where?"

"I'll pick you up. What time are you done?"

She glanced at the clock. It was after four, she'd been here since eight-thirty this morning, nothing had gone well. Enough was enough.

"Half an hour." Might as well get it over with, she told herself, wishing she'd worn the blue sheath instead of this gray skirt and red sweater. At least the skirt was good and short. She'd have to put her pantyhose back on, though. She'd taken her hose off to let her legs breathe a little. Why hadn't she used that free coupon for the tanning spa?

"See you then." He hung up.

Twenty minutes later, he rang the bell and barged through the door when she pushed the buzzer. She'd used the time to wash her face and reapply makeup, and she'd struggled back into the damned pantyhose.

He looked better than he had two days before. He was clean-shaven, no bloodshot eyes, khaki pants fit snug over his butt, loose white polo shirt under a butter-soft brown leather jacket. He must work out, or else he'd had liposuction. Nobody had a stomach that flat. He even smelled faintly of something tangy, probably delayed guilt.

"Hi, Tessa. Ready to go?"

She was, more or less, but she was nervous. "Where?"

"Somewhere we can talk. Feel like a drink?"

"In the afternoon?"

"Why not?"

She couldn't think of a reason.

"Okay." She was feeling ridiculously antsy, and alcohol had its uses. "But I don't like pubs; they smell bad."

"There's a licensed café just around the corner from here."

She grabbed her raincoat, but it had stopped raining outside. Instead, it had poured down inside the office. They walked the half block in silence. The place was quiet and almost empty. They sat. He glanced at the wine list and then ordered a bottle seemingly at random.

"An entire bottle?" Maybe he'd become an alcoholic.

"This is sort of a celebration. I thought we could just put all this old shit behind us and start over, okay?"

"This old shit? This is what you meant by an apology?" She stood up and grabbed her handbag. "Right, I'm outta here. Bye."

"Wait." He was on his feet, holding her arm. "Sorry, I'm so bad at this. Sit back down, please. I'll do better, just give me a minute here."

She relented and sat. Obviously, he hadn't had any practice at apologizing.

The anxious, elegant waiter presented the bottle of wine Eric had ordered as if it were the Holy Grail, and then insisted on going through an elaborate uncorking, sniffing, stress-ridden ceremony before he finally poured two glasses and reluctantly left them alone with his pride and joy. His doleful face indicated that he knew they wouldn't really appreciate it.

Tessa lifted her glass and took a hefty slug.

"Is it okay?" Eric looked anxious now. "I figured maybe it was a dud and he was just trying to put one over on me."

She took another mouthful and pretended to roll it around in her mouth before she swallowed. "For a simple little vintage, it has an amusing undertone, a deep, penetrating bouquet evocative of aged wood."

"Wow." He lifted an eyebrow and took an experimental gulp. "It's not bad, I guess. Kinda sweet. You some kind of wine connoisseur?"

She had to grin at that. "I know three things about wine," she confessed. "Sweet, sour, medium dry."

He grinned. "That's about it for me, too. You had me worried there for a minute." He took another mouthful, swallowed, and set the wineglass down. "Look, Tessa, I really don't want bad feelings between us. Maybe we could work toward an emotional détente; start out fresh. What'd'ya say?"

"Good vocabulary." She gave him a level look. He was slippery all right. "You said something about an apology."

"God, you're a hard woman. You're gonna force me to go over it piece by piece, aren't you?"

She nodded, jaw set.

"Okay, okay. I'm sorry for what happened way back when. I should never have taken you out that first time; you were my kid sister's pal, I wasn't thinking straight that night. I'd had a couple beers; you were so damned—"

He was making excuses. She narrowed her eyes and waited, knowing he was going to work around to blaming her, and when he did he was going to wear the wine. But he surprised her.

"Pretty." He didn't meet her eyes. Instead, he fiddled with the glass, rubbing a thumb slowly around the top edge. It made her body clench.

"You were so pretty. Sexy. Soft. That mouth of yours—" He caught himself and sat up straighter. "I never intended to let it go as far as it did. It just went out of control real quick, and—well, you know what young guys are like."

"Yeah." She watched him and nodded. "Rumor has it they think with their dicks." She hadn't known that then. She'd learned it from him.

His head jerked up and down. "You got it."

"That doesn't account for the lecture you gave me afterward." It was past time for him to know how it had affected her. Remembering still made her insides shrink and her face go hot. She narrowed her eyes and gave it to him straight up.

"I felt like a slut, Eric. You treated me like a half-witted child. You told me all the nasty things your asinine friends said about girls who had sex first time out. You told me word got around. You repeated all the dirty names girls like me were called, you said"—this part still hurt like a son of a gun— "you said I wasn't fit company for Karen. Then you drove like a maniac to my house and bruised my right arm dragging me to the front door. I've never been so humiliated in my life."

He rubbed a hand over his curls. "I was an idiot. What can I say? I worried myself sick about those sisters of mine, I thought for sure one or more of them would get pregnant, or run away, or get mixed up with a real lowlife. All of which Karen ended up doing, actually."

He stared down at the table for a few minutes, and Tessa thought about Karen and felt sad. Once when they were kids, they'd pretended for a whole day to exchange lives. Karen was Maria's daughter that day, getting scolded for dirtying her new white shoes, and Tessa had big sisters and a brother who held ribbons in his teeth and scowled while he braided hair into pigtails. It was one of her best memories.

"Then I ended up seducing my little sister's best friend," he said with a groan. "I was horrified and really ashamed of myself." He waited a beat and then he looked her straight in the eye and added, "Plus, you said you loved me, Tessa. Remember that part? You said you'd always loved me. That totally freaked me out. It scared me half to death."

Tessa felt her face go hot. That night with Eric hadn't been the first time she'd had sex, or even an orgasm, but it had never been mind blowing before. She'd been emotionally overwhelmed, raw and open and astounded at the power he'd unleashed, and she'd blurted out the truth.

"I had a crush on you," she improvised. "People joke about it being puppy love, but it sure feels real at the time. I had this big thing for you, the whole time we were growing up. You were Karen's big brother, and she idolized you, so I did too." Of all things, her chin wobbled, remembering. She took control of it and added in a sprightly voice, "Well, congratulations, you sure got me over that in a hurry. I could have gone on mooning after you and missed out on my real life."

"I didn't have a clue how you felt until that night." He was giving her a strange look.

"Well, like I said, I got over it fast, there one day, poof, gone the next," she lied. Maybe he had a built-in lie detector, because he was giving her a funny look. Or maybe the wine was making her eyes go funny.

She'd polished off two glasses already; nerves were making her drink too fast. She blotted her lips with the napkin and released her death grip on the glass. When he didn't answer, she burst out, "And if you were so horrified and ashamed, how come you phoned two weeks later, said you were sorry and wanted to make it up to me, and asked me out again? Explain that, Eric Stewart."

8.

There's a fine line between pain and pleasure

Eric groaned and slouched into his chair. "Don't remind me. That was my second major mistake." He looked uncomfortable, and that pleased her.

"It was all about sex, right?" Even back then at eighteen, she'd figured that out. "You just wanted sex with me again. You figured I was easy, so why not?"

It took a minute for him to answer, and then he looked shamefaced, as well he ought. "It wasn't that I figured you were easy, Tess. Well, you were, sort of, you've got to admit that. But the sex, man alive, the sex was smoking hot; it blew me away. I couldn't believe it could be like that. I wanted more."

Hearing him admit that it had been good between them satisfied some old yearning, but they weren't finished here, not by a long shot.

"So you figured you'd take me out to Lulu's for dinner and then we'd have an instant replay in the front seat of your truck."

"My old Ford, I should have kept that baby." He

saw the look on her face and quickly added, "Hey, be honest here, you were pretty agreeable. I should have wondered about that. You planned it all, right?"

"Right." Even now it gave her a good feeling to know she'd outsmarted him. It had taken finesse and a good bit of acting, considering how furious and ashamed and hurt she was. And how fat. She couldn't believe even now that she'd ignored her extra poundage and actually worn a little blue minidress.

"You made me come to the door when I picked you up, and your mom gave me a hard time and told me to have you home before midnight."

She remembered. She'd been anything but ladylike after they got out the door. She'd brushed against him with her breasts and repeatedly touched his hand and arm.

"And you were the one who insisted we park on that deserted beach, same place I took you two weeks before."

"Yup." And she'd slid over on that shiny old truck seat before he had a chance to slide an arm around her. And then she'd kissed him, tongued him, let him touch her breasts and run his hand up under her dress. She'd reached down and stroked the bulge in the front of his jeans. And when he was breathing like a freight train and fumbling with the zipper, she'd taken revenge.

"I remember word for word what you said, Tess. You asked me what made me think you wanted another quick screw on my truck seat."

She nodded. It had been her finest moment. "And then I just parroted back to you what you'd said to me."

"You said that nothing in the world would persuade you to make out with me ever again. You said you never wanted to see me again."

"I didn't, either. Like I said, Eric, you taught me a hard lesson about men, one I've never forgotten. What men say and what they do are two different things."

"Not always. Maybe just when guys are really young."

She could tell by the look on his face that he really believed that, poor misguided idiot. Still, it was a wonder he hadn't made her walk home that night. He'd driven like a maniac, tense and silent, but this time when he pulled up in front of her house Tessa slammed out of the truck before he could move from behind the wheel. He'd peeled rubber for half a block.

He couldn't know that she'd cried just as hard that night as she had the first time she'd been out with him. It should have felt like victory, but instead it was defeat, and the end of her girlhood dreams.

"You sure did a good job of making me feel like pond scum." His mouth twisted into a wry grin. "I've gotta hand it to you, Tess, it took a good few years to get my confidence back."

It had taken her longer. She'd perfected her smart mouth and breezy manner to cover up insecurity. And she'd married the first guy who asked her before she really knew him, because her self-esteem was in the basement and she figured nobody else would be lining up.

He leaned toward her. "For what it's worth, Tessa, I still feel really bad about what I did to you. Once I got over being mad, I saw myself for the self-righteous idiot I'd been. I wanted to tell you I was sorry, but by the time I worked up nerve enough to do it, you'd moved to Calgary."

That wasn't an excuse. "You could have written me a letter, phoned me. Karen knew where I was."

"I could have, yeah. I should have. The longer I waited, the harder it got. Other stuff happened, and I guess I just shoved it out of my mind."

"Well, lucky you." It hurt, that he could do that and not look back.

He scowled. "You're not trying to tell me I ruined your entire life, are you?"

She opened her mouth to tell him yeah, and then realized it wasn't true. Nobody else ruined a life; a person did that all by themselves.

"C'mon, Tessa, it was a long time ago. We were a lot younger. Give me a break here. I'm trying to clear the air, not qualify for Guilt Award of the Century."

Part of her wanted to go on needling him, carrying a grudge and resenting him, but another part knew he was right. It really was time to lay down the gauntlet. She was on her way to Karen's in another hour. She honestly wanted them to be friends again, without Eric being a reason or a complication. He was Karen's brother; it would be tough to hang with Karen and have bad feelings for him. And there was Synchronicity to think of; it didn't look like Clara was coming back anytime soon. Tessa would have to line up his matches; it would be simpler if they were on speaking terms.

"Okay." She had another long sip of wine. It really was excellent.

"Okay. I agree. Let's shake on it."

He looked at her as if he thought there might

be a catch, and then he smiled that killer smile and stuck his hand out across the table.

"Friends?"

"Friends."

They shook. His hand was big and warm and callused, and she didn't like holding it. Or maybe she did, too much. She pulled away before he did.

He whistled, long and low. "Hey, this is good, Tessa. This makes me feel so much better; everything settled between us." He poured her more wine and took some himself. "A toast, to us."

That sounded further than she'd planned this to go, but she drank to it anyhow.

"So, Tessa, I really need to talk to you about this matchmaking. I was thinking about Karen, y'know, she was married to this real creepo, I guess you never met him, and now she needs to meet somebody who'll appreciate her. Maybe we could—"

"Maybe we could nothing." Tessa couldn't believe it. He hadn't even waited five minutes before he started asking for favors. "So that's what this whole thing was about, this crap about clearing the air and all that?" Her voice rose. "Just so you could try all over again to wangle your way out of the gift your sisters spent their hard-earned money on? You can't transfer your membership to Karen, so don't ask."

"Hold it, hold it." He held up both hands, palms out. "You got this all wrong, Tess, that's not what I was gonna say. I wanted to know about *buying* a membership for Karen, but I won't bring Serendipity up again if you're gonna go ballistic every time I try to talk to you about it. Man, you're touchy. I just thought—"

"Okay. Sorry." She'd misunderstood. "I just don't

trust you." That sounded harsh, so she added, "Yet. If you want to buy Karen a membership, I'd suggest asking her about it first. I don't want to go through that whole rigmarole again about getting your money back."

"I will ask her. I'm gonna see her in an hour or two. I promised I'd take the boys out to buy soccer boots."

"You're going to Karen's? So am I." Tessa felt more than a little annoyed. Karen hadn't said Eric would be there, but then, why should she? He was her brother, after all.

"Yeah? What time you going?"

"Six. She said to come early, so I could meet the kids."

"She probably forgot I was taking them shopping. Or maybe she figured you two would have more chance to talk with them gone; they're firecrackers, those two. You want a ride over?"

"Please. I never bring my car to work; there's a parking problem." She'd been going to take the bus home and then drive to Karen's, but the wine was making her a bit dizzy. "I'd appreciate that." What harm could a ride do?

"You hungry?" He tipped more wine into her glass. "Let's see if they serve anything edible here."

"Well—okay." She'd planned to skip dinner, not smoking more than one a day had put four and three-quarter extra pounds on her hips. But wine always made her ravenous. She finished another glass and thought what the hell. She could always diet tomorrow.

"Karen's boys play soccer?" They were his nephews. She'd never really thought about him having nephews. "You're an uncle, lucky old you. I'll bet if my parents had tried harder, I could be an aunt right

now." The wine was loosening her tongue. "Sometimes I get so pissed off at them only doing it that
one time." Although come to think of it, they might
be going for twice, tomorrow night.

He laughed. "I coach Simon's soccer team; he's
catching on. The kids on Ian's team are still having a hard time figuring out which end they aim
for."

"I wish I had nephews." She felt as if she might
cry. Wine did that to her, too. "Or nieces. I'd like
nieces. I'd take either, but I'd prefer both."

"You didn't want kids of your own? When you
were married?"

"Of course I did. Why do you think I got divorced?"

"Beats me." He shook his head and held up his
palms. "Maybe because the two of you couldn't
have kids?"

"Because he *wouldn't* have kids." It made her
mad and sad all over again. She had almost finished the wine. She tipped more into her glass.
Talking about Gordon made her tense. "Don't you
want your own babies someday, Eric?"

"Nope." He shook his head. He said it casually,
but without room for compromise. He was looking
at the menu. "Raising my sisters was enough for
me, and now I've got Karen's boys to worry about.
I figure I've had enough of raising kids to last me a
lifetime."

Something inside of her contracted and then
hardened. She was going to have to make a nota-
tion on his file. No point lining him up with someone whose dream was to get pregnant. It was such
a waste; he had the most beautiful eyelashes. What
was wrong with men? She really felt like crying
now. Her chest hurt. Her stomach cramped. She'd

had way more wine than he had, way too much wine. She had to pee. She tried to get to her feet, to find the bathroom, and the carpet tipped.

"Whoops." She grabbed at the table, missed, and connected with his shoulder. It was solid, reassuring, warm. But he didn't want kids, the rat.

He got up and helped her find the bathroom. She took a long time because she was so dizzy. She kept forgetting what she was supposed to be doing. She washed her face with cold water and then realized she hadn't brought her purse in with her. No more makeup. Oh well, so he'd see her bare-faced; she certainly wasn't trying to make an impression on him anyway. He didn't want kids.

He was waiting with her coat and bag when she came out.

"Let's take a walk, clear our heads, maybe find a burger place. Unless you want four courses and sauce on everything—that's what's on this menu."

"Nope, no courses." She was just sober enough to figure out that he'd suggested walking for her sake, because she was really tipsy from the wine. In fact, she might just be a tiny little bit drunk.

He put his arm around her when they got outside, which was a good thing because the sidewalk kept moving up and down. It felt safe, having his arm around her. It felt sexy.

"Wine makes me feel sexy; it has absolutely nothing to do with you," she told him just in case he thought otherwise.

He laughed. "Thank you for sharing."

They walked, but the fresh air didn't sober her up. She couldn't keep to a straight line. She giggled when he steered her safely past people and signs and fire hydrants. She blew kisses to a policeman in a cruiser, and to a couple of babies in strollers. Once, overcome with good feelings, she made Eric stop and she pulled his head down and kissed him, not on the lips, though. Her aim was off, and she missed, getting his warm, scratchy cheek instead.

But then he turned the tables and took her face between his palms and placed his lips smack on hers. Her knees buckled and somehow her tongue got in his mouth and the heat made her dizzy. Eric made her dizzy, and she wanted more, but then he pulled away.

"This beats snarky all to hell," he said, but his voice was shaky.

His skin smelled good. He hugged her tight for a long, sweet moment, and she thought she could feel his heart banging, but it might have been hers. Wine made her heart bang. Then she pulled away, because she remembered he didn't want children.

"There's a city ordinance that forbids making out on the street," she told him in a stern tone. "We could get arrested."

He said he thought it was worth it, but then she thought of more stuff she needed to tell him. Friends should know things about each other, even if they weren't going to have children together. She told him about Gordon, how he ate the same breakfast day after day, and had lists for everything, and never read anything but newspapers, and didn't remember his dreams.

"So what did you want from the guy?" Eric sounded puzzled.

"I wanted him to buy tickets for Cuba some Friday afternoon, or take guitar lessons, or study yoga, or start wearing a kilt. I wanted him to buy a red car, and make me an ice-cream sundae and bring it to bed. He didn't want babies because it would disrupt his schedule. And everything was always wrong. The dry cleaners put starch in his collars, other drivers cut him off, the waiter at the restaurant was rude. Call me Pollyanna, but I want to see the right things about life."

She knew she was talking too much, but she also knew she was a brilliant conversationalist when she drank wine. Next she told him about trying to stop smoking before it yellowed her teeth and gave her wrinkles and made her breath smell bad. "Besides, it puts guys off sex in the morning, and I really like sex in the morning, don't you?"

"Oh, yeah." His voice was husky and he cleared his throat. "Afternoon, evening's okay, too. And then there's holidays; holidays are good." He grinned down at her and gave her a long, speculative look with his eyebrows raised. He took her arm in a gentlemanly fashion.

"Would you consider yourself highly sexed or just ordinary, Eric?"

He definitely found her as funny as she figured she was. "Is this a quiz, Tess?"

"I'm doing research. For my job." Wow, she was inventive when she'd had too much to drink. It made her pulse kick up, too.

"I've never really run a comparison survey."

"My boss says sex is biology. We should use it for courtship."

"Instead of pleasure? Your boss has obviously spent too much time making out with the wrong kind of lovers."

"Only one wrong one." Tessa told him about Bernard and the Christmas party, but he didn't find it funny the way she expected him to.

He growled, "Dumb ass needs his butt kicked."

For some reason that made her deliriously happy.

"A guy like that could cause you real trouble, Tess."

She opened her mouth to tell him that blundering Bernard was too busy making out with his assistant to bother with her, but just in time she remembered that was privileged information. So instead she told him about Clara's resistance to computers, and how much easier it would be to do her job if Synchronicity was computerized.

"You should come over to my office and talk to Henry, my office manager. He's a whiz at computers. He computerized my entire business, and he just finished setting up an astrology program for Anna. Which wasn't the best move he ever made."

"Why not? I'm gonna get Anna to do my chart; I want to find out when I start to live happily ever after." She was sort of happy right now, though. She jumped over cracks in the sidewalks and said she hoped her mother appreciated it. She quoted Jabberwocky and then cried when an ice-cream truck drove by. "It reminds me of being little and having that excited feeling, like anything was possible. And then you grow up and find it isn't."

He handed her tissues and hugged her until the tears stopped.

"I'm enjoying the hell out of this, but I think you need something to eat, Tess." He bought them burgers in a fast-food joint because that's what she said she wanted.

"Grease, the grease will settle my stomach," she insisted. "Or was that olive oil? Grandma Blin always claimed it was a cure for hangovers. But maybe you had to drink it before you drank." Famished, she wolfed down a veggie burger and fries and a vanilla shake

But she realized afterward that it was the coffee that did it. After the second cup, she burped twice, really loud, and then suddenly wasn't drunk anymore, but man, she was embarrassed. She covered her eyes with her hands and moaned.

"Headache? I've got Tylenol—" he started fishing in his pocket.

"No headache. I'm just mortified. I was drunk. You got me drunk."

He nodded. "Oh, yeah. But I didn't take advantage of you, did I?"

Not that the thought hadn't crossed her mind. That must be what any port in a storm meant. Damn wine made her horny. How could she have kissed him that way, leaning into his pelvis right there on Granville Street? Why couldn't she be the kind of drunk who didn't remember anything?

"Is it too late to go to Karen's?"

"Nope. I'll call and tell Karen we're on our way. They'll be waiting."

She noticed his hands on the cell phone. He had workman's hands, big, with veins showing, nails broken, knuckles swollen. Clean, though. It was so refreshing to be with a guy who didn't have manicures.

He also didn't have the sports car she expected.

"Here she is, my pride and joy," Eric purred, opening the passenger door to an orange Volkswagen van with a white top. "She's a classic, nineteen seventy-two, super reliable, great for carting things around. Henry's mother, Gladys, had her sitting in her garage, mint condition. Gladys wanted to buy a red Cadillac, if you can believe that, so she let me have this baby for a song."

Tessa hoped it wasn't a very long song, because this baby was downright ugly. It, too, was clean, and about all you could say for it was it got them where they were going. But who was she to criticize his taste in transportation? Personally, she was with Gladys, she'd have gone for the red Caddie in a heartbeat.

There were cracks in the sidewalk leading to Karen's condo, and someone had used spray paint on the wall. Karen's adorable sons dove at Eric the moment the door opened, crawling up his legs, wrapping their arms around his waist, shouting for his attention.

Simon was a big, muscular boy, tall for five, with Eric's blue eyes and Karen's smile. Simon was thin and angelic looking. Both boys had masses of curly red hair. Karen introduced them to Tessa, and after a bit of prompting they released Eric and shook hands formally with her.

Simon gave her a suspicious look. "Are you one of my Uncle Eric's girlfriends?"

"Heavens, no." Tessa gave a nervous little laugh and her face got hot. "He just gave me a ride over to your house."

"Cause Uncle Eric has lots of girlfriends. Auntie Sophie says he does catch and release," Simon told her. "Like with fish, but Uncle Eric does it with ladies." He burst into giggles and Ian did, too, both of them chanting *"Catch and release, catch and release."*

"Boys, put a plug in it." Eric picked them up, one under each arm. "We're outta here, see you later. Bye, ladies." He didn't quite meet Tessa's eyes.

"Sorry about that," Karen said when the door closed behind them. "They've just got so much energy. Come and sit down, I've got fresh coffee made."

"That's what's great about kids," Tessa managed in a feeble tone.

Lots of girlfriends? Catch and release? Lucky she didn't have any feelings for *him* anymore. Eric Stewart was obviously the desk clerk at Heartbreak Hotel, and she'd be wise to remember it.

Just before ten, Eric unlocked the street door and walked along the dim hallway to his apartment. What had Karen told Tessa in the two hours he'd been out with the boys sending shoe clerks batty? He'd gone from getting kissed brainless on the street and asked about his sex drive to frostbite that damned near took his nose off when he stuck it out and offered her a ride home. He'd actually been looking forward to being alone with her again. He'd heard Tessa and Karen laughing when he came in the door. And then he'd suggested the ride home, and she'd given him that look that would have frozen his blowtorch in midflame.

"I've called a cab, thanks anyway," she'd snapped at him. Maybe she was getting her period. Maybe she had personality disorder. Women, who knew? She'd managed to knock the hell out of a perfectly good mood, so he'd stopped at a pub on the way home just to confirm that barbunnies still found him irresistible. They did, but it must be his age, because tits and ass just didn't appeal the way they once had.

His building was so old there wasn't even an elevator, which made him glad he'd chosen an apartment on the main floor. At least nobody complained about all the junk he dragged in. Hauling tons of scrap iron in and out also saved him what he'd have spent on a gym membership, so there were lots of perks to both the place and his hobby.

He unlocked his door and went in, flicked on a couple of lights, and gulped down a glass of water. He looked at the dog he was building and decided not to make life-altering changes tonight. The message light was blinking on his machine, but he wasn't in any mood to listen. Whatever it was would keep till morning. He was heading for the shower when the phone rang.

"Eric?" It was Karen, and the tension in her voice set alarms off in his head. "Eric, where were you? I've been calling and calling. The police came here just after you left." She took a quick little gulp of air, and he waited for the worst, heart hammering.

"Eric, Jimmy's dead."

9.

I don't know whether to kill myself or go bowling

It took a moment to sink in, and then a horrible thought struck him. Could a guy die from a broken nose? He didn't think so. He'd never heard of it happening, but he wanted desperately to call Sophie and find out. Could it take a whole week to happen?

His throat tightened. "How—what did he die from?"

"He was just walking along the street. The detective said that they're—the police are treating it as a suspicious death. The coroner has to do the—the autopsy before they can say for sure what happened."

Jesus. "I'll be right over."

"Anna's here now. It's okay, you don't have to come. I just wanted you to know."

Would Anna be able to calm Karen down? She'd probably spout some crap about karma, and things being written in the stars, and it all being for the universal good, and souls choosing their destiny. Was that going to be much help?

Karen was still talking. "I called her when— when I couldn't get you. She's staying tonight." Karen sounded like a small, frightened girl. "I have to work tomorrow."

"No, you don't, sweet pea. Take the day off. I'll call the witch for you right now, tell her why you can't make it."

"No, no, I have to go to work. There's this thing with a customer. I need to talk to Junella." She sounded hysterical, so he dropped it. Maybe it was better for her to work, keep her mind off it.

"What about the kids? Want me to take them somewhere, give you a break?"

"Sophie's taking them to Science World. Anna called her already."

"What else did the cops say, sweet pea?"

"They asked a lot of stuff about the fight you had with Jimmy; they already knew about that. And they asked if I'd seen Jimmy this week. The last time I saw him was at the pub a week ago."

Even dead, Jimmy Nicols was managing to make waves.

"Anna's doing my weekly horoscope on her laptop. She says this is a difficult transit, but it's coming to an end soon."

"That's great, Karo." Eric closed his eyes and shook his head. Somebody oughta tell the cops to talk to Anna. They could get her to do one of her fancy charts and figure out exactly what was what, save the coroner a lot of trouble.

"You didn't—they didn't ask you to identify the body or anything like that, did they, Karo?"

Now Nicols had become the body. It didn't really have a bad ring to it.

"Bruno went."

Good old Bruno. Thank god he'd married Anna.

"You sure you don't want me to come over to-night?"

"I'm fine, honest. Anna brought me some melatonin. She says it'll help me sleep. Sophie said it was okay to take it."

"Let me talk to Anna for a minute. And you call me if you need me, anytime in the night, whenever. Do you want me to come over early and talk to the boys?"

"Oh, Eric, yes, please." He could hear relief in her voice. "I'll tell them myself about Jimmy, but I'd like you to talk to them, too. Come early and I'll make blueberry pancakes."

His eyes filled with tears. The kid knew they were his favorite, and in spite of everything, she wanted to please him.

Sweet pea, what am I ever going to do with you?

Karen handed over the phone, and while Anna talked to Eric, she tried hard to figure out how she felt about Jimmy being dead.

Shocked, horrified—no one should end up murdered, if that's what had happened. But there was also an overwhelming sense of relief, and that was followed right away by terrible guilt.

Jimmy was the father of her sons. She'd slept with him; she knew exactly how he snored and farted, how he moaned when he came. At first, his lovemaking had mesmerized her with its intensity, swept her along with its wild, uncontrolled energy. She'd been so happy, knowing that he wanted her. And she'd believed in him, in his dreams of getting rich, of buying a wonderful house for them to live in. "I'm gonna be somebody," he'd say, his fierce dark eyes glowing. That was in the beginning, when he was working steady, when they'd go riding along the dikes on their bicycles. She had those good memories.

Simon barely remembered his father, Ian not at all. She thought of them, asleep upstairs. Jimmy hadn't exactly been a doting father. "Take him, I'm not good with kids," he used to say when Simon was a baby. They'd fought over that, too, because he didn't cherish the boys the way she did. He hadn't cared enough to come back and see them, after that last terrible fight.

He was out of work, and he'd gone out drinking, dropping the kids with the sitter. She was exhausted when she came home and furious when she found out the kids weren't there. He'd come home and fallen asleep on the couch, and she woke him up and raged at him. And he'd hit her, hard.

Eric wasn't around, so she called Sophie. Her sister had barged in the door within twenty minutes, taken one look at her, put ice on her nose, and called the police. Then Sophie had phoned Eric, ignoring the threats Jimmy was mouthing, the fist he kept shaking in her face.

"Don't try that shit on me, Nicols. You'll end up in jail so fast it'll make your head swim. And if I were you," Sophie had said in a deadly voice Karen had never heard her use before, "I'd get out of here before Eric arrives. And I'd stay gone, if you know what's good for you."

Jimmy had rammed some clothes in a gym bag and roared off in their old Toyota, just ahead of the cops. And he'd never come back. Now, he never would.

Anna was off the phone now, brewing a fresh pot of chamomile tea.

"I did Jimmy's chart once, when you two were first together," Anna confessed, her white blond hair swinging as she reached into the fridge and brought out cream. Anna was the only person Karen knew who put cream in chamomile tea.

"It was so bad I figured I'd made a mistake." Anna poured the tea into two mugs and handed one to Karen.

It was good that Anna had come over, but now Karen wished she'd go, because now she had to talk, answer questions, think of words, pretend she wasn't about to fall apart.

"The planets indicated violence and tragedy, and I never told you, Karo. I should have. I blame myself."

"The police asked if I knew who might have wanted him dead," Karen remembered. She gave Anna what felt like a smile and lifted the cup to her lips. She was still shaking so much the hot liquid slopped over, so she set it back down. "I told them that apart from my sisters, and especially my big brother, I couldn't think of anybody."

Anna's round blue eyes widened and she whistled between her teeth. "Good going, kid. I always did want to know what the inside of a cell felt like."

"I didn't really say that," Karen confessed. "Even though it's the truth. I said I couldn't think of anybody. They asked me a lot of questions about the fight in the pub, about Eric hitting Jimmy. Whether I knew Jimmy was coming there that night, whether Eric did. I told them of course I didn't know. I wouldn't have gone if I thought he'd be there. And Eric didn't know either. How could he?"

"There are no accidents; everything happens for a reason."

Somebody was going to kill Anna one of these days if she kept saying things like that.

"They can't think Eric had anything to do with it, can they, Anna?"

Anna bristled. "Whatever they think, it won't change the truth. Eric doesn't have it in him to really hurt anybody, he's a peaceful soul, his chart shows that clearly. Right now there's a lot of disruption, but it's all connected to Venus, which is the planet of love," she said. "There'd have to be lots going on with Mars if he was going to get in trouble with the law, and there isn't."

Karen felt relieved, even though she knew Anna could be making half of it up. She wanted to ask what her chart showed. She wanted Anna to tell her that she was going on a long trip, that there was a handsome stranger in her future, that she'd wake up one morning knowing how to manage the boys without hollering or dissolving into tears when they used her economy-size can of mousse to make snow on the living room rug, or plastered four-hundred Band-Aid strips along the walls in the upstairs hallway, or poured an entire box of laundry soap into the machine and turned it on, laughing with glee when the soap bubbles reached the ceiling.

She loved them, but they scared her. She didn't know how to handle them. She didn't want them growing up like Jimmy. But she didn't want them growing up like her either, loving but never feeling good enough, strong enough.

"Simon's kindergarten teacher told me this afternoon that Simon's a gifted child. She's recommending him for special classes."

"I could have told them that years ago."

Tears came to Karen's eyes when Anna said that.

She knew her sister loved her nephews, but Karen had wondered at times if she really liked them. She never offered to baby-sit; she never took them places the way Eric did. It was always Bruno who did things with them, not Anna.

She and Anna and Sophie were close, but they were very different. Basically, Anna and Sophie were smart; Karen wasn't. Sophie had breezed through medical school. Anna had graduated with honors in education, whereas she'd barely scraped through high school.

What would happen when Simon had homework that she couldn't begin to understand? He'd think he had a stupid mother.

Karen had also told Tessa what the kindergarten teacher had said. Tessa had never been brilliant in school either. Both of them squeaked through agreeing that rocket science and brain surgery were probably boring as hell anyway.

"Simon's lucky he's got you," Tessa had said, and she meant it. "You can teach him the really important stuff that lots of smart guys never learn, like hugs and surprises and compliments and laughter."

"Love," Karen said, nodding. Tessa made her feel better in a way that her sisters couldn't. "If I had a choice," she confided, "I'd want my boys to grow up to be just like Eric. He's good at loving."

Tessa nodded, but Karen could see that she wasn't convinced. She would be, though, it was just a matter of time.

Then Tessa had made Karen laugh telling her about the guy she'd dated right after her divorce. He'd invited her for dinner and then came to pick her up in a motor home. He'd bought steaks and potatoes and expected Tessa to cook them.

"What'd you do?"

"Told him I needed salad things, got him to stop at a supermarket where the produce guy let me out the back door and called a cab for me."

"Ever see him again?"

"Trailer trash? Never. I did date the produce guy a couple times."

Karen wondered if the time would ever come when she'd want to date anybody. Eric had asked her about a membership to Synchronicity and she'd refused. She was a widow now; that was different from being divorced.

She sort of wished Tessa was here instead of Anna right now. Maybe together they could figure out how a smart mother would go about telling her boys that their father was dead.

10.

Hatched, matched, and dispatched

Simon and Ian met Eric at the door on Friday morning. It was barely seven, and they were still in pajamas. Simon's were blue with Batman, Ian's yellow with Teletubbies. They each took one of Eric's hands, jumping around with excitement. "Uncle Eric, guess what?"

Eric waited for them to tell him, trying to figure out how to answer.

Simon didn't wait for a response. "Auntie Sophie's taking us to Science World. There's a big mouth that you climb in and slide down into a stomach and then you get to come right out the bum part. Just like poop."

The two of them laughed uproariously.

Simon added, "And Mommy said a policeman came here. He said my daddy died. We won't be seeing *him* anymore. You don't see people anymore when they get dead."

"Yeah, your mom told me. I'm sorry, guys." He herded them down the hall and into Simon's bedroom. He'd spent half the night awake, wondering how to talk to the boys about this. It was a traumatic moment in their young lives. He'd decided that honesty was best, although he wasn't sure what to do when they asked about heaven. It was tough to imagine Jimmy in anything resembling heaven.

He sat down on the bed and they leaned on his knees and looked up at him, all innocent eyes and auburn curls.

"How do you guys feel about that, about your daddy dying?"

"Okay." Simon shrugged. "He didn't live here with us, not for a long time. And Mommy can get a new one. Jenna's mommy got her a new daddy."

"Get a new one," Ian echoed, nodding sagely and swinging on Eric's leg.

"Yeah, well, that does happen, guys, people do marry again." Usually not before the body's buried, though. "After a while, that might be the case, but not now. Not for a while."

Simon was already off in another direction.

"Did he had 'surance, Uncle Eric? My friend Kyle's daddy got 'surance, and if he dies Kyle gets to have lots of money, maybe even a hundred dollars. Kyle's gonna buy a new Game Boy."

Eric felt a little dizzy. How had this discussion gotten so far off-track?

"I don't know about insurance, Simon. I don't think so. But it's not good to just think of money when somebody dies."

"Why not? Our teacher said dead people can't use money anymore, so other people gets to use it for them."

The kid's teacher obviously was the down-to-earth sort. "Yeah, well, that's true, but it usually makes us sad when people die, so we feel sad more than wondering about their money."

"Are you sad 'cause my daddy died?"

He'd talked his way straight into that one. Lucky there was a time and place for lies. "Yeah, I am."

"Now we don't have to watch for him through the pee hole, right?"

"No more pee hole," Ian agreed emphatically, and both of them burst into helpless giggles.

God. Eric rubbed a hand over his eyes. His heart felt like a bucket of rocks, lying in his chest. How come he'd never talked to the boys before about Jimmy? He should have tried; these two had picked up some really strange ideas. He'd try again, but right now he couldn't take anymore of this, not on an empty stomach.

"Did you guys have breakfast yet?"

"Nope, Mommy made us wait for you. She's making blueberry pancakes. And we got maple syrup, and real butter."

"Let's get you washed and into your clothes, so we can eat."

"Auntie Anna's here. She and Uncle Bruno brought us maple syrup. Auntie Sophie's coming, too. Last time she brought us ice-cream bars. Did you bring us anything, Uncle Eric?"

The best of intentions, guys. I was going to explain about your daddy dying and feeling sad and how life goes on. I was going to sugar-coat it all for you. How could I forget about not being able to fool kids?

"I didn't bring anything, but tomorrow I'm gonna take you guys to the park so I can show you how to throw a football."

"We don't got a football."

"We'll go buy one."

Screams of joy.

Hello, football, good-bye Jimmy Nicols.

Monday morning, Tessa decided it was time to
say a firm, kind but definite good-bye to Alistair
Farnsworth, the dot-com millionaire she'd been
out with Friday and Saturday evenings. It was either that or die young from terminal boredom, in
spite of Clara's enthusiasm.

"He's wealthy; he's attractive. He's got to be smart
to have made all that money," Clara had enthused.
"He seems sincere, committed to finding a mate.
Give him an honest try, Tess. What have you got to
lose?"

At the moment, her right ear. Tessa balanced
the phone on her shoulder and sorted through female profiles, searching for someone to sacrifice
to Eric as she listened to Alistair bemoan the fact
that one of his company shares had dropped from
four figures to something behind a decimal point.
They'd been on this news flash for over seven minutes before he switched gears, if you could call it
that.

"Byron Burbank, the North American expert on
blue chip investing is in town tomorrow, Tessa.
He's giving a lecture at the Hyatt. I picked up tickets for us. It'll be very enlightening. You'll get
good advice about where you could invest that divorce settlement you mentioned. I'll pick you up
at eight."

"Thanks, Alistair, but I can't make it."

What was wrong with the man's head—besides
thinning hair—thinking she'd want to go with him
to listen to some poor unfortunate soul named
Byron Burbank go on about the market's ups and

downs? She might be able to pretend a smidgen of interest if Alistair was sexy or if she had a single investment to track, but she didn't and he wasn't.

She had her wonderful house, which she owned outright, which still seemed like a miracle, an '89 white Beretta with red upholstery, and a paycheck that almost covered her monthly expenses, as long as she didn't buy lingerie. And her divorce settlement was perfectly safe stashed in the bank in a savings account, collecting minute interest. Despite Alistair's advice, she wasn't about to risk it on stocks. By her own standards, she was well off. Grandma Blin always said that money was only worth the enjoyment a person got out of it, and by that criterion, Alistair Farnsworth was a pauper.

It was a desert out there. Where had all the heroes gone?

"Aren't you concerned about your retirement, Tessa?"

No. Her ovaries, yes. Retirement, no.

"I'm sorry, Alistair, but I'm busy tomorrow evening." She was busy. She had to cut her toenails and clear away rampant bits of hair that insisted on growing in visible places. Did she want to see him ever again in this lifetime? The simple answer to that was an unqualified no. It was time to cut him loose. She sighed, and wondered how to tell him. They got so upset when you dumped them, begging and promising.

"You know, Tessa," he was droning in her ear, "you're a wonderful woman and some man is going to be very fortunate to spend his life with you, but the chemistry just doesn't seem right between us."

Tessa almost dropped the phone. He was using one of Clara's best lines on her, before she'd had a chance to remember it herself. The little weasel. how dare he dump her before she had a chance to dump him! And he didn't even have the decency to wait five minutes and pretend to be heartbroken before whining, "Do you think you could arrange a date with someone else for me for the weekend? After all, I'm a member of Synchronicity. The understanding was that you people would find me a suitable companion."

Tessa crossed her eyes and stuck her tongue out at the telephone receiver, giving him the finger with her left hand as she exerted superhuman effort and kept her voice perfectly polite.

"Absolutely, Alistair, I'll make certain we locate someone compatible right away. I'll get back to you." She waited until Alistair hung up to smash the telephone down. *The miserable creep.* He could at least have been gentlemanly enough to let her let him go. She snatched up the files, determined to find a perfectly despicable unattractive gold digger who'd take Mr. Dot-Com dipstick on the ride he deserved. It shouldn't be hard—there were a surprising number of members who fitted that profile exactly.

But there were also messages to return, prospective clients to charm, and this nagging need to find someone for Eric. And today was the tenth business day Clara had been absent. It seemed strange that Clara didn't care anymore if her clients dated or not. Each time Tessa phoned her, she seemed to be lying down with a cold cloth on her head. Why didn't she just cut up all Boorish Bernard's best suits, toss him and the scraps out on the driveway, and get on with her life?

She flipped through the female possibilities and

paused at Margaret Westwall, a perfectly despicable, unattractive gold digger. *Yes, Alistair.*

Margaret was a widow, and going by the snapshot on the file, she was okay if you liked the bulldog look, square jaw, lots of mouth, big teeth, droopy eyes. She didn't seem to drool, which was definitely a plus. Clara's notes indicated that Margaret was interested in wealthy men who knew about the stock market. Probably didn't want them to lose money before she had a chance to get her paws on it, Tessa concluded. Margaret wanted to travel, and she considered herself a good conversationalist. The good conversation bit was iffy with Alistair, but the stock market thing was positive.

Tessa called the number on her file. The female voice on the answering machine was starchy and abrupt. Well, maybe the market wasn't doing too well the day she recorded it, Tessa reasoned. Margaret would be a perfect match for Alistair. Although she didn't have firsthand knowledge, she just knew that his penis reacted in direct relation to the Dow.

With hardly a twinge of guilt, Tessa left a glowing and flattering description of him on Margaret's machine, a lot of which centered around his bank account, adding, "If you think this fascinating gentleman would interest you, Margaret, please call Synchronicity and leave a message, and we'll give him your number."

There. She blew out a breath and fished in her purse for a cigarette before she remembered she'd flushed them all down the toilet this morning. It was the third pack she'd wasted that way. Alistair would have pointed out that she could have used the money to invest in a cigarette company.

Now she had to find some unsuspecting fellow

female to offer as a tidbit to Eric, the catch and release king. Out of the mouths of innocent children came truths she might otherwise never have
known. He was good at deception. She'd even been
starting to trust him before Simon summed up his
track record. Hell, she was even liking him a lot.

Poring over the files, she finally located a photo
of Sylvia Delecroix.

Lithe blonde, good teeth and hair, smart busi-
ness suit. Banking specialist, whatever that was.
Clara had noted with her usual optimism that
Sylvia was intelligent, attractive and sophisticated.

She dialed the number on Sylvia's file, and in a
sugary voice that almost gave her diabetes, she ex-
tolled Eric's virtues. To her eternal shame, she
made him sound like a cross between Mel Gibson
and Superman. She didn't add that he thought
women were disposable—*what was wrong with her
head, what else would a garbage man think?*—or that
he wasn't about to use his precious sperm to produce progeny. Sylvia wouldn't care about that anyway; she didn't sound the motherly type. She
might have something to say about Eric's ugly old
van, though. They'd deal with that when the time
came.

When Tessa hung up, she symbolically washed
her hands with scented soap in the bathroom and
then sucked hard on a toothpick, squinting her
eyes at the imaginary smoke she blew out in invisible puffs.

All she had to do now was wait for a call from
poor Sylvia, and with the bio she'd created for
Eric, that call was inevitable. Then Tessa would call
Eric with the good news. She made a bet with herself that she'd hear from Sylvia before noon; God

help the sad woman. This must be what it felt like to slaughter lambs, and what was lung cancer in the face of that? She was just about to lock the office and race out for a new pack of cigarettes when the door opened and Clara walked in.

Tessa immediately gave Clara a guilty hug and sent up a prayer of thanks for delaying the cigarette run. "Clara, honey, how *are* you?"

She looked like hell. The short white hair, usually softly waved and puffy, hadn't been washed or set. Her eyeliner was on crooked, her mascara smudged. She gave Tessa a wan smile.

"Not my best, dollink."

No kidding. And if Clara were anyone else, Tessa would have found her boring, because every sentence in the next half hour began or ended with Bernard. Bernard this, Bernard that, Bernard the next thing until Tessa wanted to gag.

"Bernard's moving out of the house," Clara confided while Tessa was trying to give her a rundown on which clients were seeing which. "He's starting divorce proceedings, he's asking for a ridiculous amount of money from me."

"That's bullsh—" Tessa caught herself. "That's a load of crap. What does your lawyer say?" Tessa had relied totally on her lawyer, Sheldon Winesapp, during her own divorce. "What men think they can get and what they do get are two very different things, Clara," she quoted. "The law does protect women more now than it did years ago."

Like when Maria divorced Walter, for instance. Tessa's mother had sworn for years that she got cheated on the settlement. Tessa couldn't help but wonder what would happen if those two got married again and divorced for the second time. Lord, they'd both be in care facilities arguing about who got the dining room set long after Tessa sold it to pay for their maintenance.

"I'm going to see a lawyer, but I need to talk with you first, Tessa." Clara paused dramatically. "I've decided I have to sell Synchronicity. And I want you to buy it. You're the only one I'd trust with my baby."

11.

Always look a gift horse in the mouth

Openmouthed, Tessa stared at her employer. "Sell? But you love Synchronicity. Don't do anything hasty, Clara. You'll change your mind once this is all over with."

Tears shone in Clara's eyes, but she shook her head. "My mind is made up." She put a hand on her ample bosom. "My heart is broken. I just can't believe in romance anymore. Promise me you'll treat this as a confidence, because if Bernard knows I'm even thinking of selling, he'll insist on even more money in the divorce settlement. And Synchronicity is mine, not Bernard's. You and I can come to a private agreement, honorable, a handshake between friends." Clara's tears spilled over and she dabbed at them with a lace-edged handkerchief. "This is so hard for me, I wouldn't sell to just anyone, Tessa, but for you, dollink—I'll give you Synchronicity at a special price, just because you're you and I love you. And no one needs to know."

Tessa's head was swimming. She hurt for Clara, but wouldn't it be illegal to buy the business and not let Bernard know? There was something called disclosure, she remembered that. But this was Bastard Bernard they were talking about here, she reminded herself. Serve him right to get screwed. And a selfish, greedy little part of her was already thinking of how it would be to be her own boss. She could make this place zing, install a computer, start an astrology link, advertise on the Net. And she had her own divorce settlement just sitting there in the bank. Didn't Alistair say it ought to be working for her?

But the last thing she wanted to do was take advantage of Clara at a time when she was down.

"Did you have a figure in mind?"

Clara named one. Tessa gulped. It wasn't exactly a gift. In fact, her entire savings would barely meet it. There might just be enough left over for a computer, if she got a deal on one.

"It's an established business," Clara said.

And it was one Tessa could get really good at, she just knew it. It was hard not to write a check right then, but she forced herself to say, "I never make major decisions on the spur of the moment, Clara." Marrying Gordon on the spur of the moment had at least taught her that much. "Can I think about it for, say, a week or so?"

Clara didn't look happy about it, but she finally agreed. "But keep it our little secret, promise me, Tessa."

Tessa promised, knowing that her nose was growing.

Clara left. Tessa instantly snatched up the phone and called lawyer Sheldon Winesapp in Calgary. She'd dated him twice, and although he wasn't the man for her, they'd parted on good terms because she hadn't had to dump him, she'd moved to Vancouver instead. When he came on the line, she didn't waste time.

"Sheldon, is it illegal to sell a business and not tell your husband? I mean when he's a total sleazeball and planning on divorcing you because he's screwing everything that moves? And the business doesn't belong to him anyway?"

Fortunately Sheldon had experience listening to her when she was excited. "Hi, Tessa, long time no see. Is there a separation agreement? Are lawyers involved?"

"Not yet. Maybe on his side, I'm not sure, but for sure not on hers."

"Transactions don't count before a triggering event."

"What's a triggering event?"

"An order for divorce, a separation agreement signed by both parties."

"So there's nothing wrong with her selling me the business and not telling him? Nothing could happen to me if I bought it?"

"Not a thing. There might be a slight problem for the wife if the other lawyer finds out *after* the triggering event and no funds have been disclosed, but beforehand, *nada*. And you're in the clear regardless."

Tessa felt like jumping up and down and squealing with joy. Instead, she thanked Sheldon, realizing too late that she'd been way too effusive.

"I'm missing you, Tess. I'll be in Vancouver for a trial in a couple weeks," he said. "Maybe you could show me the sights?"

"Absolutely." Hell and damnation, he was a good lawyer, but he was also a twenty-four-carat bore.

And the sights he wanted to see were covered by her underwear. Well, she'd worry about Sheldon later.

She got off the phone and glanced at her watch. It wasn't even noon yet, and already she'd been dumped by a millionaire, hit on by her last lawyer, and she was going to buy a business. And oh yeah, she'd betrayed a fellow female by lining her up with Eric

When you're hot, you're hot.

By noon on Monday, Eric was wearing down. He hadn't slept much since he heard the news about Nicols's death, so he'd come to work extra early.

He'd spent the weekend teaching the boys football, hanging out with Karen and his sisters, and then going to bed and wondering how long it would be before the cops came calling to accuse him of murdering Jimmy Nicols. His rational mind told him that was ridiculous, but in the middle of the night, reason wasn't his strong point. Lots of innocent guys went to jail.

He spent the morning doing paperwork in his office and listening to Henry and his mother holler at each other in Cantonese. He'd hired Gladys three days a week, but she volunteered the other two. It was a good thing he loved the van the way he did.

He'd been going to tell them about Jimmy dying. Henry and Gladys knew his family probably better than he did. But this morning he hadn't been able to face the feeding frenzy that would follow, so he put it off

They'd want to know every detail, and they'd go over it and over it, and Eric had already had enough of that with his sisters.

Just before noon, the smell of something deliciously pungent and Asian lured him into the kitchen, where Henry was slumped over the table, a bowl of food in one hand, chopsticks in the other.

"Hey, boss, how's it going?" Henry's eyes disappeared into his chubby cheeks when he smiled. "Want some lunch? Mom brought fresh wonton. You see Vince yet?"

Eric spooned wontons into a bowl and added broth.

"Nope. What's up with Vince?" Klavinski was a good driver; he'd worked for Eric for three years now. He just wasn't very smart, but that was an employee problem Eric encountered a lot. After all, how many brilliant little kids dreamed of driving garbage trucks when they grew up?

"Ahh, some weirdo punched him. Vince says customer filled the drop-off bin with rocks covered over with tree limbs, truck couldn't move it. Vince told him take some out; guy went ballistic. That's what Vince says."

Eric knew there was probably more to the story. Vince was six-two and built like a tank, with a temper that spilled over without much provocation. "So what did Vince do then?"

"Hit him back. Busted some teeth. Guy's suing us. Good thing we took out that insurance you bitched about."

Eric nodded and spooned in wonton. Henry had fought him over the insurance, and not for the first time, Henry had been right. The premiums were astronomical, but it looked like they'd be worth it.

At least the guy Vince hit wasn't related to him by marriage. Eric wondered if the policy extended to hitting ex-brother-in-laws in bars and having them die a few days later.

"I'll talk to Vince; we're maybe gonna have to let him go."

Henry shook his head. "Cut him some slack, boss, he told Ma his wife took off with a telephone man. Vince is all cut up over it. Ma's counseling him. Don't worry, when the insurance people call, I'll handle it."

"Better you than me." It was, too. Henry would query them on every single tiny detail, not once but millions of times, until they simply wore down and paid the claim. The adjustor would probably quit and apply for mental disability, but that was the insurance company's problem. Henry was good at his job. He was born to be obstreperous.

"Where's Gladys?"

"Watching *Young and Restless*. She'll be here in a minute."

Five years ago, Eric had bought the lot he'd been leasing up till then, as well as an adjoining property. He'd had this spacious office built and hired an assistant for Henry, who'd been complaining, legitimately, that there was too much work for one guy.

That first assistant lasted three days, the next three one day each. Henry claimed total innocence when it came to why no one could work with him. The applicants told Eric that Henry was controlling, manipulative, nosy, bossy, and impossible to work with. One complained that he ate all day and as a result, she'd gained seven pounds.

Henry Wong was all the things they said. He was also totally reliable, smart as hell, loyal to a fault. He knew everything there was to know about the junk business and had set up the entire computer system single-handed. He was the only one who really understood it, so that made him impossible to replace. Eric had put Henry in charge of finding his own assistant, which was how Gladys came on board.

At sixty-four, Gladys Wong was as tiny as her son was large. Part of the time, they fought like wild dogs, screaming at each other and slamming doors. But in between wars, they ran the office like a finely tuned machine and brought in new contracts in a steady stream due to their connections with the Chinese community. The Wongs were a major pain in the ass, and Eric was grateful for and to them.

"Boss," Gladys hollered as he was finishing his food. "Anna's on the phone."

Eric went into his office and took the call, wondering if the cops had been around again. They hadn't, which was a relief.

"I just checked your natal chart, and Saturn's still messing around with it," Anna reported. "That's what this thing with Jimmy is; Saturn's causing every unresolved issue in your life to surface. I was thinking a deep tissue cleansing would help. I've got a friend who sells herbal stuff and does coffee colonics."

"*Coffee* colonics?" He knew what a colon was, and it didn't take a whole lot of imagination to figure out what adding *ics* to the end might involve. But—coffee?

"Since when did people stop drinking the stuff and start putting it up their butt?"

"It's very effective, Eric. Don't knock it unless you've tried it."

He thought of telling Anna that he really didn't think pouring coffee up his nether regions was going to make a whole lot of difference to the unresolved issues in his life, but he knew that would bring on a lecture about the ignorance of the general populace when it came to alternative healing. So he just thanked her and got off the phone, shaking his head and wondering if she'd managed to talk poor old Bruno into having one of these colonic things. One could only pray that Bruno was tough when it came to resisting Anna and her idiotic ideas.

He was getting a headache. He needed to get the hell out of the office for a while, and he liked driving his own garbage trucks. The grass roots of his business was garbage. He had no qualms about getting his hands dirty, so he found a work order and a truck and got behind the wheel.

It was comforting to take the unit to the site and load up. By the time he'd made the slow trek through rush hour traffic out to the dump and back, he was feeling pretty good. He turned the stereo to a Western station and sang along with someone who didn't want to live if she didn't love him, which was a little extreme, Eric figured.

And just like that, Tessa walked into his head uninvited, long black curls tousled as if she'd just gotten out of bed, brown eyes sleepy and heavy lidded as they'd been when she'd had too much wine last Thursday. Too bad she couldn't just stay drunk all the time; she was a great drunk. Sober was another story.

And with Tessa on his mind, his good mood went south. He swore and tried to shove her back into limbo where she damned well belonged, but she was as stubborn in imagination as she was in reality.

At last, he gave up and grudgingly let her stay. And damn it to hell, she started taking her clothes off. At least she wasn't cutting him down with that mouth of hers, but her breasts were doing a good enough job of making him uncomfortable even without the audio turned on.

The thing that surprised him was the sexual impact the image held. There he was, in bright June sunshine on the Oak Street Bridge, having desperately horny thoughts about a woman he really wished would join the Peace Corps and move to Africa.

He got back to the office, and the day took another turn, right in synch with his fantasies.

"Lady called for you," Gladys reported. "Never called before; this is a new one, huh?" Gladys shook her head and clucked her tongue. "Here's the name and number. Said for you to call back as soon as possible." Gladys handed him a yellow reminder slip that read, *Tessa McBride, 439-9934,* and he cursed himself for giving Synchronicity his business number. The cell had just seemed too intimate that day.

"This Tessa your new squeeze, boss?" Gladys prided herself on her slang. "You're getting smarter, dumping Nema was a good idea; she was bad news, Nema."

"What makes you think I got rid of Nema?"

Gladys's unlined face, round as the moon, split into a grin. "She hasn't been around wearing that black raincoat for over a week now; she's history. She had bad *chi,* that one."

The raincoat thing had started to wear thin. Nema never wore anything under it, and his office was anything but soundproof. He didn't bother asking Gladys what *chi* was. It probably had something to do with colonics, and there was no point telling her to stay out of his personal business, he'd tried before. She just pretended she didn't understand the English word *nosy.*

He took the memo into his office, surprising Henry, who was sitting at Eric's desk, size fourteen extra-wide trainers propped on a stack of invoices, reading letters whose envelopes were clearly addressed to Eric and marked personal.

"Out." Eric glared at him and jerked a thumb at the door.

Henry moved fast for his size.

Might as well get it over with. Eric made sure the office door was shut and dialed the number.

"Synchronicity, Tessa speaking."

She did have a voice that vibrated in his loins.

"Eric here. How you doing?" Maybe he should tell her about Jimmy dying. Maybe she was over whatever bug had bitten her the other night.

But she wasn't. Without any greeting, and in a chilly, snappy tone, she said, "I have a lovely woman named Sylvia who's willing to meet you." She made it sound like a small miracle that anyone would agree to that, and he decided against telling her his brother-in-law had been murdered. He didn't need a pity party.

She gave him a rapid rundown on a beautiful, animated, interesting, warm, physically fit, ambitious female who, if she was anything at all like her bio, should need bodyguards to fend off the hundreds of men hitting on her.

"Sylvia enjoys the finer things in life," Tessa went on, obviously reading from a tip sheet. "She loves fine dining, the theater, symphony and classical music. Her hobbies are petit point, sketching, and working for the Vancouver Symphony as a fundraiser."

What the hell was petit point? "So what's the catch?"

"*I beg your pardon?*"

"If she's a perfect ten, how come she needs a matchmaker?"

"Has it occurred to you that perhaps she's simply *discriminating?*"

He grinned. He had her now. "So *that's* what it is. Well, no wonder you lined her up with *me*, Tessa. Perfect match. Gosh, you're good at this."

She mumbled something.

This was getting to be fun. "Gee, Tessa, I thought I heard you say *fuck off* just then, but I must have heard wrong."

She sounded about ready to explode. "Sylvia's number is 926-5926. I've already given her yours. Strain yourself and try to be polite if she calls." Without another word, she hung up in his ear.

He immediately pressed callback. It was fun tormenting her. It sure beat waiting for the police to come and haul him off to prison.

She had the answering machine on. After the beep, he purred in a suggestive tone, "Sorry, but I didn't quite catch that number, Tess. And I'm really hot to make the call. Sylvia sounds like my kind of gal."

Three seconds later, the phone rang.

"The number you requested—" a man's deep, cultured voice repeated it slowly. "Ms. McBride is not available at this time." When he was done, he broke the connection without waiting for a response.

Eric shook his head with reluctant admiration. Tessa was sly and way too clever for her own good. Who the hell was the voice-over? Did she have guys just hanging around waiting to make obscene phone calls whenever she asked?

There was a tap at the office door, and Henry stuck his head in. For once, his eyes were not only visible, but popping from their sockets.

"Holy doodle, boss, there's a Vancouver city *detective* here to see you." His voice vibrated with excitement. "Name's Michaels, what's up? You murder somebody?" He gave out with his high-pitched *hee hee hee* at what he considered a good joke.

And the last of the fun went leeching straight out of Eric's day.

12.

Napoleon to his valet: Dress me slowly;
I'm in a hurry

"Thanks, Kenneth." Tessa grinned at the sweet older man sitting across from her. "I owe you one for making that call for me."

"I enjoyed it, even if you won't tell me what it's about." Kenneth Zebroff's green eyes twinkled. His white wavy hair was perfectly trimmed, lean, lined face tanned, casual khakis and checkered blue shirt immaculate. At sixty-two, Kenneth was handsome, funny and intelligent. He'd been a pharmacist before his retirement three years ago. Retirement had been forced; it came as a package deal along with the car accident that had left him with one leg that buckled unless he kept a tight grip on his steel cane.

To top off his string of bad luck, his third wife had died suddenly a year ago. He'd had rotten luck with wives. He'd been made a widower three times; his first two wives had also died, the second six years ago, the first seven years before that. He was special to Tessa, because he was the very first client she'd signed up all on her own after she came to work for Clara.

And she'd done her best to find him a companion, but his age and disability were causing problems.

Clara had explained it. "All the attractive women on the over-sixty list are on estrogen, with sex drives that have kicked in big-time all over again, and exercise programs that would exhaust women half their age," she'd said after five women refused to even consider Kenneth. "They're looking for younger men. And women under sixty won't consider a man over sixty, they're having midlife crises, age is a huge issue, and even if it weren't, a guy with a cane is out of the question."

In desperation, Tessa had started matching Kenneth with women from the challenged list—chronic complainers, congenitally unhappy, grossly fat, or physically disabled themselves. Quite a few of them, in Tessa's private opinion, were just plain old wacko.

"Thank you for my rose." Tessa put it in a glass and set it on her desk. "I'm really sorry about Olga, Kenneth."

Olga should be glad to be matched with someone still breathing, Tessa figured. She was as rich as she was plain old miserable, and true to form she'd called and complained about Kenneth. "He gave me the willies," she'd said. "And to top it off he tried to kiss me, I'm looking for a *companion*, not some geriatric sex maniac."

"Did you happen to mention on your sheet that you're only interested in platonic relationships, Olga?"

"What other kind are there among older people?"

Tessa had pulled out Olga's file and, with a red

marker, scribbled FRIGID across it in big block letters.

Poor, dear Kenneth. Tessa longed to find him a
warm, passionate, funny lady of a suitable age; there
had to be one out there somewhere. After he'd
shared a coffee with her and left, she wondered
why she didn't just date him herself. There was the
age difference, though. Well, after she bought the
business, got this place computerized, and hired
Anna as an astrological consultant, she'd run a
check on every single applicant and by hook or by
crook she'd find someone for Kenneth.

There was gonna be a whole lot of shakin' goin
on around here.

"Nothin' to get shook up about, boss," Henry
said. "So you hit Nicols and broke his nose. Week
later he turns up dead. What part's your fault?" He
shook his head, crossed his arms on his chest and
leaned back on the chair in Eric's office. The chair
was one Eric had made from steel rebars, so even
with Henry's considerable weight, it held up fine.
"Guy was a loser, no support for Karen's kids,
broke her nose."

Eric appreciated Henry's loyalty even though
his logic wasn't perfect.

"I wish Detective Michaels thought the way you
do." The detective had gone back and forth and
up and down the pub fight. "I asked Sophie how
often a punch in the nose caused death. She said it
was rare, but it had been known to happen.
Cerebral hemorrhage, she called it."

"Detective said the coroner's doing the autopsy
this afternoon."

Eric nodded.

"Until then they're on a fact-finding mission, that's what he said, right? Should'a let me sit in when he talked to you, boss. I would'a told him what kinda straight-up guy you are."

Why remind Henry that the reason he knew so much was that he'd been listening at the door?

"Well, the good news is they haven't arrested me yet." Eric tried to keep his tone light, but the fact was, he felt horrible. No matter how much he'd detested Jimmy Nichols, he'd never wished him dead.

"The cops can't arrest you without probable cause." Gladys was now standing at the office door, arms crossed on her skinny chest, listening to every word. "Just watch *Law and Order*, you'll see." Her voice was scornful. "Those cops are barking up any tree. They've got nothing; they're just trying to pin the rap on you. Clearing case loads, that's what this is all about." Gladys watched way too much television.

"You need a good criminal lawyer, we know this guy, cousin of Ma's sister-in-law," Henry said. "He got that politician off when they said he'd murdered his wife."

But Gladys shook her head and rattled something in Cantonese to her son, who disagreed and hollered something back, and the war was on.

When the phone rang, the noise level in Eric's office was deafening, and with both his office staff arguing over his criminal career, there was no one left to answer it but him. He waved them out, but they ignored him.

"Morning, Junk Busters." He had to raise his voice to hear himself over the din.

"Eric Stewart, please." The female voice was brisk, cool and businesslike.

"Speaking."

"Sylvia Delecroix here, Synchronicity suggested I call you. I think we have a bad connection, shall I call back?"

Eric made sweeping motions and ferocious faces at his staff and pointed at the door.

Henry and Gladys moved at the speed of turtles, and of course they didn't close the door behind them. Once they were outside, total silence fell. Eric knew they were lurking in the hallway, listening.

"I think the line's cleared by itself." He took the portable receiver with him as he slammed the door and then locked it for good measure. What the hell was he supposed to say next?

"Thanks for calling, Sylvia." Brilliant. He sounded like a pathetic, needy wimp. He wanted to murder his sisters for this. Nope, nope, he didn't. He was going to wipe every reference to murder out of his vocabulary.

"Synchronicity gave me your number. You sound like an interesting man," Sylvia said.

Interesting? Oh, lady, you don't know the half of it.

Maybe she should. Maybe he should tell her right up front he was involved in a murder investigation. It was tough to work it casually into the conversation, though, particularly because Sylvia seemed to be no-nonsense, no small talk.

"When would you like to meet?" She got right to the point.

"How does this evening sound?" Might as well get this over with fast. They could have a coffee at Starbucks. He'd spill the beans about the cops and probably be home in time to watch the last of the rugby game on the tube. Italy was playing Scotland; it would be a good match, take his mind off things.

"Oh, not tonight, I have meetings every evening this week, except for Thursday. We could attend the symphony that evening. They're guest hosting the Russian National Orchestra. I have season tickets. You could reimburse me for them if you so chose."

If he so chose? He was getting a real bad feeling here. What did she think, that he was some cheapskate who didn't know the first thing about dating etiquette? Talk about an agenda. Unless he missed a guess, this lady was a class A ballbreaker. Which accounted for her joining a matchmaking service; any guy he knew would bolt fast right about now. Which was good news, because he'd have a conscience like clear glass when he dumped her on her bossy ass right after the concert.

"I guess Thursday's okay with me."

"Good. I'll just make a note of that here." He could hear her scribbling him down in her Daytimer, as if he was somebody she'd forget unless she wrote him down. She added, "It's probably best if we meet at the Queen Elizabeth Theatre; the program begins at seven. We could dine afterward; there's quite a nice little French restaurant around the corner from the theater, The French Laundry. Have you heard of it?"

At least she had good taste in restaurants. It was one of his favorite spots, but he didn't say so, because he didn't want her to know much about him just yet. He was still figuring out how to play it.

"Sounds fine to me."

"I'll be in the lobby at six-forty-five, wearing a black cocktail suit with a large diamond pin in the shape of a star on the left lapel. I'll leave your ticket at the kiosk, ask for it in my name."

"See you there." He hung up, blew out a breath,

and saluted. "Yes, *Ma-am.*" Making out with Sylvia would be like joining the Marine Corps.

Not that foxhole. Farther down. I told you, don't go there. Aren't you listening, soldier?

Not that it would come to making out. Ms. Sylvia Delecroix was gonna be a one-off. The murder angle was good, but another idea had started forming in Eric's head. If he was going to have to go along with this dating crap, he might as well have fun. It would supply a few laughs to his cell mates.

He walked stealthily across and jerked open the door, but Henry was already several feet away, doing his best to make his ass look innocent. Damn, the guy was good.

A black cocktail suit, huh? Eric sat back down at his desk and gave serious thought as to what to wear on his date. After a few minutes, he called Bruno.

"I need to borrow some clothes." There was a lot of untapped potential in cowboy boots.

Later that afternoon, Eric tried on a shiny turquoise shirt with silver snaps instead of buttons, a string tie Bruno called a bolo, a white Stetson he'd gotten at the Calgary Stampede several years before he married Anna, and a black coat whose cut and style were pure Johnny Cash. The coat was a bit tight in the shoulders and chest, but Eric figured that it wouldn't hurt to look as if he was busting out of the thing. It added to the image he was aiming for.

As Bruno hauled stuff out, he filled Eric in on the visit he'd had from Michaels. "He asked questions about the fight we had that night at Riley's, whether you'd ever made threats against the prick. I told him apart from hearing you say Nicols oughta be drawn and quartered and then castrated, you'd never said a word against him."

"Thanks, I owe you one."

"No problem. Seriously, how the hell you figure Nichols ended up dead?"

"Beats me." Eric was trying the Stetson at different angles and thinking that he was fed up to the teeth with hearing about Nicols, dead or alive. Henry and Gladys were driving him nuts with it.

"At least they haven't arrested me yet."

"I asked Fletcher if he thinks that's likely. He said no way until the autopsy reports come in. You heard anything yet?"

"Not a word, and in the meantime, I don't want to talk about Nicols. I'm gonna enjoy myself planning this date."

"Sort of like a last meal, huh?"

Eric gave him a look, and Bruno took the hint and dropped it. "I'll bet this lady has a thing for cowboys; most women do."

Which was obviously the reason Anna didn't let Bruno wear most of this stuff. "It's not the clothes they're after, Bruno, it's the body underneath."

"You should know, you're the one beating them off with rebar." He waited a moment. "So, did the cops talk to Sophie? Rocky was asking."

"Why doesn't he call and ask her himself, he's got her number." Frustration made him snarl. He'd had it with the whole cop thing, and sometimes Rocky could be dumb as a rock. "Sophie made him those cookies for his birthday, and does he take the hint? It would serve him right if she gave up on him and married some cardiologist who'd bore us all cross-eyed talking about cholesterol and heart disease and diet." Hell, what business was it of his? This matchmaker thing must spread like a virus.

"Yeah, well, maybe diet's got Mercury and Pluto beat all to hell."

Eric shot him a glance. Bruno looked a little down at the edges. "Anna giving you grief?"

Bruno shrugged. "Maybe she's right; maybe I don't read enough. She never said that before we were married, though."

"Look." Eric was about to say his sister was a weirdo, but he stopped because it was Bruno's wife they were discussing. "Women keep changing; they can't help it, it's their nature. Just ignore this astrology thing as best you can, she'll be on some other kick before you know it."

"Yeah," Bruno said in a doleful tone. "That's what really scares me." He reached into the closet again. "Wear this belt, it goes good with the tie. The buckle's a collector's item, pure silver. I got it that time I was in Reno."

The buckle was shaped like a tombstone. On it was engraved, *Rest In Peace*.

13.

BITCH-babe in total control of herself

Tuesday morning, Sophie called before Eric left for work.

"You can rest easy, bro. Nicols died of an aneurysm. A defective artery in his brain ruptured. I called in a favor from a friend in the coroner's office. She just read me the autopsy report. It had nothing to do with him getting punched."

Tension seeped out of Eric, and for a moment he was euphoric. He was finally free of Jimmy Nicols. "So what happens now? With Karen." A nasty thought was surfacing. "She and Nicols weren't divorced. Is she gonna have to fork out to bury him?"

What he really meant was *he* going to have to fork out to bury the guy. Funerals were expensive, and Karen didn't have any money.

"I don't think she's legally responsible, but you know Karen. She's liable to feel it's her duty."

"You're right." He sighed. "Well, at least that'll be the end of it."

"Unless Anna's right and the spirits of the troubled dead hang around."

Sophie had a perverted sense of humor. "By the way, Eric, how's it going with the matchmaker?"

"I've got a date on Thursday that I'm looking forward to."

"Way to go." But for some reason she didn't sound all that enthusiastic. "Maybe you're about to meet your destiny."

If destiny was a pair of black trousers that fit snug around his butt and thighs, as well as the pair of cowboy boots he'd bought on a whim and never worn, then he was on the right track. Eric buffed up the boots and on Thursday afternoon, put on Bruno's finery. He'd remembered to buy a huge cigar, and he stuck that in his chest pocket.

He'd watched enough reruns of *Gunsmoke* to mimic the way a cowboy walked. He parked outside the Queen E and stuck the unlit cigar in his mouth as he swaggered in the doors. He felt like a dork, and the stares he got when he retrieved the ticket and entered the lobby told him he maybe looked like one, too. This was good.

Just as he'd known it would be, the lobby was filled with refined-looking people wearing sophisticated evening dress, the men in suits or tails and the women in formal gowns. He spotted Sylvia Delecroix right away and made his way across the crowded room, directly toward her. She looked elegant, and Eric had to admit she was one good-looking lady, blond and tall and slender in her short black cocktail suit. Her eyes flickered over him, up and down, and away. It was hard to keep from grinning.

He strode right up to her and lifted the Stetson.

"Miss Sylvia?" He replaced the hat and held out his hand, talking around the cigar. "Eric Stewart. A real pleasure to meet you, ma'am."

Her pupils widened, and he saw shock, horror and dismay flicker over her face, but give her credit, after the first moment of awful recognition, she managed to collect herself. "Eric. Eric Stewart, *ummmmm,* how do you do?" She touched his hand and tried to jerk away, as if he had a skin disease.

He grasped hers and held on, giving it five or six hearty up-and-down shakes. "Really fine, Sylvia, really fine." He pitched his voice louder than normal. "Nice to get hooked up with a pretty lady like you. Before I forget, we need to get straight with that little money deal; here we go." He made a show of dragging a wad of bills out of his pocket, whipping off several, and holding them out to her. "I think this'll cover our little agreement, right?"

People nearby were watching. A scarlet stain crept up her neck and suffused her face. She had narrow lips, and they were pressed together so tightly they almost disappeared.

"Not *here.* Not *now,*" she hissed.

"Oh, but I insist, ma'am." He shook his head and waved the money in the air. "Us Stewarts are real fussy about paying our bills, specially when a pretty lady's involved." He gave her what he hoped was a lewd wink.

Her eyes went from side to side, assessing the attention they were attracting. Eric was delighted to notice it was considerable.

She was the type who got red patches when she was upset. She snatched the money from him and furtively shoved it into the little silver bag she wore hooked over one wrist.

"Pretty fancy crowd, huh?" He gestured at the bar with the cigar. "Can I get you a beer or something?"

"No. No, thank you. That bell means the program is about to begin, I think we should go up to our seats."

"Is that what that dinging means? Feature that." He stuck the cigar back in his mouth, took her arm and tucked it firmly under his crooked elbow. "You just hang tight there, Sylvia, and I'll herd us through this crowd of heifers."

A strangled yelp was her only response as he bulldogged their way to the carpeted stairs. The seats were excellent, front and center in the lower balcony, about the same place he usually sat several times a year when he came to the symphony. Eric grinned, touched the brim of his hat, and apologized in a booming voice to as many people as possible as he shouldered his way to their seats.

"This was one damned fine idea, this symphony thing," he said as soon as they were seated. "I been to concerts before; last time was at the Pacific Coliseum, where they have the hockey games? Man, I do love hockey. How about those Canucks, eh? Anyhow, I saw good old Garth Brooks out there. You ever see Garth live on stage, Sylvia?"

She gave her head a slight shake. She was huddled in her seat, slumped as low as she could get without sliding right off onto the floor.

"We'll have to take him in next time he's in town. He's a sight for sore eyes."

Fortunately, Bruno had filled him in. "The man's a living legend. He got lowered to the stage by a crane, and he smashed his guitar when the show was over. I got me a little piece for a souvenir."

"How nice," she croaked, staring straight ahead.

She flicked her eyes at him just once, staring at the cigar. "You do know there's no smoking in here?"

"Oh yes, ma'am, I just like to sorta munch on the end, if you know what I mean. I enjoy a chew of snuff, but I guess there's no place to spit in places like this." He started to wonder if he was overplaying this just a little.

She closed her eyes one long moment. "Don't you think you better take that hat off so the people behind can see?"

He gave her an astounded look. "Yes, ma'am. Don't usually, but anything to please you, Sylvia." With a show of great reluctance, he removed his hat. He placed it on his lap just as the lights dimmed and the symphony director began his introduction.

Eric made sure he clapped harder and louder than anyone else when the man was finished, and he also put his fingers in his mouth and whistled.

When he did that, Sylvia put her hands over her face and muttered, "Oh, dear God." Her face was more mottled than ever, and Eric sort of hoped she wasn't one of these women who had heart attacks early and easily.

As for him, he was having an interesting evening. He hadn't thought about Nicols or Karen or even Tessa for a good hour or two, and the Russian music was superb, filled with fire and passion. But when the haunting strains of the love theme from *Zhivago* filled the theater, his spirits plummeted and a sudden bolt of pure loneliness shot through him.

It would be fine to sit here beside someone he cared about, hold her hand, share this breathtaking music. It would be fun to talk about it afterward over an intimate late night dinner. It would be exciting to drive home and make love with the melodies still alive in their minds and their cells, enhancing the raw physical need for each other. And how come the lady in every one of his fantasies these days resembled Tessa McBride?

Maybe he ought to give this Sylvia an honest chance, tell her that he'd been teasing, laugh a little with her and make the most of what was left of the evening? He turned toward her and changed his mind.

She was sitting as far away from him as she could get, arms crossed over her quite nice perky breasts, shapely legs in dark hose angled so that no part of her touched any part of him. Her narrow mouth was clamped tight as a vise, and she looked mad enough to bite the heads off small animals.

He'd thought earlier that if she was quick witted and had a good sense of humor, she'd see straight through his elaborate charade and they could have some fun with it, but she'd fallen for it, shiny shirt, boots, and cigar.

He wasn't surprised, when intermission came, to have her say, "I have a migraine. I'll skip the rest of the program and go straight home."

"Can I give you a lift?" It was the least he could do, considering.

"Oh no, no, no." Her vehemence left no doubt as to how eager she was to get rid of him. "I'll take a cab, thank you."

He waved one down right outside the theater, handed her in, and gave the cabbie a twenty. He lifted his hat to Sylvia, who ignored him. When she was safely out of sight, he meandered back inside. The bell was tolling for the beginning of the second half. No point wasting the seat. He sat back and allowed the heart-rending music to transport him.

It made a nice change from talking about Nicols. And he had an interesting conversation to look forward to with his own personal matchmaker.

Before Tessa could get the office door shut on Friday morning, the phone was ringing. She picked it up.

"*Good* morning, Synchronicity." She was feeling chipper, even though she hadn't slept much. She kept thinking about owning Synchronicity, and finding more of her own clients.

Sylvia Delecroix was on the line, and she was definitely having a queer spell—queer as in raving, spitting mad.

"—how *could* you be stupid enough to match *me* up with a *drugstore cowboy!* I've never been so humiliated in my *life.*"

It didn't sound right, but this had to be Eric they were discussing.

"—not only turns up looking and sounding like John Wayne, with that *stupid, asinine* cowboy hat and that humiliating jacket, he had a *cigar* in his mouth."

Tessa frowned. Since when had Eric traded garbage trucks for horses? She'd vowed not to touch a cigarette, lit or unlit, until at least noon. Sticking a pencil in her mouth, she sucked hard on the wood as Sylvia spewed invective down the line. She was in full rant.

"How could you *do* such a thing to me! I knew I should have *insisted* that I deal only with Clara. I registered with Synchronicity because she assured me the service had a number of *quality* gentlemen, and then you line me up with this loud mouthed, crude, rude—why, he shoved *money* at me right there in the lobby. People must have thought I was some kind of, of *paid companion*. I don't know how I'll ever face the Symphony Committee again. I blame you personally for this, Bessie."

"Tessa." She bit the pencil in half and put the rubber end back in her mouth. This one was a proper bitch, and for five cents—

She thought of the business that would soon be hers and held her tongue. Sylvia was still rolling along, gathering steam.

"—never been so humiliated in my *life*, he was wearing cowboy boots and this—this horrible *turquoise* satin shirt, and he had a *cowboy hat* on, at the *symphony*, and there are people who *recognize* me—"

Tessa made sympathetic noises, horrified noises, placating noises, and tried to keep herself from grinning at the mental images Sylvia's words created. She propped her feet on the desk and admired her ankles as Sylvia ran down.

By the time Sylvia petered out, Tessa had a clear picture of what Eric had pulled, and an even clearer one of why four men so far had flatly refused to date Sylvia Delecroix a second time. It sounded as if she'd spelled out where, when and how to Eric, which didn't excuse his asinine Hopalong impersonation, but it did point up how totally, utterly dismally dumb Ms. Delecroix really was.

And the amazing thing was that the daft woman had not a clue that he'd been acting. If there was one thing Eric wasn't, it was stupid. He'd set out to piss Sylvia off, and he'd succeeded in spades. The way he'd done it might have been downright funny, but what made her temper sizzle was the

To start your membership, simply complete and return the Free Book Certificate. You'll receive your Introductory Shipment of 3 FREE Zebra Contemporary Romances, you only pay $1.99 for shipping and handling. Then, each month you will receive the 3 newest Zebra Contemporary Romances. Each shipment will be yours to examine FREE for 10 days. If you decide to keep the books, you'll pay the preferred subscriber price (a savings of up to 20% off the cover price), plus shipping and handling. If you want us to stop sending books, just say the word… it's that simple.

FREE BOOK CERTIFICATE

Yes! Please send me 3 FREE Zebra Contemporary romance novels. I only pay $1.99 for shipping and handling. I understand that each month thereafter I will be able to preview 3 brand-new Contemporary Romances FREE for 10 days. Then, if I should decide to keep them, I will pay the money-saving preferred subscriber's price (that's a savings of up to 20% off the retail price), plus shipping and handling. I understand I am under no obligation to purchase any books, as explained on this card.

Name _____

Address _____ Apt. _____

City _____ State _____ Zip _____

Telephone (___) _____

Signature _____

(If under 18, parent or guardian must sign)

CN093A

Thank You!

lll..l..lll...lll.l.l.l.l..l..l..ll.l.l.l.l..l..ll.l..lll..l

Zebra Contemporary Romance Book Club

Zebra Home Subscription Service, Inc.

P.O. Box 5214

Clifton , NJ 07015-5214

PLACE
STAMP
HERE

way he'd made a fool out of Synchronicity, and more exactly, out of her.

Well, maybe he could piss in Delecroix's ear and tell her it was raining, but it wasn't going to work with yours truly.

She dialed Junk Busters without having to look up the number.

A woman with a lilting voice answered. Wouldn't you know he'd have some slavering little schoolgirl working for him.

"I'll see if he's free to take your call, miss," she caroled, and then Tessa jumped when she heard her holler, "Boss, one of your lady friends wants to talk to you, you here or not?"

Maybe the voice was deceiving.

"Hello?"

One of your lady friends? Not bloody likely, Cowboy.

"Just exactly what kind of game do you think you're playing with me, Stewart? I go out of my way for you to meet a perfectly nice woman, and you treat the entire thing like a stupid childish joke, one that only your pathetic little pea brain can appreciate." She was building up a nice thundercloud and it felt great. "I know exactly what you're doing, you know, and it isn't gonna work, so give it up." She snatched a breath. "Just on principle, and out of respect for your sisters, Synchronicity is *not* refunding the money they paid, no matter what. I'm going to do my best to find you a suitable match, and if you had a whit of consideration or respect, you'd stop acting like a *total bloody jerk.*"

"Hey, cool it, Tessa. I was maybe a little out of line with Sylvia. It wasn't that I didn't respect her; I just thought a few laughs would do her good. She's pretty uptight. Did you notice? Who'd ever think a

bright lady would take a little bit of teasing that seriously?"

"Teasing? As in *cowboy boots? At the symphony?* Get
a grip, Stewart. And what's with the cigar?" She
snatched up the paper he'd filled in. "It clearly
states right here on your info sheet that you *don't
smoke.* I *told* her you didn't smoke. She specifically
said she didn't want anyone who *smoked.* None of
our clients, men or women, want anybody who
smokes. No one with even a trace of brain cells
smokes nowadays." Which was exactly what had reduced her to chewing on pencils.

"Well, you didn't tell me that when you gave me
her bio, did you? And anyway, I haven't smoked
for years. I gave it up when I was twenty-three, it's a
filthy habit. But it doesn't say anywhere that I can't
hold an unlit cigar in my mouth, does it?"

Filthy habit. That was hitting way too close to
home. Tessa yarded the pencil stub out of her
mouth and threw it violently into the garbage.

"If you think for one moment that I'm going to
spend my precious time lining you up with sincere
women just so you can act out your juvenile fantasies, bean brain, you've got *another . . . think . . .
coming.*"

One moment's silence. A deep, heartfelt sigh
from him, phony as hell.

"Sorry, Tessa. It was an innocent joke. And how
come I spend most of my time apologizing to you
when I haven't done anything wrong?"

"Beats me," she snarled. "Do you think it could
possibly have to do with your devious, twisted personality?"

"So does this mean I get kicked out of the dating pool?"

She knew he was grinning. *Don't you wish,*

Stewart. Damn the man, he knew she had to find him another date, it was part of Clara's ridiculous contract. The first thing she'd do when Synchronicity was hers would be to change that asinine contract.

"I'll find you another lady fast, and so help me, Stewart, you'd better try a little bit harder next time."

His voice was liquid honey. "Or what, Tessa? That sounds like a threat."

"It is a threat. I'll call your sisters and tell them exactly how you're wasting their money."

"Ouch. You really know how to hurt a guy. Okay, I'll be on my best behavior from now on, cross my heart."

"You haven't got one," Tessa snorted and then gave up even trying to talk like a lady. "I've more faith in a fart in a hurricane than I do in your promises, Stewart."

14.

Good girls go to heaven.
Bad girls go everywhere.

Eric laughed. "I'm so glad you haven't lost your way with words, Tess. You had me worried there for a while." He'd been wondering how long it would take before she called and reamed him out. He'd been looking forward to it. The only other thing he had to look forward to today was paying for Jimmy Nicols's funeral.

There was charged silence, and he figured she was gnashing her teeth and trying to get hold of herself. It must have worked, because in an entirely different tone she said, "You still interested in that gift membership for Karen? Because you were right, she needs something in her life. Do you want to go ahead with it?"

"I did ask her, she said no. But even if she'd agreed, I don't think that's a good idea right now, Tessa."

"I wasn't thinking this minute. I was thinking maybe in a couple weeks. Maybe she'll change her mind, I could talk to her about it. Not all our male clients are like you, you know. I'd find someone who's perfect for Karen."

"You haven't spoken to her recently." Suggesting a dating service before the funeral wasn't something Tessa would do.

"Not since I was over there."

"Well, her husband died; a blood vessel burst in his brain. The service is Saturday morning at ten. Would you like to come?"

He wasn't joking. Having Tessa there might take some of the sting out of footing the bill. He'd gone for the small economy size, with cremation, but it still bugged him to have to bury Nicols. Just as Sophie figured, Karen had decided it was up to her. And Anna had reinforced the decision, telling Karen it was a good idea, because it would give Karen something Anna called closure.

Of course, he'd agreed, even though he figured that kind of closure was right up there with the colonic, but he didn't say so to Karen. She'd been distracted and nervy and upset enough all week.

"This is the husband who broke Karen's nose?"

"Yup."

"I'm surprised you didn't murder him yourself."

"Why, thank you, Tess. For a while there, the cops thought I had. We had a fight, I broke his nose, and a few days later, he died. At first, the cops thought the two events might be closely related."

Silence. And then, in a small, contrite voice, she said, "Sorry. Me and my smart mouth. I had no idea. I didn't mean that I thought you'd ever murder anyone."

He was getting a vote of confidence from Tessa McBride?

"You were always good about protecting your sisters, though," she added. "I remember when Sophie and I were about nine and that Patterson kid threw rocks at us, you chased him down and scared him half to death and then made him apologize. I always envied Sophie, having a big brother who watched out for her."

"Yeah?" This conversation was blowing him away; she was suddenly being so nice to him. He should have told her about being a suspected murderer sooner. "Patterson ended up playing second string for the Lions. I always hoped he wouldn't remember that little incident."

She giggled.

He wanted her to giggle more; it was infectious. But she sobered and said, "I shouldn't laugh; the thing about Karen's husband isn't funny. Is there anything at all I can do for her?"

"Maybe just drop by. Make her laugh. She really had fun with you the other evening."

"Sure. I could even tell her about this guy who pretended to be a cowboy at the symphony." There was a smile in her voice.

He smiled back and drawled, "Go ahead, make my day."

She laughed. "Okay, Clint. And I'll sort through the files and find you another babe."

"There's a better way, y'know." He'd been giving this a lot of thought. "You could come out with me yourself, sort of like an educational thing. You're an expert at this matchmaking stuff; you could give me pointers on what I'm doing wrong. A school for the romantically challenged. What do you think?"

She made a noise that could be called a snort. "You're a devious man, Stewart. I shudder to think what you'll come up with next."

"It would be a kind thing to do, Tessa. Altruistic.

You could start maybe tonight. We could do something easy, like go to a movie, have a pizza. What'd'ya say?"

"If shoes were clues, you'd be barefoot, Eric. I'm not on the menu."

He was still laughing as he hung up, and almost immediately the phone rang again. He snatched it up.

"I knew you'd change your mind, I'll pick you up at—"

"Eric." Sophie's voice was tense. "Can you come over to Karen's right away?"

Adrenaline shot through him and he shot to his feet. "What's wrong? Is she okay? Are the kids—"

"Nobody's physically injured. There was a bad scene at Junella's and Karen's hysterical. I've given her a shot. Anna's on her way over, Bruno, too. We need to have a family conference."

Twenty-three and a half minutes later, Sophie met Eric when he came charging in the door of Karen's condo.

"What the hell's going on?"

At first glance, everything seemed calm enough. Ian and Simon sat at the table eating peanut butter–and–jam sandwiches, one on either side of Bruno. Anna was pouring tea.

Sophie said to the boys, "You guys take your sandwiches in the TV room and watch cartoons, okay?"

Simon shook his head. "We can't eat in there. We're not 'lowed cause Ian spilled Spaghettios on the rug."

"You can this once. I'll take the blame if anything spills," Sophie declared, placing the food on small plates and escorting the boys out of the room.

Eric sat down in the chair where Simon had been and shot to his feet again when he hit a puddle of milk.

"Damn." He scrubbed at his rear with a towel Anna tossed him. "Okay, what's happening? Where's Karen?"

"Zonked out in bed," Anna said. "She was screaming and laughing and crying all at the same time, so Sophie gave her a shot. It calmed her down, in fact it knocked her cold. I don't really agree with tranquilizers. It's better if the person can get in touch with their emotions and ask what's really wrong, or simply watch the feelings as they happen; that way it's easier to embrace them and just gently let them go—"

"Anna, can you just cut the crap and tell me what exactly happened here?" Eric's head was starting to pound.

Sophie came back in. Relieved that at least one of his sisters was still sane, Eric turned to her.

"What gives, Soph?"

Sophie flopped into a chair and heaved a sigh. "I got a call at work from Junella at Scissor Happy. She screamed at me that Karen had gone nuts and I'd better come and get her or an ambulance would pick her up. I found someone to take over for me and when I got to the salon, it was some kind of nightmare." She shook her head and ran her fingers through her hair.

"Clients were running around with towels and rollers on their head, Junella was hyperventilating, and there was this half-bald woman in the middle of it all crying and screaming about a lawsuit. I finally got the story out of Junella. Karen had been working on the woman's hair. Her name is Myrna Bisaglio, and my guess is she was giving Karen a hard time over the cut or color or something. Anyhow, according to one of the other operators, Karen just suddenly snapped. She grabbed electric clippers and cut a wide swath right down the center of the old bat's head. The woman was too shocked to move so Karen did another one. Good job, too, she cut a bald strip about four inches wide, smooth as a baby's bum."

There was silence as Eric digested Sophie's words.

It was Anna who giggled first. She put a palm over her mouth, but she couldn't hold it back, and within seconds they were all laughing.

Eric was the first to pull himself together and think of the logistics.

"Junella must have insurance to cover stuff like this, but she's going to try and make Karen pay, you can bet on that. I'll give Fletcher a call and find out what the legal ramifications are."

Sophie nodded. "Good idea. Junella hollered as we were leaving that Karen's fired, not to show her face in the salon again. Bet she tries to hold back on the wages she owes her, too."

Eric said, "We'll just see about that."

"If she's fired, maybe that's the best thing that could happen," Anna declared. "The universe has obviously arranged this so that Karen can make a new beginning, find a place where she's appreciated, where there's potential for spiritual growth. There wasn't at Scissor Happy. Junella was always jealous of her. Junella really projects her own inadequacies on everyone around her. I mean, we all do, but she's *extreme*. It helps so much to know that projection is perception."

Sometimes Eric wondered if Anna was on the same planet as the rest of them, never mind the same page. Bruno rolled his eyes and exchanged a look with Eric.

"Karen needs a holiday. She needs to get away by herself for a while," Sophie interpreted.

That made sense to Eric, and he nodded. "She's had an emotional meltdown; that's for sure."

"So what can we do?" Always practical, Bruno's concern was mirrored in his face.

"How much time do you figure she needs in order to get it together, Soph?" A plan was beginning to take shape in Eric's head, but it would take the cooperation of all of them to implement it.

Sophie said, "Ideally, six weeks. At the least a month."

"This is just a suggestion; see what you all think," Eric said. "Karen still misses Mom and Dad—why I'll never know, but she does. So I'll pay for a plane ticket to Mexico and make sure she's got enough money so she doesn't have to rely on those two for anything when she gets there. I'll cover her mortgage and expenses here while she's gone, so she doesn't have that to worry about. But that leaves the boys. She has to know they're taken care of, or she won't agree to go."

"I've got leave coming from the hospital," Sophie said. "I'll take Simon and Ian for the next week or ten days. Simon's kindergarten is finished for the year. We can visit parks and do fun things."

"Great." Eric turned and looked expectantly at Anna, sitting on his left. After all, she was the only one who didn't have a nine-to-five job. She was peeling polish off her nails with her head down and her hair covering half her face, and she didn't look up.

But Bruno leaped eagerly into the gap. "We'll take them for the rest of the time, right, Anna?"

Anna didn't answer, and Eric saw her fingers curl into knots on her lap. "Well, I do have that spiritual intensive I registered for months ago. I can't really cancel now; it's a two-week course. And I'm not convinced that sending Karen away is the right answer, because wherever you go, there you are."

That bit of philosophy went sailing right over Eric's head. He knew better than to question it. Instead, he stuck to the practical.

"When is this course of yours, Anna?" He was trying to figure out whether he could possibly manage Ian and Simon on his own. Maybe he could get Gladys and Henry to pitch in, because he'd need all the help he could get. He'd watched his nephews in action, and it wasn't pretty.

"The first two weeks in August." She sounded sullen.

Eric was studying his pocket calendar. "That means the kids can spend a couple weeks with you, and then I'll take them."

Anna was still staring at her damned nails.

"Well, I don't know—" she sounded as if she was about to refuse, but again Bruno jumped in with both feet.

"I'll make sure I'm at home. I can do a lot of my work away from the office. I'll take care of them."

"Great. Thanks, Bruno." What the hell was wrong with Anna? Eric had expected her to offer to take the boys for the whole summer.

Bruno added, "We can take them away on a holiday, Anna. We'll go camping. We can go to that lake where we went on our honeymoon; the boys would love it there."

Anna looked unhappy. "I'm not sure if I can get away, I do have appointments for readings all summer, Bruno."

"Anna, for God's sake, this is a family emergency." Bruno gave his wife a disbelieving look. "Call those people and tell them to come in before we go or after we get back. The planets aren't going to go on strike just because you change around a few astrology readings."

"Honestly, Bruno, that really shows how little respect you have for what I do." Anna's face was getting red, her voice rising, her eyes narrowing. "Just because I'm not doing a nine-to-five job anymore doesn't mean I'm not working. Just because I'm doing something outside the box doesn't mean it's not important."

Bruno eyes narrowed. "I know that. Don't get going on this again, Anna. We've been over it and over it." He crossed his arms on his chest and got a stubborn look on his face. "I want those boys, I want to take them fishing; I want to play catch with them. I want to take them camping and roast wieners and tell ghost stories." He glared at her. "I want to take them to matinees, go swimming with them."

Anna huffed out an exasperated sigh. "It sounds to me as if you don't just want to get in touch with your inner child. You want to actually be a kid again yourself. You ought to take a good look at that, Bruno. Where is that coming from?"

To Eric's amazement, malleable old Bruno gave his wife a killer glare and said, "That's enough of that shit, Anna. Your theories are one thing, but this is family we're talking here."

And just like that, she caved, but not with good grace.

15.

Tulips are the vodka of flowers

"Okay, okay, we'll *take* them. But I want to be back to go to the intensive. The instructor already said I have a lot of potential for channeling, I just need to develop it."

Jesus. Eric figured his dotty, selfish sister could use a course in family relations and generosity taught by her husband, but he wasn't about to say so and have her change her mind again. Instead he gave a sigh of relief and said, "Okay, it looks like we've got this sorted. As long as Karen agrees, I'll book her a ticket to Mexico. The damned funeral is tomorrow. You think she's in any shape to go, Sophie?"

"We'll let her decide."

Eric nodded.

Sophie said, "You gonna call the parents and tell them she's coming, or you want me to do it?"

"I'll do it." It probably wouldn't do any good to tell them Karen needed their help, but he'd do it anyway. "Maybe you could talk to Karen, though,

Soph? She's liable to get it in her head that she won't go away without the kids."

Sophie thought about it. "I don't think so. I think she's exhausted, physically and emotionally. She's overwhelmed with everything. She's asleep right now, but the shot I gave her will wear off in a couple hours. I've got to go back to work, but I'll come back about six and stick around for the weekend."

Bruno shot Anna a defiant look. "I'm gonna take the kids to the park now for a couple hours and then we'll go for burgers. We might see that movie that's on, the one about dinosaurs. I've been wanting to see it. You coming, Anna?"

"Bruno, you know I can't. I've got to meditate, and then I've got my yoga class."

"I'll take the kids on my own."

The doorbell rang, and Anna shot to her feet. "I'll get it. I'm leaving anyway. Bye everybody."

She waved a hand in Bruno's direction, but she didn't look at him. There was silence as she grabbed her handbag from the counter and hurried down the hall to the door.

"Everyone's in the kitchen, just go straight through," Eric heard her say, and a moment later Tessa walked in.

She was carrying an immense bouquet of red and yellow tulips, and Eric could see she was ill at ease when she found them all there. Her eyes went from one to the other and met his full-on.

"Hey, Tessa, give me your coat." He got to his feet and waited as she slipped her raincoat off. He hung it in the closet.

Sophie said, "You remember Anna's husband, Bruno Lifkin?"

Tessa shook her head, so Sophie made the introductions. "You want a coffee? I'm about to make a fresh pot. And let me take those tulips. They're totally beautiful. Karen's gonna love them."

"Where is Karen?" Tessa handed the flowers over.

"Asleep. Come sit down and we'll explain." Eric patted the chair Anna had vacated, right next to him.

She sat, and he could smell her perfume. Her hair had shiny raindrops hidden in the thick dark curls. She was wearing a short denim skirt, and no stockings. She crossed her legs, great legs. He noticed her hand when she reached down to put her handbag on the floor beside her chair. She had good hands, strong and long-fingered. No rings. Damn, she was one sexy lady.

Her voice was hesitant. "Is—is anything wrong? I decided to drop by after work, I tried to reach Karen at the hair salon, but maybe I had the wrong place because the woman who answered said Karen wasn't working there anymore."

"She isn't." Sophie poured a cup of coffee for Tessa. "Karen sort of lost it at work today and her boss fired her. She's sleeping just now."

"What can I do to help? Can I take the kids for the weekend?"

Classy, this lady. Anna could learn from this.

"Thanks, I think we've got the kids sorted, but if you and Eric could maybe stick around for a while?"

Tessa tensed, but then she nodded. "Absolutely."

Sophie glanced at her watch. "I have to get back to the ER, Bruno's taking the kids out, but somebody should be here when Karen wakes up. I didn't give her a very strong sedative. I'll be back about eight-thirty, nine."

Bruno went to get the kids.

Sophie left, and the excited boys burst into the kitchen, searching for shoes and jackets. Eric and Tessa helped. After a short, frantic, noisy time zipping zips, fastening shoes, and locating an action figure Ian insisted had to come with him, Bruno got them out the door and silence fell in the small yellow-painted kitchen.

Eric hadn't noticed till now that there were plants in the window, crumbs on the counter, fingermarks on the cupboards, Lego pieces scattered around, artwork on the door of the fridge. The tulips blazed. And there was him and Tessa and with any luck at all, Karen would go on sleeping till Soph got back.

A little block of time with the lady. What would she do if he came on to her? "More coffee?" Eric lifted the pot and set it down again when she shook her head.

"I've had too much caffeine today." She gave him a look. "Rough day at the office, lots of complaining."

"Yeah, I heard." He winked at her.

She smiled and shook her head, then waited until he sat down, across from her this time because it seemed silly to take the chair right beside her when they were all alone, even though he really liked it there.

"Eric, can you tell me exactly what happened with Karen, or is it confidential?"

"Nope, it's the sort of thing that ought to be posted as a warning to nasty customers on the walls of beauty salons." He related the story, enjoying the way her dark eyes widened and her mouth dropped when he got to the head-shaving bit. He liked her with her mouth open.

"Omigod." He could see her struggling with the

urge to laugh and losing. A giggle bubbled **up and** out, and she put her palm over her mouth.

"Sorry, sorry, I just keep seeing—" she lost the battle. Between chortles she gasped, "It's perfect, good for Karen." She sobered and added, "Maybe not so good, though. She lost her job. Will she have trouble getting another one?"

"Who knows?" He hadn't got that far yet. "Losing her job isn't the worst part. Losing her cool is what has me worried." He explained what the family had decided to do.

"I love the way all of you support one another."

He shrugged, pleased but also a little embarrassed. "Hey, it's business as usual. All families hang together in a crisis."

"Nope." She scowled and toyed with her coffee mug. "Mine doesn't, not in the same way. But I guess it's harder when there's only one kid."

"Doubly hard when your folks are split up."

"It wouldn't even be that bad if they'd only just make up their minds once and for all to *stay* divorced." Her voice and her face reflected her disgust. "Would you believe that as we speak, my mother is probably somewhere on the freeway on the back of a motorcycle driven by my dad? Who, I might add, has two citations for speeding already on that thing."

She did righteous really well. "What's Maria doing riding around on the back of Walter's motorcycle?"

"They're *dating*. After years and years of hating each other, now they've decided to *date* again."

He wanted to laugh at the appalled, outraged expression on her face, but he didn't dare. "So what do you think brought on the peace settlement?"

She held out her hands, palms up. "Who knows? For years I've listened to Maria go on about Walter's faults, how she was way too young when they met, how he took advantage of her, how she should never have married him—this, you understand, even though she was five months along with me at the time. Which always made me feel responsible for the whole mess." She blew out an exasperated breath. "Then she suddenly broke the news that they were seeing each other again." She paused and then added, "It really bugs me." Her voice dropped and she leaned toward him.

Her shirt was high necked, which was a real shame.

"I think they're even having *sex,* Eric. They go across the border to this pub and then they don't come back until the next day. Mom even told me the name of the motel they stay at, in case I need to get in touch with her. It's absolutely gross."

"Sex, huh?" He clucked his tongue. "At their age. What are they, in their fifties now? That is revolting." Eric tried to keep a straight face and couldn't manage it. He broke up, and after a minute, she did, too.

"Well, the very idea of my parents in bed together is enough to send me running to a nunnery."

He gave her a long, lazy look, imagining her in bed instead. "I'd give that more thought if I were you. I don't think it's a step you ought to take as a protest gesture. Why not try burning something instead?" *Like your underwear?*

"That's a thought. My birth certificate, maybe?"

"I'm with you there. I knew early on that having kids should be a licensed operation."

"Your parents weren't around much, were they?

I always thought it was so romantic, you guys having musicians for parents. Mine were so boring: salesperson, insurance adjuster."

Eric snorted. "I'd have traded Sonny and Georgia for almost anybody else's folks. We grew up with a string of sitters, because they spent most of their time traveling with the band, playing gigs in every small town in B.C. The only times they stayed home for any length of time was when Georgia had a baby. Thank god somebody clued them in about birth control after Karen was born or I could still be raising kids."

"Didn't you have a woman staying with you? Flaming red hair, long black dresses. Karen used to call her Auntie Mo."

"Yeah, our aunt Maureen, Sonny's sister. She never married, fancied herself an artist. She painted, never sold a thing. Dad talked her into living with us when I was fourteen. It meant there was an adult on the premises, so social services couldn't step in, which I think they were threatening to do by that time. Maureen was a token babysitter; she had a major drinking problem, spent most of her time in her room. Poor old Mo, Soph says she was suffering acute depression as well as alcoholism."

"She still alive?"

"Nope, dead. She died of liver cancer when I was in my early twenties. She'd been sick for a while; she and I were the only ones living at home by then. The girls all moved out. Sophie and Anna were living in residence at university, and Karen had an apartment with three other students from the School of Hairdressing. I was just getting the business started, running it out of the house. But right after Maureen died, the parents sold it, so I had to find somewhere else to set up shop."

"Wow. Weren't you pissed off at them?"

"Big-time. I still am, matter of fact."

She propped an elbow on the table and leaned her chin on her hand.

"I mean, first they leave you to raise your sisters, and then they boot you out of the house. That's straight out of Dickens. What's up with them, anyway?" She watched him, brown eyes big and sympathetic.

He didn't want to think about Sonny and Georgia, and he really didn't want to talk about them. It always made his gut burn. "It's pretty simple. Some people should never have kids."

"Well, they stayed married; that has to count for something."

"Maybe it's easier to stay married when you have no sense of responsibility."

"You have, though, maybe they knew that. You did such a good job raising your sisters. It's amazing, when I remember how you were with them. How you still are."

He shook his head. "You remember wrong. Mostly, I ran the household by bullying the girls into submission." The memory made him squirm. "No fourteen-year-old boy can do a proper job of parenting. That's why Karen's so screwed up now. And look at Anna, out there in la-la land."

After tonight's performance, he wondered if Anna had more than a little of her parents in her. He was also starting to worry about her marriage.

"Is that why you don't want kids? Because you figure you wouldn't do right by them?"

She really went for the jugular. He really didn't want to talk about this. Damn women, anyway. There were the Nemas, who didn't want conversation at all, and then there were the Tessas, who wore a guy's skin off with talking. He'd far rather she was rubbing it off another way.

"I've never thought about it much; it's just a gut reaction." Dangerous zone. *Change the subject, Stewart.* "Hey, enough about me, Tess. How about you, what about this matchmaker thing, you like it? Is it gonna be a long-term career move?"

She sank back in her chair and crossed her legs. The skirt hiked up higher and for a minute his mind went blank.

"Well, before you came along, I was even liking the rough parts." She didn't smile, but her eyes were sparkling. "It's not the way I thought it would be, but there's always action, it's got typing legal briefs beat all to heck. So yeah, I really like it." She gave him an assessing look. "How are you at keeping secrets?"

"Hey, I've got sisters. If I couldn't keep secrets, I'd be dogmeat."

She leaned toward him and clasped her hands. "I'm buying the business. Clara is having marital problems, and she's offered to sell to me."

"Well, congratulations. That's a big step, buying a business."

"I'm a little nervous about it, and I'd like to talk to your office person to see about getting a computer. I'm gonna modernize the business, I've got so many good ideas—" she stopped and bit her lip. "I probably shouldn't be telling you this; after all, you're a client."

Not for long. "I'm also a friend, I'm honored you'd confide in me." How was that for gentlemanly? Even when he was feeling more and more like jumping her, right here in his sister's kitchen. On the table. Or the floor, the floor was fine. Although there was the couch.

"Eric, you know so much about running a business, and I do need advice. How'd you build yours into what it is today?"

He didn't answer right away, because he had to stop thinking about having sex with her first. "I'm not exactly a billionaire yet." He planned to be, though. "I guess I just took advantage of every opportunity that came along, took chances, lived on the edge." It was strange to try and put it into words. He hadn't really had a plan, not in the beginning. "I moved furniture, cleaned up apartments nobody else wanted to touch, went door to door asking if there was junk I could take away for a price. I put every cent I made back in. I've been careful not to overexpand. Bruno's my accountant; he's been a big help. He'll give you financial advice if you need it. I'm going to buy the garage that services my trucks because I can't find one that's reliable." Where had that come from? He'd never told anybody that little dream.

"I worked out of my apartment until I could afford the big lot I'm on now. I found people I could trust and paid them what they're worth. When do you want to come down and meet Henry? He'll find you the best deal in town on a computer."

While Gladys does a number cross-examining you.

She shrugged. It made her breasts push against her shirt. "I'm running Synchronicity alone, I can't just close it during office hours and take off."

"We're open tomorrow. Saturdays are big days for yard cleanup." He remembered Nicols. "I'll be there after the funeral." Usually he didn't work on weekends anymore, but if she was coming, he was going.

She frowned and thought about it. "I probably should go to the funeral, too. For Karen, for emotional support. Then I'll come over to your office afterward, if that's okay."

"Very okay. You want me to come and get you, take you to the chapel with us?"

She shook her head. "I'll bring my car; it's easier that way."

He found a paper and scribbled down the address, gave it to her, and for an instant he felt the tiniest bit grateful to Jimmy. She wasn't exactly dating him yet, but this was a start.

"Eric? Hi, Tessa." Karen, wrapped in a tattered blue terry robe, leaned on the doorframe. Her face was pale, her eyes dazed and glassy. "Where are the boys?"

"Hey, Karo, you okay?" Eric got to his feet and went over to his sister, wrapping a supporting arm around her. "Bruno has the kids at the park. Tessa came by to see you but you were having a nap. She brought you those flowers. You hungry?"

Karen spotted the tulips. "Oh, they're gorgeous. I always loved tulips, you remembered, Tessa." She tried to smile, but her face crumbled and she started to cry instead. "I'm—sorry, I—I just can't—"

"Ahhh, Karen." Tessa hurried over and wrapped her arms around Karen. Eric took his own arm away, but he was close enough to smell Tessa's perfume and her hair, close enough to be surprised at the powerful hum she generated just under his skin. He wanted those long, strong arms around him.

"I'm so sorry you're not feeling good," Tessa crooned. "This isn't a good time. I'm going to go home and then another time we can talk, and if there's anything at all I can do, you just let me know, okay?"

Karen nodded.

Tessa went to the closet to get her coat. There was this incredible sweetness to the woman, when she wanted to let it show. Eric didn't want her to go. "Stay and have something to eat with us? I make gourmet scrambled eggs."

She smiled at him and shook her head. "Thanks, but Karen needs time alone with you." She picked up her handbag. "Bye, Karen." She looked his way and their eyes met. "See you tomorrow, Eric." Something hot went zinging back and forth between them, and there was more color in her cheeks when she finally looked away.

Then the door closed behind her, and he felt a sharp disappointment, a sense of loss and emptiness. He was missing her, and she hadn't been gone five minutes. What the hell was that about? He didn't go around missing women. He was usually relieved when they walked out the door. Mind you, that was after they'd screwed his brains out. He really needed to get Tessa started doing that so he could stop missing her.

16.

His absence is good company

Eric sat Karen down with coffee while he scrambled them both some eggs and toasted bread. While he devoured his and Karen moved hers listlessly back and forth on her plate, he told her about the plan he and the others had come up with.

"Oh, Eric." She dropped her fork and started shaking her head no. She put her hands over her face. She started to cry again, harsh, tearing sobs that hurt his heart. He held her, and his spirits sank. They'd have to come up with plan B, because obviously A wasn't going to work.

"Hey, sweet pea, you don't have to go, it's only an idea."

She rubbed at her bleary, bloodshot eyes and then looked straight at him. "I—I *do* have to go, my life is a mess. I don't know what to do about it anymore; this might give me a chance to figure it out." She hiccupped. "I'm—I'm crying because it's such a fantastic thing, such a generous, good thing, and I've—Oh, Eric, I'm so *scared*. I've been scared for so *long*. Oh, Eric, thank you." She flung her arms around his neck, holding on as if he were the only solid object left in the universe.

He patted her back and let her cry. He lifted the tail of his shirt a couple of times to dry her face off. This type of female tears was productive; he'd learned that much from his sisters. He'd learned quite a lot from them, when you came right down to it. Relief spilled through him. It was going to be all right. Karen was going to get better. Anna wasn't going to get any worse. Tessa was beginning to like him. There was no need for a costly divorce because they'd cremate Jimmy Nicols in the morning and that would be the end of that chapter.

Yes, sir, his life was swinging around to near normal again. He could just feel it happening.

Sitting in the small chapel at Jimmy's funeral, Karen wondered if she'd ever feel normal again. She wasn't totally wrecked the way she'd been yesterday, but she was shaky, inside and out. She'd decided against bringing the boys because they barely remembered Jimmy. Granted, there was no casket to upset them; he'd been cremated so this was more of a memorial service, and a short one at that, but still, she figured it was better that they weren't here. Sophie had taken them swimming.

There weren't many people present. There was Eric, Bruno, Anna, her. And Tessa. Karen was touched that Tessa would come. And the man who'd been with Jimmy that night at the pub, along with two other men, probably from the docks where Jimmy worked. He hadn't made many friends in his life, and he'd had no relatives.

They'd sung a hymn, and the resident pastor said a prayer, and then read a psalm, and then he said, "Does anyone want to say a few words about the deceased?"

Awkward silence stretched, and he cleared his throat.

"Then we'll repeat the Twenty-Third Psalm—"

Karen was on her feet, wondering how she'd gotten there, walking to the front, turning around to face her family, her friend. She was shaking so hard she could hardly stand up, and she wondered if her voice would work at all.

"Jimmy—" her voice trembled and her chin wobbled, and she tried again. "Jimmy was my husband" she managed. "Because of him I have two sons, and Anna says—" she looked at her sister, and it helped. Anna smiled at her and nodded encouragement, and after a moment Karen was able to go on, figuring it out as she went.

"Anna says there aren't any accidents, that people come into our lives as teachers for us, even when the things they teach us aren't, *ummmm,* very happy." She sniffled. Her tissues were in her bag, on the chair. Her nose was running, but she made herself go on. "I think that's what Jimmy was for me, a teacher. I'm not sure yet just what I was supposed to learn, and it's hard to thank somebody who's"—she almost lost it, but she managed to go on—"who's hurt you, but I do anyway. I thank him for Simon and Ian." She started to cry, and everyone got up and surrounded her, and the piped-in organ music started, and then it was over.

Tessa was still crying off and on as she drove over to Junk Busters. Karen might be having problems, but she sure had guts. And she also had a family who stood by her. She'd watched Eric hold his sister in his arms, use his handkerchief to wipe away her tears, kiss her and whisper something in her ear that brought a tiny shaky smile.

And then he'd come over to Tessa and given her a big hug, and there was that sensation again, the one she had every time she was around him, like every last one of her endorphins were being released, but the little buggers were directionally challenged, heading straight for her groin instead of her brain.

"Thanks for coming, Tess," he'd said, giving her that blue-eyed *whammo* look. "It means a lot to all of us. We're taking Karen home now. Bruno and Anna are gonna spend the day with her. See you at the office in a while?"

She'd managed to nod. Eric in a black suit, cream shirt, and blue tie was a heart-stopping sight. He ought to carry a dangerous goods sticker. But beneath the image, there was the substance, and that was what was starting to really bother her.

She was being forced to see him differently than she had before. She didn't want to, she wanted him to be shallow and selfish, a womanizer who trampled on female hearts as if they were grapes.

Instead, she kept seeing a hero. She was reverting straight back to herself at eight, twelve, fourteen, when he'd been her best friend's big brother, the guy who drove her and Karen to their first school dance in his beatup old Ford pickup, the one who caught them smoking in Karen's room. Instead of bawling them out, he'd made them finish the entire pack, and they'd both been deathly sick as a result. She hadn't smoked again for years. Why the hell she'd ever started—but she knew why, she remembered why.

It was the first week after her wedding, when she

woke up in the morning beside her new husband, feeling warm and sensual and loving. She'd put her arms around him, snuggled into his back, touched him down there. He'd removed her hand, then slid out of bed.

"It's not a good idea in the morning," he'd said, as if he was chastising a child, and Tessa knew right then she'd made a gigantic mistake. She got up, pulled on clothing. She walked to the corner grocery and bought a carton of cigarettes. Gordon hated women who smoked.

Gordon was long gone, and she was now a nonsmoker again. For two whole days, she hadn't succumbed. Each time she was tempted; she'd visualized kissing Eric and having him gag at the taste.

Tessa blew her nose as she turned into the side street where Junk Busters was. The sign on the gate was strange, obviously made from reclaimed material. The words JUNK BUSTERS INC., formed out of thick cable, were welded to what looked like old iron bedposts. There were three huge disposal trucks parked in bays at the back of the property, and dozens of bins. A covered storage area held neat stacks of sorted metal. The office was unimpressive from the outside, a single-story brown-brick rectangle.

She parked, tried to fix her smeary eye makeup, and finally gave up and went in. The small space was carpeted in what looked like indoor-outdoor industrial gray. The only items not strictly utilitarian were an enormous jade plant on an upturned barrel in one corner, a huge stylized green–and–neon pink–satin fish suspended from the ceiling in the other corner, and a television on a portable stand, tuned to a soap opera. There was also a really ugly lamp, made out of twisted pieces of metal, with a hubcap for a shade. Eric hadn't spent much on interior design.

A tiny Asian woman in a purple tracksuit sat behind a desk. She had a telephone clamped to her right ear, but her eyes were glued to the TV.

"You tell him we'll do the job, real good price," she was saying in a singsong voice. She raised a hand and waved at Tessa without looking her way. "Best deal in town, you tell him. He's crazy to go anyplace else."

She hung up and reluctantly looked away from the television where two half-naked people tumbled on a bed. "Afternoon, miss, how can we help you?"

"I came by to see Eric. He's expecting me."

"I'll see if he's here, should be, he just got back from his brother-in-law's funeral, good riddance to bad rubbish, I say." She jerked a thumb at a chair that might once have been a car seat. *"Young and the Restless* is on. Watch and tell me what happens."

She scurried off down the hallway just as a man carrying two large bags of Chinese take-out food shouldered his way through the entrance door. He was short and wide and smiling, his eyes hidden away behind rolls of flesh.

"Hi, I'm Henry. Anybody helping you?"

Tessa nodded. "Thanks, someone's gone to tell Eric I'm here." She couldn't resist adding, "What does he do, escape out the back door?"

He came over close to her and said in a low voice, "Sometimes, you never know with the boss; he's kinda slippery." He glanced down the hall and grinned. "Ahh, but you're in luck, here he comes. Hey, boss, I got lunch. That new place just opened is great; cheap, too. They gave us a deal. I told them about the funeral. And I said we'd hand out some business cards for them."

Eric ignored him. "Tessa, I was watching for you, and then Sophie called in a panic. She lost Ian at the community center, she was a little upset. But she's found him. He was hiding under the exercise mats in the gym."

The wide, welcoming smile on his face was reassuring. He'd changed into chinos and a short-sleeved shirt. She mourned the suit for a moment.

"I see you've met Henry Wong, my office manager. This is Henry's mother, Gladys. Tessa McBride," he introduced.

The wizened woman smiled and shook Tessa's hand, her eyes gravitating back to the television.

"Ma's a soap fiend." Henry winked and hefted the take-out bags. "Good thing I got enough for an army. You'll stay for lunch, Tessa? C'mon in the kitchen; we oughta eat while it's hot."

Henry led the way into a small kitchen. He began putting plates and cutlery out on a wooden table. Gladys came in after a few moments and set out cups, pouring boiling water from an electric kettle into a fat white teapot.

"Green tea, good for cancer," she said cheerfully. "You got any cancer, Tessa?"

"Not that I know of." She felt more than a little dazed, first a funeral and now Eric's staff. She was gratified when Eric held a chair for her and then took the seat next to hers. She had a feeling if Gladys sat there she might reach over and start examining Tessa's breasts for lumps.

Gladys poured tea as Henry removed the covers from one container after the other. There seemed an enormous amount of food for just the four of them, but when Henry began heaping his plate, Tessa understood that there probably wouldn't be much in the way of leftovers.

Gladys, too, had a massive appetite. She took generous amounts of everything, eating through the questions that poured out of her.

"You know the boss long, Tessa?"

"Since we were kids. I grew up a couple blocks away from his house."

"Ahhh, long time friends, huh?" She gave Eric a speculative look. "Was he a good kid, or bad?"

Tessa raised her eyebrows at Eric. "When he was good he was very good, and when he was bad he was horrid."

Gladys found that funny and chortled. "So, are you married?"

"Divorced."

"How long you been divorced?"

"Four years now."

"You got kids?"

Tessa was having problems finding time to chew. She swallowed and shook her head. "Nope, no kids. Someday, though, I plan to have at least four." Might as well lay all her cards on the table.

"Ahhhh, lots of kids, smart woman. Me, I only had Henry, female problems, couldn't have any more, worse luck. So what do you do for work?"

"I'm a matchmaker's assistant at a place called Synchronicity. We find suitable companions for lonely people." Tessa noticed that this turn in the conversation was making Eric visibly uncomfortable. He shifted in his seat, passed a container of noodles to Gladys, made slight negative motions of his head at Tessa.

She ignored him. It was fun to watch him squirm.

How much did the staff know about his connection with Synchronicity?

Gladys answered that. "So this is how come you dated that Sylvia woman, boss. Henry told me, all that crazy cowboy stuff." She shook her head. "That's bad luck, boss, making fun of people that way."

Gladys rattled off a long string of Cantonese to her son.

"Ma wants to know is this like Internet dating, E-Love, like on television," he explained.

Tessa shook her head and used tea to wash her food down. "We don't use computers yet. I think we should but my boss doesn't believe in them."

She needed to talk to Henry about that, and she wondered how to get around telling him about buying the business. What the heck, what were the chances he'd ever have any contact with either Clara or Butthead Bernard? It couldn't do any harm to just mention it, as sort of a possibility.

"In fact, I might be buying the business, and I wondered if you'd be able to help me find a computer at a good price?"

"For sure." Henry stopped shoveling in food. "What you want to pay?"

"As little as possible."

"What you want it to do for you?"

Tessa explained about a database for clients, and a way of matching them that combined astrology with basic compatibility.

Henry nodded and said, "You know of a program like that?"

"No, but I'd like to set one up."

"I could help." Henry was looking animated. "So, how much you paying for this Synchronicity?"

"A fair price." This was a person with no boundaries.

Gladys said, "How much is fair?"

These were two people with no boundaries. Tessa shot a *save me* look at Eric.

"It's not settled yet," he said. "And it's bad luck for Tessa to talk about it now."

Gladys nodded. "Superstitious, huh? Superstitious is good."

Tessa nodded, bewildered.

Gladys said, "Chinese people are very superstitious. And we have always used astrology for matchmaking. I tried for Henry." She scowled and waved a fork at her son. "My friend Susie has a daughter, not much older. Astrological charts fit. Nice girl, good cook. Smart. What more is there?" She flung the fork down in disgust. "He said she was too fat. Look at him. How can he say she was too fat? Talk about a double standard. You ever come across a nice woman for him, you let me know, okay?"

Henry said something in Cantonese and Gladys gave up on English and went on at him in a loud, shrill voice for some time. Henry was unaffected. He shrugged his heavy shoulders and bent over his second loaded plate, methodically eating his way through his mother's tirade.

Tessa gave up on food, expecting blows at any moment.

"You had enough, Tess?"

She wasn't certain whether Eric meant the food or the company. She nodded to both.

"C'mon then, I'll show you around."

"Thanks for lunch, Henry. Nice meeting you, Gladys."

Both stopped in what appeared to be midsentence. Henry got to his feet and gave Tessa a half bow, and Gladys smiled sweetly.

"I'll get back to you on the computer," Henry promised.

"Come again soon," Gladys said. "Nice meeting you in person, now I know who the boss is talking to when you phone."

"And isn't that a big plus, now she can inquire about your bowel habits before she gets me on the line," Eric muttered as he led Tessa down the hallway. The argument in the kitchen had begun all over again.

Tessa glanced back and whispered, "Are they always like that?"

"Always. Makes for a tranquil work atmosphere, huh?"

"Why did you hire them both? And where's Mr. Wong?"

"I didn't hire her; Henry did. And Mr. Wong died years ago, relieved beyond measure to get away from those two." Eric opened a door and stood aside so she could enter. "This is my office."

"Wow." It was all she could think of to say. The massive desk was oak, his chair was leather, and there was another weird lamp made from pipefittings beside it. A two-seater couch along one wall was actually the resurrected front seat of a car, placed on a frame concocted from drainpipes. Under the single window a leafy green plant spilled from a hubcap mounted on a twisted metal frame. Live fish swam in the screen of an ancient television cabinet, and on the wall behind the desk, photos of Eric's sisters and nephews smiled out from frames made of pipes.

"Eric, where'd you get all this—this stuff?" It was truly hideous.

17.

He who hesitates is a damn fool (Mae West)

"I made it. It's my hobby, making stuff from valuable secondary material. Junk art," he added with a grin, closing the office door behind them, and then locking it with a bolt.

"Why the heavy security?"

"Because Henry is a snoop, and Gladys's worse."

Tessa walked around. The furnishings looked just as bad close up. "Have you ever exhibited at shows?"

"God, no." He sounded horrified, thank god. "I find stuff and weld it together for my own pleasure."

"Do you have a studio?"

He shook his head, and her heart sank. He did this at his *home?*

"My apartment. I had to redo the wiring and knock out some walls, but now there's space there for junk and my welding equipment." It was all she could do not to shudder.

"Your landlord didn't object?"

"He appreciated the rewiring."

"You didn't mention this on your form at Synchronicity. I'll have to start matching you up with someone artistic." Actually, blind would be better.

"You and I match, Tessa. I told you before. How about you dating me?"

He kept asking, and she kept thinking about it. There was chemistry, no doubt about it. But he'd be detrimental to her health. He didn't want babies. He drove an ancient orange van. And now there was his hobby.

"I'd rather we just stayed friends."

"What, friends don't date? I thought you told me that friendship was one of the things most important between couples."

"It is. I just think it would hurt too much when the hook came out."

He waited a minute, frowned, and then shook his head. "You lost me with that one."

"Catch and release, Eric. Meet 'em, date em, drop 'em."

"C'mon, Tessa, you gonna hold my past against me again? Maybe it wouldn't be that way with us."

"But probably it would, and I'm an old-fashioned lady, long-term, commitment, marriage, kids. The whole nine yards. I told you that."

"So what's wrong with having some fun along the way?"

"It's a detour. There's only so much road ahead for me, and I've already taken too many wrong turns."

"You do random acts of kindness, though, right?"

He was truly devious. "Where are you going with this one, Stewart?"

"Karen's flying out tomorrow. I got her a ticket on an excursion thing. Sophie has the boys, but she has a meeting Tuesday evening. I promised the kids I'd take them to the fair, but I'll need help. You can't call that a date, can you, coming along with me and two kids to a fair? It's more like an act of mercy."

Say no, Tessa, say no, say no, just say no.

"The kids would love it; they like you. They asked me if your hair was really real or if it was extensions." He reached out and took a strand between finger and thumb. "Hairdresser's kids, I ask you."

Did hair have nerve endings? She could swear she felt it like a long, slow shiver. She moved away a little.

"It's real. My hair." Well, apart from a little color to cover a few strands that were growing in a lighter shade of pale. *Karen's kids. That beautiful energy, those amazing minds, that innocence. Those missing front teeth. Their uncle.* He fought dirty.

"You did offer to do whatever for Karen, I heard you, and I could lose them on my own, all those people. They're gonna be missing their mom, too, poor little beggars."

"Eric, that's outright blackmail."

"It's the only way to get ahead in this cutthroat world."

She puffed out a breath and said in an exasperated tone, "Oh, *all right.*"

He grinned and made a thumbs-up gesture, and came over to her, way too close all over again. "Well, Tess."

"Well what?" She should move away.

"Well, I'll look forward to seeing you Tuesday."

He smelled good. He must have one hell of an internal thermostat, because she could swear he was giving off waves of warmth. Or was that her?

She had a couple days to get ready. She could

try that new sugar stuff she'd bought and get all
the hair off her legs. And there was her bikini line
to consider. And there were always her eyebrows,
and her toenails. Maintenance was a real pain. She
wasn't doing it for him, either. It was for Simon
and Ian.

Yeah, right.

He was a kind man, though. Dogs probably followed him everywhere. Female dogs, anyway. If
only she didn't know what he felt like naked and
swollen.

"I'll pick you up at four."

She'd have to close the office early. He was
standing way too close. The room was too small.
She edged away. Did he still make those noises
when he came?

"How long since you went to a fair, Tess?"

She cleared her throat. "Not since I was a kid."
She thought of the Ferris wheel, and cotton candy,
and tilt-a-whirl. Did they still have tilt-a-whirl? She
felt as if she was on one right this minute.

"We can grab junk food at the fair, and then after
we drop the kids off we'll go out for a decent dinner afterward, okay? We'll need to unwind, they're
pretty high energy, those two."

"You just keep pushing, don't you?" Being close
to him caused a physical reaction, a tightness in
her throat, an ache in her chest, a fullness and
heat in her abdomen that spelled out plain old
lust. Besides, she couldn't back up any farther; she
was against the desk.

"I do when I want something."

Going out for dinner without the kids was a bad
idea. What the heck, going out with him *with* the
kids was a bad idea. Being in here alone wasn't the
smartest move she'd ever made, either.

"Okay, dinner. But that's it."

"Thanks, Tessa." The crooked killer grin came and went. "It'll be fun, I promise."

Was I promise right up there with trust me?

18.

A lady never shows her underwear unintentionally

He was sort of touching her arm, just with his fingertips, running them up and down her bare skin and pretending it was absentminded and he didn't know what he was doing, the jerk.

Oh, the hell with it. What if she just went ahead and scratched this itch that drove her nuts each time she was around Eric? What if she treated it the way guys did, just a quickie, no emotional attachment, sex for the sake of sex, for old times' sake? Could she do that?

She could try. What would he do if she wrapped her arms around his neck and her legs around his waist right this minute? There was a lock on the door. She was wearing a midcalf dark cotton dress, and she'd stripped off her pantyhose in the car, and she wasn't having her period. She had lovely French underwear. Navy, with pale pink flowers.

Never mind matching underwear. Was he strong enough to hold her up if she jumped him? What if he staggered? She'd be humiliated. She'd never done that, wrapped her legs around a guy. She'd lost weight when she divorced, but she probably still weighed too much to attempt it. She'd never wanted to before like she did now.

He was strong, Eric was. That chest. And she could see the muscles in his arms. And then there was that bulge in the chinos.

It seemed a good time to start if she was ever going to; she wasn't getting any younger. He was looking at her with those blue eyes, and he stopped stroking and put his hands on her shoulders instead. "Tess, you make me crazy," he said with a resigned sigh. "I've been trying not to make a move on you, but it's out of my hands."

He pulled her forward, and she went willingly. His hands dropped from her shoulders to her waist, and she let herself touch him with her breasts and hips and thighs, and her breath came shallow and her heart pounded when all of her places pressed against all of his. Hers were soft, but his weren't.

She breathed in a long, trembly breath. Her nose was near his neck, and a subtle, natural smell, not aftershave, not men's cologne, but pure essence of Eric, took her instantly back to his beaten-up old Ford truck, and the way it had felt to have him inside her. He'd smelled this exact same way that night. Other things might age, but apparently smells stayed just the same.

He kissed her. He tasted like soy sauce from the food they'd eaten, and she figured she must taste the same way, salty, dark, fermented. And then she stopped figuring anything at all, because kissing him made her so hungry, the texture of his tongue, the way he cradled her face with his palms—his hands were hot; her skin was hotter.

He slid one hand over her breast, cupping her

through her dress and her nice bra, using the other down low on her butt to press her crotch against his. She sighed and looped her arms around his neck and opened her eyes.

He was looking at her, looking straight into her eyes, and it was the heat in his that pushed her over the edge.

"God, Eric."

"Yeah. I know. Me too." His voice came in jerks from deep in his chest.

It seemed the ideal time for the leg thing, because she simply had to get closer, tighter, or die. She lifted her right leg high and got a death grip on his neck, and he made an eager, encouraging noise, cupped her bottom and hoisted her up. She gulped and wrapped her other leg around him, high as she could reach, and understood right away why women liked doing it this way. Tab A was in instant unopposed contact—except for her best panties and his chinos—with Slot B. But she could see that those navy bikinis and thick chinos presented a problem. With him valiantly holding her up, and her holding on for dear life to his neck, there were no hands left to get their clothes off.

He took two big steps, holding her up with no visible effort—she thought of the game she used to play, take a giant step—and then her rear was resting on his desk.

"Radio." He flicked a switch, and she jumped a little when Chuck Berry was right there with them, doing "Let's Twist Again." And she knew Eric was remembering the way she'd moaned the last time they'd twisted.

"Golden Oldies. Henry eavesdrops." He was kissing her again, and her legs were still wide apart, and her breath wouldn't reach down into her chest. Now he was standing in between her thighs, undoing her zipper, sliding her dress up and over her head.

"Eric."

"Yeah, Tess. I know, honey."

This was okay; this was a one afternoon Saturday stand. It didn't mean a thing. Oh lord, he'd unhooked her bra. The way his mouth felt on her nipple, how did he know to flick his tongue that way? Lots of practice. *Don't think about that—suck your belly in, Tessa; sitting this way your fat's going to bulge.* But she was bulging between her legs, all of her pushing and pulling in and pulsing and longing, and wet, she was so wet. *Get with it, Tessa, strip him, no fair having a fat bare belly alone.*

Her fingers were deft on his buttons. He wasn't wearing anything under his shirt except curly golden chest hair, and his skin, god, his skin, smooth and salty on her lips and then his belt came open really easy. Damn, she had good hands.

She shoved at the jeans, they were tight, so he took his hands away from her skin and pushed at his clothes impatiently, and then the part of him that she'd tried hard to forget and never could popped up hard into her hand, hot, veined, thick. She tightened her hold on him and he thrust and groaned and stopped and shuddered, and now Jerry Lee was singing "Great Balls of Fire."

"It'll all be over if you keep doing that."

The visual was graphic, but she was greedy. She felt herself go up too many notches to wait.

"Now, Eric. Now, okay?" So she was begging, what did it matter if she got what she was after?

"Okay." He didn't take her pants off. Instead, he slipped his fingers under the crotch part and pulled them to one side, and she'd never wanted anything more, but he was pulling away.

"Hey, you can't—don't stop—"

"Damn, I almost—"

She had to lie almost flat while he mashed her into the desk and flicked up the lid on a small wooden card index box. He came back with a condom—no babies—*he kept them right on his desk?* How often did he do this here?

Don't go there, Tess, stay focused—

"Hurry, please, hurry—"

He did and then he used his fingers again, testing her wetness, easing the panties away even more, and then, oh my, he slid into her, and it felt the same as it had that one other time. Heaven.

He reached around behind her and tugged her closer still, impaled her on him, and her legs closed around him by themselves, and then her insides closed on him, too, and they rocked and it was a little clumsy and she didn't care. She was making noises and her head was rocking from side to side. Had he had other women this way, in his office, here, on his desk—

Stop. Pay attention. This is for now, Tessa, this is for you, there's nothing but now, now, NOW.

"NOW." She heard herself moaning it, over and over, louder and louder, and she didn't care if every employee he had heard it and burst through the door, she didn't care if the whole world heard it, because she was coming and coming, oh, she couldn't stand it, but she did.

And he was making that sound, like an engine revving, the sound she remembered, and she opened her eyes and his head was tipped back so she could see the underside of his chin. He'd missed a place there shaving, and he was shuddering. When he stopped, he slowly tipped his head back down and looked at her for a long moment.

"You're so good at this," he said in a reverent tone. Then he sort of shook all over, and shoved her back until her bottom was more firmly placed on the hard edge of the desk. They'd knocked papers and a jar filled with pens to the floor, and she hadn't even noticed.

When she figured she could put two words together, she said, "You're not so bad yourself." Heaven help her, she'd violated the very first rule of serious matchmaking: *Sex is biology. Use it to encourage courtship.*

"I need to get down." It was one thing to be spread-eagled and horny. It was quite another to fully appreciate that it was afternoon, and sunshine was pouring in his window, and she had on black medium-heeled sandals and a pair of bikini panties, which were a little the worse for wear.

Fortunately, he had blinds on the window, and although they were open, none of his employees were pressing their noses to the glass.

She slid her feet to the floor, and realized that he was in worse shape than she was. He'd done away with the condom, but his jeans and a set of red underwear were down around his ankles. *Red?* Just when you thought you knew someone.

He had his shoes on, too, white and blue trainers. He gave her a weary grin, bent over and pulled his pants up as she retrieved her bra and dress and wriggled into them.

"Bathroom's right in there, Tess." Fastening his belt, he walked over to the door, slid the bolt back and flung it open. "Henry, goddamn it," he bellowed. "Get away from my door."

Feet pounded off down the hallway.

"I'm gonna fire him." Eric's face was blotchy and red, but she figured that was from sex. "I'm gonna fire him, the pervert, listening at the door."

Tessa was shaking, but that, too, was the aftermath of sex. Damp, eager parts of her were still throbbing, slow to acknowledge history.

"Don't fire him until he finds me a computer." She was having trouble being an emancipated woman. She'd just had great sex with a man she didn't want to date, and she was going to have to walk past Henry and Gladys to get out of here, because she'd stupidly left her handbag on the front counter.

They'd both know what she'd been doing, and she was feeling a little low on chutzpah. The mirror in the bathroom reflected a dazed slut with a satisfied expression, swollen lips, and blurry eyes. There was nothing she could do to repair anything. She'd just have to brazen it out.

"I'll walk you out to your car."

He looked as done over as she did. "I think I can find it myself."

"I'm being a gentleman; don't discourage me."

Tessa straightened her spine and tried to look innocent when they got to reception. She needn't have worried. Gladys's attention was totally on the soap unfolding on the television. Tessa's purse was on the desk. She snatched it up, looking around for Henry. He'd disappeared.

"Bye, Gladys."

"Nice meeting you, Tessa," Gladys said, not even glancing her way.

Eric walked out beside her and held his hand out for her keys. He unlocked her car door and she got in.

"Tessa, we still on for Tuesday?" He sounded less than certain, and this was the moment when she should bail. Sex was one thing; going out with him was another.

He must have read her mind. "A promise is a promise."

"Okay, four o'clock, Tuesday. Pick me up at work."

She decided in a brilliant burst of afterglow that she'd maybe forget about the courtship thing for a little while and just go for sex, especially when he bent over and pressed a kiss on her mouth.

19.

The less things change,
the more they remain the same

Eric watched her nearly sideswipe a car on her way out of the lot. He should have given her hot sweet tea or something; he was feeling a little shaky himself. That had been—he searched for a suitable word. Explosive? Phenomenal? Feeling weak in the knees and low in vocabulary, he tottered back into the office.

"So, boss." Gladys was waiting, black eyes snapping, mouth pursed into a tight knot, arms crossed on her skinny chest. "Finally, a lady with a brain on her, and you treat her the same as that Nema treated you."

He opened his mouth to object, but he had to admit that he'd had sex with Nema in his office, on his desk. Numerous times, in fact, which of course Gladys knew about, thanks to Henry.

"Like *Sex in the City* around here," Gladys hissed.

He couldn't really argue that. Nema used to turn up in a raincoat with nothing on underneath, and she'd never said two words to Gladys. She hadn't said many more to him, come to think of it.

"This one's smart, funny, little bit plump so probably a good cook. Got some money; gonna have a business. Likes you even when she's known you long time. Your problem is you don't know a good thing when she turns up, boss. I think you need to talk to that Doctor Phil guy on Oprah; he counsels sex addicts."

He tried his best glare, but it didn't work on Gladys. "Tessa's nothing like Nema."

"Maybe *she's* not, but you are," Gladys snorted. "Maybe it's true nobody changes, they just get more like themselves."

God. He was surrounded by wackos. Did Gladys and Anna have long conversations when he wasn't around? Probably. He slunk off to his office. It smelled strongly of musk, and he enjoyed it for a while and then opened the window to clear his head.

Sex was good. Sex was necessary for good health. He hadn't had any since Nema walked out, so it was past time. He was no addict. He picked up the stuff that had gotten knocked off the desk and closed the lid on the condom container.

Sex with Tessa was way over the top on the Richter, in fact. But it had been pretty spectacular with Nema in the beginning, too, before—

Before what? Before he'd ended up feeling used, feeling as if he were just an appendage attached to a penis. He never wanted to feel that way again. He didn't want to make anybody else feel that way either.

Tessa made him laugh, she surprised him, she intrigued him, she made him think. She also made him terminally horny, but that was good, wasn't it? He felt hot all over again thinking about those navy panties, but once he really got his brain functioning, he started feeling not so good about the sex on the desk.

Maybe he was getting old, but he was starting to want more than just sex these days. Well, with Tessa, anyway. He could talk to her; she was funny and smart and open and caring. Sure, he wanted sex with her. Who wouldn't? But it looked as if, for some glitch known only to the female mind, the two might be mutually exclusive: friends or lovers, was that the way it worked? Come to think of it, he hadn't really had any female friends, apart from his sisters.

Maybe the sex thing should go on the back burner for a little while. He didn't want to be just another notch on her bedpost.

On Sunday afternoon he drove Karen to the airport, and it dawned on Eric on the drive home that for the first time in years, he was a little strung out about a date. He'd told Tessa Tuesday wasn't a date, but it was, and she had that bad impression of him from the cowboy thing. And maybe from the other thing, too. He'd stick to the friendship thing on Tuesday.

He called The French Laundry and reserved a table by the window. He checked the long-range weather report. If it was going to rain, the fair wasn't the place to go, and Vancouver was having one of its wet summers.

The prognosis was sunny with possible showers. What the hell did that mean? He'd have to play it by ear, see how it looked. If it rained, he'd have to come up with Plan B, whatever that was. Just in case, he bought a new big, black umbrella and stowed it in the trunk of his van.

Sunday evening he cleaned the Volkswagen inside and out, washing, waxing, vacuuming, even emptying out the glove box and the console, which was a lucky thing because he found a black lace bra stuffed in there.

Nema again; she'd enjoyed stripping off clothing while they were parked in traffic. He'd hated to rain on her parade, but each time she did it he got really nervous and yelled at her to quit it. He had visions of the cops arresting him for aiding and abetting nudity. He dropped the bra in a Goodwill box when nobody was looking and drove away fast.

That potential catastrophe made him think about his apartment.

What if Tessa asked to see where he lived? He wasn't going to have sex with her, but what if there was more lacy stuff under the bed or somewhere else he never looked and she did? It took seven phone calls and a hearty bribe to get a cleaning service to come and clean the place on short notice, and then the three women almost walked out when they got a good look around. The stacks of metal and the welding torch seemed to get to them.

It cost him double their usual wage to get them to stay, and when he found out what their usual wage was, it made him wonder if setting up a cleaning service designed for desperate singles shouldn't be his next smart business move.

He didn't want to be late, so he went for the kids twenty minutes early.

Sophie met him at the door looking frazzled.

"Eric, those nephews of yours just peed off the balcony onto the heads of the people who live directly downstairs. They were going to a wedding, and believe me, they weren't amused. I offered to

pay for dry-cleaning their clothes, but they said
that this was vandalism, and that I'm obviously not
fit to have children living with me, and they're calling Social Services. I hate to make you the bad guy,
but would you speak to the boys for me? I was so
mad I couldn't go near them without wanting to
beat them. And they *laughed.*"

"Where are they?"

"In their bedroom. And for god's sake don't
threaten them with staying home. I'm not ready
and I have to make this meeting. The docs are de-
ciding whether to strike."

"Okay." Eric glanced at his watch. If this took
long, he'd be late picking Tessa up. He went into
the bedroom.

Simon was playing with his Game Boy, and Ian
was seeing how high he could bounce on the bed.

"Hi, Uncle Eric." Simon sounded happy, ful-
filled, and totally unconcerned.

"What kind of bullshit is this peeing thing,
young man?"

Simon clapped a horrified hand over his mouth.
"You're not supposed to swear at us. Mummy says
swears are not allowed."

"Yeah, well, you're not supposed to pee off
Auntie Sophie's balcony, either. I want you to apologize to her, and I want your word that you're
gonna behave yourself from here on in, or else."

"Or else what?"

The cockiness in the kid's voice was unbelievable.

"Or else I confiscate the toys you like the best."

"Okay, Uncle Eric. I promise."

"You better be a man of your word, Simon. Because if you're not, that Game Boy is coming to
live with me. Same goes for Bay Blades."

"I'm really sorry, Uncle Eric."

He sounded as if he was this time.

Eric went through the same drill with Ian, except that Ian was a lot tougher customer. Threatened with the loss of his toys, he said, "I don't care. You can have them if you want."

"You won't feel that way when you have nothing to play with."

"I'll just tell the policeman you're 'busing me."

The kid was diabolical. "Where did you hear that?"

"At my baby-sitter. She said always tell the police if we were getting 'bused." His chin wobbled and he whined, "When is my mommy coming for me? I wanna go to my house."

Eric caved. He took the kid in his arms and held him close.

"Mommy's gonna send you a letter really soon."

"With the mailman?"

"Yup."

For some reason that seemed to mollify Ian, and he promised he wouldn't pee anywhere except in the toilet.

By the time he'd wrestled the kids into their shoes, found jackets and the action figure Ian wouldn't leave behind, and waited fifteen minutes while Simon had a leisurely bowel movement, Eric had fifteen minutes left to get to Tessa's, and it was a twenty-minute drive.

He considered calling and telling her he was running late, but he decided not to. He'd chance running a few red lights before he'd give her the impression he didn't figure being on time was important.

Except he couldn't run lights, not with the kids in the van. He drove with caution, using the time to lecture Simon and Ian on how they were to behave—no whining, no complaining, no deliberate burping. No farting. That still left time to think about Tessa and wonder if she was thinking about his desk the way he'd been all day, although she didn't have to work on it the way he did. He wondered what to say to her when they met, whether she'd be self-conscious. He'd make an extra effort to put her at ease.

They'd all have a great time, he assured himself. The kids would be worn out early, and they'd take them home and then have dinner at the Laundry. They'd talk, and then he'd ask her up to see his creations in his clean and tidy apartment. She'd actually seemed to like the stuff he had in his office; he couldn't wait to show her Dog. That would be it, though. No sex, even though it made him sweat to remember how she'd wrapped those long legs around him.

When he got to her office, he rang the bell and waited for what seemed a long time. She wouldn't have given up on him and gone home, would she? Ten minutes late wasn't that bad.

The outside door finally opened, and he hauled the boys on the elevator and up to her office, but Tessa wasn't there. A woman in black leather pants that accentuated astonishing hips and a black T-shirt that said BIKER CHICK in gold glitter was sitting behind her desk. She had hair cut in a brush cut and dyed a funny shade of orangey red. She also had a lot of mascara and purple lipstick.

Eric stared at her. He figured he ought to know her, but he couldn't for the life of him think who the hell she was.

20.

The best-laid plans of mice and men

She remembered him, though. "Eric Stewart, right?"

And suddenly it clicked. "Mrs. McBride, how are you?" God above, it was Tessa's mother, looking as if she'd taken up with the Hell's Angels. He remembered her now; she'd had on an apron and a blue housedress last time he'd seen her, and her hair had been up in rollers under a chiffon scarf. She'd given him this same disapproving look, as if he had snot stuck to his nose. Her gaze went to the boys, cowering behind him, and she smiled.

"Are these fine fellows your sons, Eric?"

"No, no, they're my nephews. Ian, Simon, this is Mrs. McBride, what do you say?"

Ian stared up at her. "Are you a witch?"

Eric quickly said, "Is Tessa ready to go?"

"She's in the bathroom; she'll be right out."

The buzzer rang, and Maria pushed the appropriate button. When the door opened Tessa's father, Walter, came in. He smiled and stuck out his hand, and Eric took it.

"Hey, great to see you again, Eric, how's it going?"

Eric liked Walter McBride. Before he and Maria divorced, the older man had always taken time to talk. Walter, too, was wearing leathers, and he must have had them custom made because the waistband fit neatly around his sizable potbelly. His hair, mostly white and thinning on top, was pulled back into a skinny ponytail tied with a leather thong. He jerked a thumb at the door. "Did you happen to see my mean machine out in the street? I was just out checking on her; you can't be too careful nowadays."

Eric hadn't noticed, but it seemed polite not to say so. "That bike yours? She's a real beauty."

"She is, isn't she?" Walter beamed. "Maria and I were out for a spin; thought we'd drop in and say hi to Tess."

As if her father had paged her, Tessa came out of the bathroom.

Eric tried to make eye contact. He gave her what he thought was a reassuring smile.

She scowled at him. "You're late, Eric. Hey, guys, how's it going?"

Simon took that literally. "It's going pretty bad, Tessa. We peed on Aunt Sophie's neighbors, and they all got really mad. Uncle Eric did, too; he said he's gonna take all our toys away if we do it again. And we can't fart."

"Some people have no sense of humor."

"You look great, Tess. Ready to go?" She had on soft gray pants and a hot pink, silky jacket thing. Under it was something tight and black and low cut, so the tops of her breasts just about showed. And now he knew exactly what they looked like showing, which didn't do much for his blood pressure. He was still trying to figure out what the protocol was with her parents when she said, "We're off, Mom, and I have to lock the office."

"Time we were on the road anyhow. Don't want to be out on the open road if that rainstorm hits," Walter said.

"Rain?" The sun had been shining all day, and Eric had more or less forgotten about possible showers. He felt a twinge of foreboding. "It's not gonna rain; it can't. We're going to the fairgrounds, there's a carnival on."

For some reason, Tessa shot daggers at him for revealing that.

"Supposed to have showers later on this evening. But maybe we'll be lucky and it'll pass right over," Walter said. "Carnival, huh? That's a thought, haven't been to one in years myself. Wanna go to the carnival, Maria?"

"Not if it's gonna rain," she said. "Tessa, you should be wearing something more than that flimsy jacket."

Tessa ignored her. She was already in the elevator, the boy's hands in hers. When they reached the ground floor, she whizzed them through the door and down the street. She said over her shoulder, "Are you coming, Eric?"

He said a fast good-bye to her parents and caught up with her beside the van. She was stowing the kids in the back. "Hurry *up*, Eric. Let's just get out of here before they decide to come with us."

He hurried, and when they were a couple blocks away and there was no sign of a motorcycle behind them, she slumped back against the seat and let out a huge sigh.

"Can you *believe* that scene? Did you see my

mother's hair? And those pants, she *really* shouldn't wear those *pants*. If that's what menopause does to you, I'm having a sex change before it happens."

Simon said, "What's a sex change?"

Tessa shot Eric a horrified look.

He gave his head a reassuring shake and said to Simon, "It's just an operation people sometimes have."

"Because they're sick?"

"No, it's called elective surgery, which means they decide to have it."

"Are you gonna get one?"

"Nope."

"Can I have one when I'm big?"

"Only if you really, really want to," Eric said. "Now, you guys be quiet for a while so Tessa and I can talk."

Silence, back and front.

"Your folks look happy, Tess." He didn't know what else to say; they were sort of beyond description.

"Happy? *Happy*? They're senile. They ride around on that death machine; they hold hands all the time. They seem to have moved in together, having totally forgotten how *really* well that worked the first time they tried it. I've spent years of my life listening to them rant and rave about each other, and now this."

"Maybe it'll wear off when winter comes, snow and ice, and they can't ride the bike anymore. Maybe the novelty will wear off." It had with him, countless times. He wondered how long it was going to take with Tessa.

"Yeah, maybe. But that's a long ways off, and in the meantime, I keep worrying that Mom's going to get preg—" She stopped abruptly.

"Uncle Eric, we're not farting," Simon announced in a righteous tone.

"My daddy died," Ian commented.

"I heard," Tessa said. "I'm so sorry."

"Don't be sorry, Auntie Sophie told Auntie Anna it was a blessing in disguise. I know blessing from church, but what's disguise, Uncle Eric?"

"It's the opposite of dose guys. Now how about counting red cars for me? Ten cents for every red car you spot."

They got into it, and Eric started to relax, but it only lasted until they approached the fair grounds. Parking was obviously going to be a problem. Eric circled block after block in widening circles. Even the kids selling space in their backyards had nothing left.

"I'm going to drop you and the kids at the gates, Tessa. I'll be along as soon as I find parking." He handed Simon twenty dollars. "You be the gentleman and pay at the gate for me, okay, sport? I'll meet you by the hot dog stand just inside."

"Okay."

Eric dropped them, and finally located a parking space eleven blocks away. He locked the van, and he'd trotted six blocks when it started to spit rain and he remembered the brand-new umbrella he'd left in the back of the van. He sprinted the last few blocks, hoping his deodorant was as good as the ads claimed. It was only sprinkling when he reached the entrance gates.

"Good night for the fair," the ticket vendor said. "Not too crowded, I guess people are scared it's gonna rain."

"It's not," Eric declared, handing over the money for the ticket. "It's stopped; it was just a shower."

"Hope you're right."

He saw them from a way off. Simon was talking as fast as his mouth could work, and Tessa was laughing, so maybe the kid wasn't saying anything really horrendous for once. The boys already had balloons. Ian was twirling around with his. Eric's chest expanded and he thought, *Damn, I'm happy,* and then he thought, *This is what it would feel like to have a family of my own.* It lasted a moment until he came to his senses.

Get a grip, Stewart. Take an aspirin and lie down till the idea goes away.

"I love the smell of popcorn," Tessa said when he reached them. "The taste, too." Her eyes were shining, and her curls sparkled with raindrops.

"We'll have to get some, then." Eric bought it, and they wandered from one concession to the next, munching. He won a teddy bear and a beach ball throwing rings, and he felt like a hero because Tessa applauded.

The boys lost handfuls of quarters on the nickel toss and the digger machine. They went on Mad Mouse's Wild Ride and the Corkscrew. Eric bought foot-long hot dogs, and when Tessa got mustard on her chin, he waited until the boys weren't looking and then leaned over and licked it off. She didn't pull away, so he figured she didn't mind.

"You've got a sexy chin," he whispered. "I noticed that Saturday." He really needed to know how she felt about that.

"I'll bet you say that to all the women you do on that desk."

He should have had a snappy comeback to that, but instead he felt his face get hot. She couldn't have talked to Gladys, could she?

They rode the tilt-a-whirl, and the octopus, but Tessa took Simon with her and Eric took Ian, so there was no chance to hold her close when she got scared and screamed. Simon was doing that for him. Who'd have thought he'd end up jealous of his five-year-old nephew?

Simon said, "Can we go on the roller coaster next?"

"I want the Ferris wheel," Ian argued. "I'm scared of the roller coaster." Eric was secretly grateful. He wasn't exactly scared of the thing; he just didn't like being that far out of control.

"I get to sit by Tessa," Ian declared as they lined up, and Eric felt like arguing the point, but decided against it. He'd get his chance at Tessa's attention when the boys were safely home with Sophie.

Strapped in beside Eric, Simon talked nonstop all the way to the top. Tessa and Ian were in the next car, and after admiring the view for a while, it dawned on Eric that they'd been sitting up there looking at it for quite a long time.

He wasn't the only one who thought so. People behind and ahead of them started to holler at the attendants on the ground, and soon it was pretty obvious that something was stuck.

Simon yelled out, "It's broke, Ian, we're gonna fall down."

Ian let out a bloodcurdling scream.

"No, we're not," Eric said, although at that moment he wasn't too sure himself. "Be quiet, Simon. Don't scare your brother that way."

It was too late. Ian was howling, and Tessa was leaning over him.

There was a breeze and the seats rocked. It was cold so high up, and as if that wasn't enough, it started to rain again, not just a little. A lot. A cloud-burst.

"What an adventure," Tessa called to them, but her voice wobbled.

Some guy on the ground with a bullhorn apologized and said that there was nothing to be concerned about, just a slight problem with the gears; mechanics were working on it. Two teenage girls three chairs away started to scream, and a woman with a good pair of lungs hollered that she had to get down; she was afraid of heights, which made Eric wonder what the hell she was doing on the Ferris wheel in the first place.

The rain accelerated into a deluge. The seat rocked more and more as the wind increased. The rain became a torrent. Simon and Ian were wearing waterproof hoodies, and Eric's jacket kept the rain off, but Tessa was getting drenched. Her hair was smashed flat to her head, and her face was soaked when she turned around to look up at him. She tried to smile, but her eyes were scared.

"We're gonna die, I know we're gonna die," a man was shouting, and now Simon started wailing in earnest.

Somebody else hollered, "Shut up, you're scarin'my kid."

Eric felt like maybe he was going to freeze to death or drown, whichever came first.

Tessa called in a small, scared voice, "Eric, do you think these things are hooked on tight?"

"Absolutely. They have to comply with safety regulations. They check them everyday." She'd never know he was lying. At least they'd die together, the four of them. He was glad that Tessa was the last woman he'd ever have sex with. For the first time, he really understood what closure meant.

21.

Good, cheap and fast—pick two

When everyone was too miserable to cry or scream or even talk, the seats jerked alarmingly and then ever so slowly started to move downward. A cheer went up from the ground, and after a week or so, they were at the bottom.

Eric's legs felt rubbery, and he had to lift Simon bodily out of the seat.

Tessa was shivering, holding Ian against her. Water dripped off her nose, her hair was flat, and her pants had huge wet patches down the front. Her silk jacket was sopping.

There was only one thing to do. "We need to take these guys home," Eric sighed. "They need a hot bath."

"So do I," Tessa said, shivering.

"We'll get you under cover, and then I'll run and get the car." Eric wondered if he could find a cab to drive him to the car. "I'll be back for you in twenty minutes, max." He took off his jacket and draped it around her, and then hurried them over to a covered concession and ordered hot chocolate and burgers and fries and fudge sundaes and everything else he could think of to keep the kids occupied until he got back.

It was still pouring.

"Take your jacket," Tessa said.

"You keep it."

There weren't any cabs handy, so he ran. He was panting by the time he reached the street where the van was parked, but at least he was as wet as it was possible to get, so that was one problem out of the way. The other problem was, the van didn't seem to be parked there anymore.

Maybe he had the wrong street. He jogged around the block, and then around two blocks, but by then it was beginning to dawn on him that he could circumnavigate the whole of east Vancouver and still not find his beloved van, because either it had been towed, which wasn't likely—there were no signs forbidding parking on this street—or some rotten, discerning bastard with excellent taste in vehicles had stolen his pride and joy.

"Damn." He thought up a string of even more creative curses when he remembered that he'd also left his cell phone on the seat, which meant he was going to have to hammer on someone's door and convince them he wasn't a mass murderer just so they'd let him use their phone and report the theft to the cops.

Except that was going to take time. He glanced at his watch. He was already ten minutes past the twenty minutes he'd promised Tessa he'd be, and the boys weren't famous for their patience.

The hell with the cops. It hurt him deeply to abandon the Volkswagen this way, but for the time being, there was no choice. He'd grab a cab, rescue Tessa, get the boys home, and then deal with cops.

Where were all the cabs when he needed one? He was almost all the way back to the fair by the time he snagged a Black Top. He asked the driver to wait while he got Tessa and the kids.

"Ten minutes," the sullen driver informed him. "Lots of fares, can't waste time."

"So leave the meter running."

"How do I know you will ever come back?"

Eric forked over ten dollars as holding money and then loped over to the gate.

"I already paid," he told the ticket vendor. "I'm just picking up my family. See, that taxi is waiting."

"Where's your ticket stub?" This wasn't the friendly weather person who'd been there a few hours ago. This bald guy looked like a Friday night wrestler moonlighting. Eric went through his pockets and then remembered that it was in the pocket of the jacket Tessa was now wearing. He explained this politely, but the guy just shook his head.

"No stub, you pay."

Eric had learned his lesson about punching people in the nose. He paid again.

Tessa was sitting where he'd left her, bedraggled and very out of sorts. "You took your lousy sweet time," she snapped. "These poor kids are freezing, and Ian got sick."

Eric saw the pool of vomit on the ground.

"I barfed on Tessa," Ian said proudly. "We cleaned it with water, but she still stinks and so do I."

What could he say? "Tess, I'm sorry. I'll explain why it took me so long, but right now there's a cab waiting, and he isn't a patient or trusting man."

"A cab? But where's the van?"

"Vaporized. Stolen. Towed. One of the above." Dragging the kids between them, he hustled them towards the gate. Thank god the cab was still there. Eric handed Tessa and Ian and Simon into the back and got in the front with the driver. He gave him Sophie's address, and the driver took off like a plane heading for the end of the runway.

"Hey, buddy, slow down, we got kids in the back."

The driver no longer spoke English. Eric glanced at the name tag on the visor and tapped him on the shoulder.

"Either slow down, Rashneesh, or stop right here and let us out."

Rashneesh rolled his eyes to heaven but he did slow. By now they were in heavy traffic, so speeding was impossible anyway. Instead he tailgated and muttered under his breath at other drivers until a sleek black Mercedes ahead of them stopped suddenly.

Rashneesh swore in Hindi and ground down on his brakes, but velocity won. They hit the other car's rear end with a resounding crash, and Simon and Ian and Tessa all started screaming.

22.

There is a tide in the affairs of men, which taken at the full . . .
                                                —Shakespeare

It wasn't much of a jolt, but Rashneesh fell apart. "Oh, goodness gracious. Oh, I am very, very, very sorry, is everyone hurt? Oh, goodness gracious, this is terribly awful."

Eric determined that no one was hurt, but both kids were howling and between them and Rashneesh the noise level was deafening. Then the driver of the car who'd been hit bustled up to the driver's window, a small, thin elderly woman with gray hair pinned up in a bun. Rashneesh's window was open and he began his goodness gracious speech, but she didn't hesitate.

She reached in and smacked him several times on the side of the head with her hand. "Idiot. Maniac. Lunatic. *Look* what you've done to my boyfriend's new car." She thrust her head in past the cowering, gibbering driver. "I'll need all your names as witnesses."

A patrol car appeared, which interested Ian and Simon enough that they shut up. The efficient cop stopped traffic until the two vehicles could pull to the side of the street, where the feisty little woman took half a lifetime writing down names and phone numbers, license numbers, business numbers, first, last and middle names, and every other detail except the size of Rashneesh's penis.

At Eric's urging, the cop called for another cab, and finally they got to Sophie's. Leaving Tessa in the cab—this time the driver was a careful, pleasant young woman, and it was definitely a better class of cab, although it had begun to smell strongly of vomit—Eric carried the boys inside, one on each arm.

Sophie opened the door.

"We had an accident. The taxi hit a lady in the rear end and she hollered and the cops came and Ian barfed all over Tessa," Simon reported.

"And we nearly died on the Ferris wheel," Ian added. "And then we ate a lot of ice cream and stuff and I think I'm gonna barf again."

Sophie looked at them and sighed. "Get in the bathroom quick."

"Uncle Eric's not getting a sex change, but he promised I can when I get big," Simon announced.

Ian began to vomit halfway down the hall. Simon came to look and started gagging, and Eric made a fast getaway.

He got in the back of the cab, relieved to find it still there. He'd fully expected Tessa to abandon him. He put a grateful arm around her shoulders. She closed her eyes and leaned her head back.

"Don't get close to me; I stink. My shoes are wrecked, my slacks are splotched with mud, I think this silk jacket is shrinking as we speak, and my hair has gone ballistic from the rain. Here's your jacket back, thanks. Be careful because I didn't get everything off it."

He tried to think of something soothing. "You hungry?"

"Are you nuts?" She shuddered. "I don't have a strong stomach. I may never eat again."

"I hope you know this didn't go the way I'd planned it, Tessa."

"You have no idea what a relief that is."

"I just wanted the whole thing to be perfect."

"It was perfect, Eric. It's the most perfectly horrible afternoon and evening I've ever spent."

"I suppose this means you won't go anywhere with me again." He tried to sound pathetic because that worked sometimes. He sighed. "Can't say I blame you."

She gave a huge yawn. "Oh, I don't know. Remember what you said about a school for the socially challenged? You were right, you do need help. I couldn't really recommend you as a match for clients, not the way you are."

"And you'll work with me on it?" This friendship thing was really tough on a guy. How did therapists manage it?

"I might consider it. At a price."

"How much?" If it was his body, he was too worn down to argue.

"I'm a little nervous about buying Synchronicity. The only lawyer I know is in Calgary, and I could use good advice."

"I have a friend who's a lawyer." Good old Fletcher. "How about catching a movie tomorrow? We could have dinner after and then you could give me pointers, and then later we'll go over your business concerns." But then he remembered his van was gone. Each time he remembered, he felt worse about it. "As long as you don't mind me picking you up in one of the company trucks?"

"A dump truck?"

"Either that, or I could always rent a limo."

"The limo's tempting, but with your track record I can't see you really pulling it off. Maybe you'd better come over and we'll rent a video instead. And we can order in. There's less chance of car wrecks and broken machinery and rain that way."

"You sure that's what you want to do?"

"I'm sure. I love watching videos."

"Okay. What time?"

"Six-thirty."

The cab driver drew up and parked in front of Tessa's house. He leaned over and kissed her slow and deep because kisses were going to have to be enough, at least for a long time. He could hold out; he was a strong, stalwart man.

"Night, Eric." She slid across the seat and he almost had it made, but then she hesitated. "I guess you don't want to come in for a while?"

He was trying hard to remember why sex with her wasn't a good idea. It had something to do with Nema and feeling used, but the details were getting fuzzier by the moment.

"Sure." He couldn't help it. He'd fought the good fight, and he'd lost.

He paid the driver off and followed Tessa in the door, and fifteen minutes later, they were naked in her shower, and he had renewed admiration for detachable showerheads.

The breaking point for Sophie was water. It came an hour and fifteen minutes after Eric had dropped off her nephews. She'd gotten most of the vomit off the rug and the walls, and they were out of the bath, angelic looking and rosy in their pajamas, watching television in the den.

The phone rang. It was a call from one of the other docs at St. Joe's. A patient Sophie had treated and released several weeks before was back in emergency claiming she'd given him the wrong drugs. The guy was obviously an addict, working the system, but the situation was complicated and the sound track on the cartoon channel loud. She walked into the kitchen and talked for ten more minutes before she was aware of muted giggling coming from the den. She'd learned in the past couple of days that giggling wasn't a good sign. Ending the call, she hurried down the hall.

Simon and Ian were on their knees in front of the gas fireplace, which she'd turned on earlier because of the rain. Each boy had a large bottle of Evian, and they were squirting the last of the water on what had been the flames.

"What are you *doing*? Give me those bottle *right now.*" She had visions of the entire building exploding. What happened when water was poured on gas? She didn't know, but now she was going to have to call the super and find out. "You two get into that bedroom and into bed, don't you dare set foot out of it again tonight. And there'll be no cartoons in the morning."

She knew her voice was shrill. She'd dealt calmly with missing limbs, torn bodies and schizophrenia, and now she was shrieking and shaking because of two little boys.

They ran off to bed, giggling like demons, and she tried to mop up some of the water, understanding for the first time exactly how children got beaten.

"We have to pee, Auntie Sophie."

"Then get in the bathroom, and make it fast."

The door closed behind them, and she heard the lock engage.

"Simon? Ian? Open that door."

Water began to run, full force. It sounded as if it was coming from both the sink and the bathtub, with the faucets on full.

"Open that door, boys, or so help me, I'll make you sorry."

She pounded and threatened and then tried bribery. Nothing worked. She called Eric, who wasn't home and wasn't answering his cell, and the super, who had a pager and didn't respond. When water began to trickle from under the bathroom door, she gave in to hysteria. The water turned into a stream, and with the last shred of her sanity, Sophie called Rocky.

He was home, he had a cell phone, and on his way over he talked her through finding the main shut-off valve, under the stairwell in the crawl space, which someone had once showed her but which she'd forgotten.

She turned the handle and the sound of water stopped, but there was now a river pouring under the door and soaking her beautiful new rugs, and they were going to mildew and stink and she'd have to replace them, and she'd offered to keep her nephews for ten whole days, and it had been four nightmarish days and three nights, and she wanted them *gone*.

When the doorbell sounded, she was sobbing. She threw the door open and tried to fling herself into Rocky's arms, but that was difficult because he was carrying a huge toolbox and several devices that resembled surgical instruments.

"Thank god, you're here; they're demons from hell," she wailed. "I can't do this anymore; someone has to come and take them away," she gabbled as he set the tools down and her arms went around his neck. "I know they're my nephews, but I never want to set eyes on them again. No wonder Karen went bonkers. Nobody could deal with those two and stay sane. They've ruined my rugs, there's water everywhere, the bathroom door is locked and they're *in there.*"

A new thought filled her with horror. "Omigod, the bathtub's full. What if they drown? It can happen in seconds. What'll I tell Karen?"

"Hey, Sophie, take it easy." Rocky's arms closed around her, and she thought, *This is what it took to get him to hold me?*

His mouth was close to her ear. "I'll get them out. I can do locks, and there's a machine in the truck that'll suck up the water. Demons from hell don't usually drown in the tub. It's going to be fine." He used his thumb to wipe tears off her cheeks and smiled down into her eyes.

"I did teach them to float, at the pool."

It felt like every one of her fantasies, being in his arms, only different. She'd never envisioned water, at least not this way. Reluctantly, she pulled away so he could get to work.

"Coming in, guys," he called to the boys. Within four minutes, using some kind of lock pick, he had the door open. Simon and Ian had discarded their wet pajamas in the middle of the lake that was the bathroom floor. They were standing beside the bathtub, stirring a large bottle of Sophie's best bath oil into the water with the end of the toilet plunger.

"We're making potions," Simon announced.

"Look, Aunt Sophie, this turns the water blue. I bet when I add this, it'll go purple." Before she could move he poured in her new bottle of Poison perfume, and Sophie's hand itched to turn parts of his anatomy red.

Simon gave Rocky a gap-toothed grin. "Hiya, Rocky, how come you're here?"

"Because you guys've made a bad mess of your aunt's nice house," Rocky told them. "That's not what good guys do, and you're good guys, right?"

Choruses of *right* set Sophie's teeth on edge. Liars, into the bargain.

"So you're gonna have to work with me to clean this up. First thing, you pull the plugs out of the sink and the bathtub so that water can go where it belongs, down the drain."

The naked demons did it with enthusiasm.

"Now we're gonna use towels and get rid of this water on the floor."

Sophie handed out a stack and they set to with a vengeance, and Rocky praised their efforts.

She escaped to the kitchen. Her hands were shaking. She recited aloud the list of calamities she'd managed with cool aplomb in the ER: car crashes, multiple injuries, near fatalities, explosions. Not once had she ever lost it this way. She actually felt dizzy, as if she was going to faint.

Low blood sugar. She poured herself orange juice, then added two good inches of vodka from the bottle she kept in the freezer. She needed it, because having Rocky here unsettled her nerves beyond what the boys had already done. She looked her very worst. She'd changed out of the suit she'd worn to the meeting into sweats, and she hadn't bothered with underwear or makeup. And she probably stank of vomit.

She heard Rocky talking away to the boys, cheerful and patient, apparently showing them what a toilet plunger was actually used for. Now why hadn't she thought of that? She could have taught them the finer points of anesthesia and had them practice on each other.

Rocky went out and came back with a vacuum that sucked up water and he and the boys used it on her hall carpet. He patiently allowed Simon and Ian turns with it. There wasn't even a fight over whose turn it was.

She was a total failure as an aunt. The only other thing she'd ever failed at was getting Rocky to notice her. Why had she ever dreamed of a time when she'd be a mother, when she couldn't even get the aunt part right? No wonder Anna was balking about getting pregnant; for once in her life, she was thinking straight.

Sophie took the glass into the study, only then remembering that the gas fireplace was out, thanks to large bottles of her Evian water. She sat on the sofa and sipped her drink and plotted.

Tomorrow morning she'd manufacture a call from work, insisting she had to go back early. Anna and Bruno could take over; after all, there were two of them, while she was outnumbered. She wouldn't have to see the boys again until maybe Thanksgiving. She might be able to extend it to Christmas if she volunteered to work the holiday.

After half an hour, the boys, still bare butt naked, came to find her. They stood in front of her, long lashes, round stomachs with belly buttons poked out, rosy, curly-topped angels. Well, she wasn't about to believe in the innocence of children, not ever again.

"Aunt Sophie, we're really sorry for what we did," Simon began.

"You oughta be," she snarled. The vodka was helping her to be strong. "I try to be a good auntie to you guys. I take you swimming and to McDonald's, and this is how you treat me?"

"We 'pologize," they chorused. "We'll never flood your house again, honest. We won't put water on the fireplace, either."

They wouldn't; she knew that. They'd just think up something else so diabolical no sane human would ever be able to second-guess it or them.

Tomorrow they were going to Anna's. Poor, poor Anna.

"Get some pajamas on and *go to bed.*"

"Rocky said we're such good helpers we can go with him tomorrow, all day. He's gonna show us how to dig holes in the ground for pipes to go through where people poop. But only if you say it's okay. Please say it's okay, Auntie Sophie?"

"Rocky says he'll get us hats like his," Ian added. "Please, Auntie Sophereeno?"

Auntie Sophereeno? She hardened her heart against Ian's charm.

Think Evian. Think carpets.

"I'll talk to Rocky about it." Tempting as it was, she was going to have to warn him about them, which meant the trip was off. They kissed her, and she hardened her heart against their soft little lips, their velvety skin, their milky breath.

"Bed." They scampered off, and she went to find Rocky.

The bathroom was pristine, the hall carpet only slightly damp, and he was loading wet towels into the washing machine.

"Rocky, I forgot there for a while, but they also

poured water on the gas fireplace, and now the pilot light is out. Is that dangerous? Is the complex going to blow up?"

He grinned. He had that great grin. "Nope. I can relight it for you." He followed her into the den and started wiping the water out of the fireplace.

She went in to check on the boys. They were both in one twin bed, sound asleep, curled up like puppies, duvet on the floor. She picked it up and tucked them in, and against her better judgment, bent and kissed them.

Karen was gone, and give the devil his due, Rocky was here, in her condo, and it was because of them. When she got back to the den, he had the fireplace dry and lit. "I don't know how to thank you." She knew how she'd like to, though. Being around him sent her hormones into overdrive.

"Would you like a drink? I'm having vodka and orange juice, but there's beer in the fridge."

"Vodka sounds good." He sat down on the sofa. He'd taken his cap off, and his hair was smashed down on the sides and sticking up on the top; it always made something inside of her go mushy, the way his hair looked. His arms were bare to the shoulder; he had the best biceps. And she knew by the way his jeans fit that his pecs and abs were just as spectacular. He had a hole in his sock, so his two middle toes stuck out. He even had great toes, extra long and only a little hairy. She knew there was no truth to that thing about men's thumbs and the size of their cocks, but maybe toes? She'd never really researched that theory.

He looked so reliable and kind and sexy and succulent. And shy. Why did he have to be so darned *shy*?

Knowing it was nuts, she'd asked Anna to do their combined charts, hers and Rocky's, and her sister had said they were totally compatible. But then, Anna would say that anyhow. "I've tried to come on to him," Sophie had confessed. "But he never picks up the ball and runs with it. I figure maybe he just isn't attracted to me."

"Going by this," Anna said, tapping the chart, "he ought to be, but he's got this asteroid in his chart that makes him feel really insecure about himself. Remember, he was dyslexic in school; that would make it worse."

"So what can I do?" She knew she was in a bad way when she ended up asking Anna for advice.

"You could visualize the two of you together, see it and feel it and really believe in it."

She'd done that alone in bed quite a lot.

"Anything else?"

Anna had looked thoughtful. "You could find a defining moment, get him drunk and just out-and-out jump his bones. Guys sometimes need the direct approach."

Sophie was full of courage in her role as physician, but in her personal life she'd always been way less than brazen. She'd always been too scared to really come on to Rocky. What if she didn't turn him on? What if he couldn't get a hard-on and she ended up so embarrassed she wanted to die? She'd have to quit her job and leave Vancouver forever.

Which, she realized, pouring orange juice and a husky slug of vodka into his glass, meant never seeing Simon and Ian again, except maybe at weddings and funerals. Right this minute, that held a certain appeal. She added more vodka to his glass and refreshed her own.

When she handed him his drink, she sat down beside him.

"The boys said you asked them to come with you tomorrow. I've got to tell you, they're bad news."

"Not much they can get into where I'm taking them. I've got a ditch to dig. I thought I'd give them each shovels; they'd get a kick out of it. Thing is, we'd be gone most of the day, but I'll make sure they eat good and stuff like that. You don't mind, do you?"

Mind? She wanted to get on her knees and thank him. She wanted to get on her knees between his knees and—she took another hefty swallow.

"I'm at my wit's end with those two, Rocky." Her voice wobbled. "I'm just not good with kids, which I never realized before now. I always thought I was, but the kids I see are sick or hurt." She felt tears slip down her cheeks, and part of her realized she was more than a little hammered from the vodka. It always made her cry.

"I guess every woman dreams of having kids of her own someday, but now I figure I'd better not try. There've been times these past couple of days when I should have been arrested"—she gulped and shame and snot overwhelmed her.

He handed her a handkerchief—who but Rocky had cloth handkerchiefs these days? She blew her nose hard and wondered what to do with the damned thing, and finally tucked it down the side of the sofa cushion.

"Don't be so tough on yourself, Sophie. You're first rate at whatever you do."

She wiped away tears and decided he deserved to know the very worst about her before she started to take her clothes off.

"We were in the car yesterday, on Broadway, after this disaster in the Safeway? You know how busy that street is, and they were fighting, punching each other, and I told them three times to knock it off. They didn't, so I stopped the car and told them to get out, that they could walk home. And they were scared and they started to cry, and I still made them get out, and then I pretended I was going to drive away. They were really crying when I finally let them back in the car." She sniffled and found another tissue in the pocket of her sweats.

"Rocky, they're five and three. It was rush hour, there's perverts around. I'm supposed to be an adult, taking care of them."

He nodded and thought for a minute. "So did they stop fighting?"

She nodded and blew her nose again.

"So it worked, don't sweat it. I remember once my dad did the same thing to me and my cousin, only he actually drove away. We were out in Surrey, miles from home. He didn't come back for ten minutes."

"Didn't it give you nightmares?"

Rocky laughed and shook his head. "We knew we deserved it. And we knew Dad would come back."

His arm was along the back of the sofa, behind her, but not touching. Even with a stuffy nose from bawling she was aware of his smell, clean male sweat. She wanted to press her nose into his armpit and lick.

"Simon and Ian would never dare do these crazy things if they didn't feel really secure with you, Sophie. You're a person kids can rely on. Eric always says you're the levelheaded one in the family."

Good old reliable, levelheaded Sophie. God, she was sick of that rep. "And being an ER doctor, I figure that must take nerves like iron." He took another slug of his drink. His voice was coming from deep in his chest. She wanted to put her forehead there, feel the curly hairs that showed under the neck of his tee tickle her nose. God, she loved hairy men.

"I've always really admired you, Sophie. I'd never have the brains to even get into med school, never mind be an ER doc."

Brains. Damn it all, she had really nice tits. Why didn't he zone in and admire those for once? There had to be a way to get him thinking in the right direction, short of ripping off her clothes and starting in on his.

"Rocky, remember when Eric got that first big contract and we went out to celebrate, and we had too much to drink and you kissed me?"

Long pause. Her heart sank. He'd forgotten, but he was too much of a gentleman to say so.

"Yeah." He sounded as if he was getting laryngitis. "Yeah, I remember that, all right. Real well."

Maybe this was what Anna would call that defining moment.

23.

I'm not playing hard to get;
I'm playing hard to hurt

Sophie's heart had developed a tachycardial rhythm, and even her solar plexus was jumpy. "So why didn't you ever do it again?" *You adorable godamned harebrained idiot?*

"I wanted to. Lots of times." He sighed. "But I've got that dyslexia thing, so I can't read too well. I'd think a lot about asking you out, and then try to figure out what we'd talk about, you know, you a doctor and me a plumber. It didn't seem to fit."

Jesus. "We could talk about my job, your job, the situation in Lithuania, whether the Lions are going to win the trophy. My sisters, my nephews, your cousins. Plumbing, surgery, athlete's foot. The time your dad dumped you and your cousin in Surrey. For cripe's sake, Rocky, I don't sit around and discuss *War and Peace*. I've never even read the damned thing."

She heaved in a breath and bared her soul. *"Rocky Hutton, don't you want to have sex with me? Don't you want to get naked with me? Am I fooling myself about this feeling I get every time I'm around you?*

Am I going to go through the rest of my life wondering why you keep running away from me?" Oh God, she was really shaking now, so hard the ice was rattling her glass.

He took it away from her and set it on the side table. His arm came down around her shoulders, and man, he was strong. She was pulled so tight against him she couldn't breathe. Or maybe that was for another reason.

He was kissing her, hot and deep and openmouthed and frantic, and inside her something was saying, *Yes, yes, more, more, faster, faster,* and he must have heard it, because then he was pulling her into his lap, and there was nothing shy about him at all. His lovely rough hands found their way under her top and she heard his breath hiss out when he found out she wasn't wearing a bra. She couldn't wait until he found out she wasn't wearing panties either.

She remembered that he was the world's most thorough kisser. He slanted her jaw with one hand. He outlined her mouth with his tongue. He nibbled and gently bit and paid attention to that vulnerable place on her neck and the lobes of her ears and her jawline.

She still couldn't wait until he found out she wasn't wearing panties, but by the slow way he lifted her top and then touched her nipples and then licked them—god, the man could lick—and then finally got around to pulling it over her head and off, she figured she might as well help him out a little with the panty thing or the kids would be getting up before they got to third base. And she wanted third base so much she felt nearly sick with wanting.

She put her hands on the waistband of the

sweats and shinnied out of them, and the sound that came out of him was gratifying. Either that or he needed the Heimlich maneuver.

His lips were close to her ear, his voice hoarse with lust.

"Do the boys wake up much during the night?"

She shook her head.

"Does your bedroom door have a lock?"

Finally, finally, they were getting somewhere. "On the inside of the door."

He picked her up and headed down the hall, one arm under her knees, the other around her back. She squealed a little and locked an arm around his neck. Nobody had picked her up since she was maybe five.

Bless those boys. Flooding the place had been such a good idea. And tomorrow he was taking them out, which meant he'd have to bring them back. She'd make dinner, and the kids would be tired from shoveling, and—and she was on the bed, and he was locking the door, and stripping off his clothes. The bed lamp was on, and she had her first really clear look at his naked body.

Oh, my. That toe business was definitely a theory worth pursuing.

Wednesday morning, Eric said, "Henry, what sort of things should you watch out for when you're thinking of buying a business?"

Eric had never bought a business. Junk Busters had just sort of developed, so he wasn't all that confident about advising Tessa.

Henry was chewing on something, but he managed to talk around it.

"Gotta be real careful, boss, can't trust anybody.

Gotta do research, find out what other similar businesses are worth, whether the financial situation is viable, if the amount quoted for goodwill is realistic. And also whether the owner's screwed around with the financial statements." He reached into a can and pulled out something that looked like a testicle without skin. "Want a lichee nut?"

"Nope, thanks anyhow." Eric knew how Tessa felt about her boss; she was fiercely loyal and trusted the woman implicitly. But ever since he'd heard about the kind of husband this Clara had, Eric had wondered how a woman with intelligence and integrity could live with such a sleazeball for so long. There wasn't a hope in hell Tessa would do any of the things Henry had suggested, but Henry would, with a vengeance.

His round face lit up when Eric asked.

"Leave it to me, boss."

Eric was glad to. He'd been on the phone with the police department's stolen car detail for over an hour again this morning. There was still no sign of his beloved Volks, and they didn't seem to be too disturbed.

"Quite an old car," the desk clerk said. "Probably get dumped in some ravine; that's what happens to those old clunkers."

Eric had felt enraged, but he was scared to holler at the guy because then nothing at all might get done.

And now to top it off he had to go and clean out the sump hole where Jimmy Nicols had been living. He'd promised Karen, and he wasn't exactly looking forward to it. He was beginning to wonder if he'd ever get free of the damned man; every time he turned around it seemed something else

came up. Nicols was almost more trouble dead
than he'd been alive.

Fletcher was dealing with the paperwork. He'd
offered to go do it, but Fletch already did way
more than his share.

Jimmy had been living in a rundown apartment
hotel in New Westminster, a good forty-minute drive
from Vancouver. All the dump trucks were out, so
after a fair amount of hassle, Eric managed to talk
Gladys into loaning him her red Caddie.

"No having sex in my car, boss," she warned. "I
can smell if you do."

"God, Gladys, what do you take me for? And
Tessa's at work anyway." He tried to feel perjured,
but he had to admit that if Tessa wasn't working,
he'd love to take her along, and he knew of this
place beside the ocean where they could park, and
the backseat of the Caddie was roomy.

That reminded him of the first time he'd had
sex with Tessa. He'd been an idiot, but he'd sure
had good taste.

He loaded up a pile of empty boxes, and the
drive didn't take any time at all with that fantasy
going on in his head. Also, the Caddie drove like a
dream. If the van didn't turn up, maybe he'd consider getting something less than twenty years old
for a change.

He had letters from Karen and Fletcher, and a
death certificate, but the super let him in without
questioning anything.

The room smelled stale and sour, but it was sur-
prisingly neat. There was a small kitchen area with
a hotplate and fridge, dishes washed and stacked
to dry. The bed was made up, and when he opened
the closet Jimmy's clothing hung in orderly rows.

"So, even psychos are tidy," Eric muttered. He started loading the clothing in boxes. He finished the closet and yanked open the top dresser drawer. A framed photo lay on top of stacks of underwear and socks, a shot of Karen cradling a newborn Ian, with Simon standing beside them, holding his new brother's tiny hand. Tucked into the corner of the frame was a smaller snap of Karen and Jimmy when they got married. Karen looked radiant, young and so vulnerable. Eric's gut clenched.

"Too bad you didn't appreciate what you had, you stupid idiot," he mumbled at Jimmy's image. He put the photo in the small box he'd set aside for anything that Karen might want.

In the bottom drawer was a shoe box with pay stubs and bills and receipts. Eric flipped through them. No bankbooks with nice fat deposits, dream on. Well, Fletcher had asked him for stuff like this; he'd let him sort through it.

It was a relief to load the last box into the car, and then dump all but the two small boxes at the local Salvation Army.

Back at the office, Gladys went flying out to examine the car, no doubt sniffing at the seats like a beagle.

"Tessa oughta phone this lady and talk to her," Henry said, handing Eric a page from a yellow scratch pad. "Mary Jo Louie used to work for Synchronicity, might be interesting to know what she's got to say."

"How did you get her name and number?"

Henry winked. "I got friends in low places, boss, you don't wanna know."

"Right." Eric stuck the paper in his pocket and forgot about it until that evening when he and Tessa were on his couch, watching *Hannibal*.

Tessa had chosen it. She'd read the book, but the movie scared her anyway, so she was nearly sitting on top of him. She had on a flimsy little red top, it was hot out, so no bra, and her nipples showed clearly through the cotton. And those shorts, wasn't there a city ordinance against shorts that flared out like that, so he could see up the legs when she curled them under her like this?

It was hot in here and getting hotter. He could feel heat building up inside him. He had to hold her close when the worst scenes were on. What else could a gentleman do when wild pigs were chasing the heroine?

Her fingers were laced with his. The light from the lamp he'd made out of a muffler picked out auburn highlights in her wild dark curls, and she was all soft, intriguing curves, cheekbones and throat and breasts and hips. She was so damned— *female.*

After a while the film ended, and he remembered the paper Henry had given him. He dragged it out and gave it to her.

"This is the woman who worked at Synchronicity before you did. It might be a good idea to call her and just talk."

"Why would I want to do that? Clara told me this"—she glanced at the paper—"this Mary Jo Louie wasn't even honest. Clara had to fire her."

"But that's just Clara's word. If you're buying the business, you want to know as much about it and its history as you can find out. Former employees maybe know things you should know. This is not the time to blindly trust anybody, Tess."

"But I know Clara. I do trust her; her word is good enough for me. I'd feel as if I was sneaking behind her back, listening to someone badmouth her."

Eric sighed. Why were women like this? "You don't have to believe Louie. But what would it hurt to give her a call?"

"I'll think about it." She shrugged and stuck the paper in the pocket of her shorts. Then she snuggled even closer and started telling him why she wasn't happy with the way the video had gone.

He, on the other hand, was entirely happy with the way things were going, wasn't he? They'd spent last night at her place and now she'd come over to his, mostly because he had no car. They'd screwed their brains out, sure, but they also talked. They talked a lot, so he felt better about things. Didn't he?

"In the book, she falls in love with him," she was complaining now. "They go off together and live happily ever after in France or someplace. Why can't movies stick to the book version?"

"Starling falls in love with Doctor Lecter?" He whistled, noting the way his breath made strands of her silky hair lift and settle. "There's hope for all of us if she falls for Hannibal."

"It's like King Kong, the Vampire Lestat, or the Hunchback of Notre Dame. It's that delicious helpless feeling that appeals to women. Those guys are powerful and dangerous and vulnerable; that's what we like. They're heroes; women want heroes."

Heroes, huh? "I can do dangerous," he growled, pinning her to the sofa and nipping at her neck. "I can carry you up to a bell tower, and suck your blood. I can even fry up some brains if you want me to." He'd felt all week as if his own brains were fried.

"Yeah, but you can't do commitment, Eric. Lecter took Starling off to Europe, spent the rest of his life with her. King Kong would have married Fay Wray if it had been humanly possible, although how that would have gone sexually boggles the mind. And the vampire made the lady his forever by turning her into a vampire too."

Commitment. Oh, shit, that again. Now was when he ought to go get them something really cold.

"But that's okay," she added. "I know this is strictly short term, and we're both in it just for the sex."

That stung. "Hey, that's sort of jaded, isn't it?" It also reminded him a little too much of Nema. "There's more to this than just sex, Tess," he said, slipping his hand down her back, feeling her vertebrae; there shouldn't be anything sexy about bones, but on her there was.

"Oh yeah? What, exactly?"

He couldn't answer because she was kissing him, her clever tongue stroking and sliding, and now she was in his lap, and his other hand had somehow accidentally slipped up under the leg of her shorts, and she was slick and wet and fiery hot under the crotch of those panties.

Nema, think Nema. Think exploited. Think dignity. Think self-respect. Think compromised.

Oh, fuck. Think condoms.

It only took one smooth, practiced movement and she was under him. The shorts came off easily, and the satin panties were hot pink, and maybe he wasn't going to respect himself in the morning, but as Anna said, that was then and this was now—

24.

Je suis migraine

Now. At last. Finally. Elation filled her. What had taken him so long? She'd begun to think the hundred thirty bucks she'd spent on French underwear was a total waste. But it was working, even without the bra part, and he was moving right along now, stripping off his jeans and then crushing her with his weight, and his leg was forcefully spreading her legs apart—*helpless*—and his fingers were probing and his mouth was on her nipple, through the tank top—*delicious*.

Just sex, Tessa, nothing serious or life threatening; men do this all the time, sex for sensation, get crazy, go mindless, be liberated.

He mumbled against her nipple, she was beautiful, something like that, how many other breasts had he said that to—

Don't think. Act. She reached down and put him inside her, arching up against him, trying to find the rhythm, losing it, finding it, gone again, *stop thinking*—

She opened her eyes and found him looking

down at her, blue eyes like a stormy sky, face stripped of all but desire, Eric, dangerous and dark and familiar for so long in her dreams and fantasies—

Dangerous, dangerous is good—

"Now?" He closed his eyes and tipped his head back and whispered it again, like a prayer, *Now?*

Yes. God, yes, because she loved him, yes, yes—

Loved him? *She loved Eric?* No, no, that couldn't be right. What was she thinking? Was that true? It was. Like a kite when the wind suddenly dies, she plummeted down just as he soared high.

He collapsed and she held him. She was numb with shock.

"Tess, hell, you didn't come. I was too quick. Let me—?" He reached a hand to touch her, but she stopped him. Wasted effort. Gone with the wind.

"Sorry, Tess." He rolled off her and fell off the sofa. He lay sprawled in a heap on the carpet for a moment and then he sat up and leaned his back against the cushions, stretched out his long, hairy legs, and rested his head on her bare belly. "I guess we need to practice more."

That's all this is to you, you rat, just practice?

So? He'd never promised her a rose garden. She'd gone ahead and planted one all on her own, and if she was getting stabbed by the thorns, she had nobody to blame but herself.

"Hey, Tess, you feel like a sandwich? I've got roast beef subs in the fridge. I'm starving."

She could go home now; she didn't like his apartment anyhow. That dog was downright eerie. Tomorrow she could find another possible match for herself in the files. She could date the sucker, and try not to swear, and be a lady in word and deed, and be bored out of her mind and dump him and then worry all over again about how she'd ever find someone she could stand long enough to marry before her ovaries packed it in.

Or she could stay here awhile, practice with Eric, give herself something great to remember when she was a lonely old woman. It was a no-brainer when you came right down to it.

"I'd love a sub." For the first time in a week, she'd also love a cigarette, but fortunately she hadn't brought any. What she had brought was an oversize handbag with spare makeup, lots of fresh underwear, and a nifty little green lyrca dress that rolled up to nothing and would unroll without a crease, ready for work tomorrow.

She made herself sound plaintive and hard done by. "Then after we eat maybe we could practice until we get this right?"

There was a silence before he answered, and she started to get nervous. But then he reached for her hand and used his tongue and lips and teeth on the inside of her wrist, sending shudders right through her.

"Hold that thought." He got to his feet and padded off to the kitchen, buck naked and more beautiful than any man had a right to be. She was crazy about his body. She put a hand over her eyes and moaned. She was crazy about Eric. She was dead meat.

Eric stared into the guts of the refrigerator, not seeing the subs, not feeling the frigid air shrinking his naked equipment, reminding himself that he didn't really like women staying here overnight. Yeah, and there'd also been his resolve about not having sex with her all the time, not letting this turn into another Nema situation.

He thought about having her beside him in his bed, warm and soft, her hair tickling his nose, her voice going on and on like a lullaby. She was one gabby lady in bed. Why should he like that in her when he'd hated it in other women?

Besides, he owed her. He must be really out of practice, leaving her high and dry that way. It wasn't fair to send her home frustrated; it was only this once, one more night. What the hell, rules were made to be broken.

Tessa made it a rule never to be late, but rules were made to be broken. She raced into the office Friday morning, to find Clara already there, sitting behind her desk with a stack of files in front of her.

"Clara, you're back. It's great to see you. Sorry I'm late; I slept in and then I couldn't find a place to park—"

The parking bit was true, but the sleeping wasn't. She'd been in bed, though, spending an hour confirming the fact that Eric was a genius when it came to oral sex.

Clara, a stickler for punctuality, didn't seem at all concerned. She gave Tessa a radiant smile. "No problem, dollink. I brought in these sale documents for you to sign. I thought we could get this settled before the weekend."

"Oh. Okay." That seemed a little premature, Tessa thought. She didn't think she'd told Clara for sure yet that she was going to buy Synchronicity. Or had she? Too much sex not only made your eyes go funny, it also addled the brain.

"And I've had a call this morning saying what wonderful matches you've been making for the clients, Tess. You're a natural at this; you're going to make such a success of the business."

This was news. "Who called?"

"Margaret Westwall. She said she's been out with Alistair Farnsworth four times and she finds him delightful."

Well, hot ziggety. *Go, Margaret.*

"There is that situation with Kenneth Zebroff. Of course, it won't affect Synchronicity, but you should be prepared just in case anyone asks."

"Kenneth? What situation with Kenneth?"

"It was in the papers yesterday. His sister-in-law is claiming that he had something to do with his wife's death, that he poisoned her. They're exhuming the body. And now the police are looking into the deaths of his first two wives; it doesn't look good. He's a pharmacist; he'd know all about poison."

Tessa was speechless. Kenneth, the guy she adored, the first client she'd enrolled all by herself. Dear, sweet, thoughtful Kenneth, a murderer?

"You never really found anyone who dated him more than once or twice, so I wouldn't worry about any nasty repercussions with the business. These things happen no matter how careful we are."

Tessa shuddered. She'd actually thought about introducing Kenneth to her mother. God. Maria could be drinking wine laced with cyanide at this very moment. Horrified, Tessa mumbled, "Has—has anything like this ever happened to you, Clara?" Was she the only one who was gullible?

"Not exactly, but there's always little glitches that we can't anticipate."

Clara seemed amazingly unperturbed, and in

good spirits. Tessa was wondering how to ask her tactfully how her divorce was coming along when the phone rang, and simultaneously a nervous prospective client arrived for an interview. It was a busy morning. Things finally slowed down just before lunch.

"Why don't you take a long lunch hour, Tessa? There's paperwork here I need to clear away before the sale is final, and you've been here on your own the past couple weeks. You deserve a break before you take over. Go and have some fun, dollink."

Go, yes. Tessa hurried out into the heat of the summer morning.

Fun, no. All morning, Tessa hadn't been able to stop thinking about Kenneth. Sure, innocent until proven guilty, but the police wouldn't be involved unless there was reasonable doubt. She'd remembered what Olga had said, that there was something about Kenneth that gave her the willies, yet Tessa had trusted him.

She trusted Clara, too. Maybe it wouldn't hurt to get a second opinion. She remembered the paper with the woman's name. She'd left it in the pocket of her shorts, and the shorts were on the floor at Eric's apartment. Maybe he had the number. She dug out her cell phone and called him.

"Henry has it. I asked him to do some research into businesses like Synchronicity. I'll put him on."

Before she had a chance to be outraged, Henry was on the line.

Fifteen minutes later, arm and ear aching, Tessa was sprawled on a bench in a tiny neighborhood park. She had Mary Jo Louie's number written on her palm, and she also had a total and complete rundown on every matchmaking business in Vancouver, and exactly what things to watch out for if she was buying Synchronicity.

"Get a good lawyer and don't do anything fast," Henry had advised. "People aren't lined up wanting to buy a business like that. It's pretty tough to dump, because all you're really selling is goodwill, whatever equipment there is like phones and computers and fax machines, and a bunch of names."

Tessa subtracted the computer and fax part. It didn't really leave one whole hell of a lot except goodwill, did it? And Clara was in an awful hurry.

Feeling only a little like a traitor, she punched in the numbers for Mary Jo. Half an hour later, she walked into a tiny shop a dozen blocks away and introduced herself to the girl behind the counter.

"Mary Jo's in the back. I'll get her."

Mary Jo was Asian; short, dumpy, with a turned-up nose and a rosebud mouth. She didn't look like a devious person, but Tessa was beginning to think maybe she wasn't that good at judging.

She smiled at Tessa, but there was wariness in her dark eyes. "So you're working for Synchronicity. You want a coffee?" She poured them each one, and when they were seated at one of the three small tables, Mary Jo said, "What do you want to know?"

The truth shall set you free. "I'm thinking of buying Synchronicity, and I thought it would be helpful to talk to you. You worked there for a while?"

"Six months." Mary Jo sipped her coffee and gave Tessa a long, thoughtful look. "Then Clara said Bernard was having an affair, and she couldn't stand it anymore. He was breaking her heart; she was divorcing him, and did I want to buy the business at rock bottom rates. When I said no, she fired me."

Tessa had to swallow several times before she could even croak, "But—but that's exactly what she told me."

Mary Jo nodded. "Yeah, I figured so. She's been trying to dump Synchronicity for a couple years; a business like that is hard to sell."

"But—her and Bernard"—Tessa stammered—"they've been married so long—he's such a total creep—I'm sure he really *is* having an affair."

Mary Jo shrugged. "He probably is, or maybe Clara is, who knows? They have some sort of agreement, not that Clara doesn't get her knickers in a knot when Bernard takes advantage of it. And maybe he does the same. Who knows what goes on in a marriage like that?"

"How do you know all this?" Tessa was beginning to wonder who the hell she could believe.

"My mother's a good friend of the woman who cleans Clara's house. You wouldn't believe some of the goings-on over there."

Actually, she would. Tessa remembered the Christmas party.

"As for the business, it's not bad, if it's how you want to spend your working life. Not at the ridiculous price Clara's asking, of course. But she does have a reasonable client base. It needs to be upgraded. She's still in the Dark Ages. No computers. It wasn't my cup of"—Mary Jo grinned her engaging grin and lifted her cup—"coffee. I couldn't take the hassle, all the complaining and stuff. I like to bake, so I started this place—coffee, pastries, soup, sandwiches, lunch crowd, mostly take-out. It's starting to break even, not bad for just a few months." She eyed Tessa. "This was a shock, huh? Don't feel bad, Clara's pretty convincing. She's not a bad person, just devious."

"Yeah." In spades.

"How much did she want?"

Tessa told her. She didn't want any secrets anymore.

Mary Jo clucked her tongue. "Highway robbery. You want the business?"

"I thought I did. I'm not sure of anything anymore."

"Think it over, offer her less than half that amount. I happen to know they've got big money problems, her and Bernard, live way beyond their means. She'll probably take it." She scribbled a name on a napkin and then got to her feet as half a dozen hungry-looking people came in. "This is a good lawyer, really knows about business stuff, helped me get started here. Talk to her before you sign anything."

Three hours later, Tessa dragged herself into Junk Busters. She'd agreed to pick Eric up after work, but he was going to have to do something about the car thing. She was worn down dropping him off and picking him up. She was worn down, period. The day had taken its toll.

Henry met her at the door. "Hey, Tessa, you talk to that Mary Jo?"

Gladys muted the television. "You buying the business?"

"Don't use your own money," Henry said. "Go to the bank, always use the bank's money, let the business pay the loan."

"I'll do the tarot cards for you, see whether the timing's right," Gladys said.

Eric came down the hallway, smiling. "Hey, Tess, how did it go with that Louie woman? Did you come to an agreement with Clara?"

"I got fired." Everyone stopped talking, which was a blessing, because she was about to scream. "I told Clara she was asking too much money, and she said she was deeply hurt, that she was giving me a special price because she cared about me. And I told her I didn't think so, and that I was going to speak to a lawyer about it, and then I told her what I was willing to pay, and she had a screaming fit and fired me."

She'd never seen Clara spitting raving mad before, and she never wanted to again. It wasn't a pretty sight. She'd actually felt the tiniest bit sorry for Bernard. For half a second.

"She'll cool off and come around," Henry said.

"She's bluffing, trying to scare you," Gladys said.

"Let's get the hell out of here," Eric said, which was exactly the right thing to say. Outside, she handed him the car keys. "You drive." She'd had enough stress for one day.

He got behind the wheel. "My place or yours?"

"Mine." She couldn't face those rusty pipes and old car seats and hubcaps, not tonight. "You start looking for a car yet?"

"One of the guys found this Fifty-two Ford. It's been sitting in somebody's garage for years. It'll take a little work, but it'll be a honey when I get it fixed."

Tessa doubted that. It was probably good that this was a short-term thing, Eric's fixation on old cars and junk made into couches was driving her crazy, along with the rest of her life.

"This thing with Clara, you want to talk about it? You want me to get Fletcher on her case? He could sue her for wrongful dismissal or something."

"No. I don't even want to think about it." She put her head back on the seat, and told him the whole story, word for word. Then she remembered Kenneth and told him about that, too. "Between Kenneth and Clara, I just don't know who to trust anymore."

He reached a hand over, took hers, and put it on his thigh, covering it with his own. "It's gonna turn out fine; this is just a little glitch." He patted the back of her hand, clumsy, comforting. Sexy, really sexy, long fingers, long muscular thigh, long— she realized she'd been waiting and waiting, but he'd never said, *You can trust me.*

It hurt like hell, but then what could she expect from him? Maybe he was doing the best he could, and the fact that it wasn't enough wasn't his fault. It was hers for expecting more. Time to get over it.

She said, "On second thought, drive to your place. I'll drop you and go on home; I think I need to be alone for a while."

"But it's Friday night. I thought we'd go out for dinner. We haven't been to a really nice place for dinner yet, Tess. And you need company, somebody to talk to; you've had one hell of a day—"

"Thanks, but I have a headache."

Stopped at a light, he leaned over, blew a raspberry on her bare thigh and murmured, "I know this great cure for headaches."

He knew all the moves, she had to give him that. She also gave him a smile and shook her head. "I'll take a rain check."

25.

She don't get the blues—she gives 'em

Rain check—what the hell was that supposed to mean? Thoroughly out of sorts, Eric slammed his apartment door behind him. He'd been looking forward to spending the evening with Tessa.

His answering machine was blinking, and he felt better. She'd probably changed her mind already, called him on her cell. He pushed play, and felt deflated, even though it was Karen.

"Could you give me a call, Eric? I really need to talk to you."

He punched out the numbers. As usual, it took three tries and intervention by an operator before the call finally went through. Sonny answered, in Spanish, and then became cheerfully hearty.

"Hey, Eric, my man, how you doing?"

There'd been a time when Eric was very young when he actually thought Sonny wanted an honest answer to that question.

Now he didn't even bother to respond. "Is Karen around?"

"She's right here; we're looking at old photos."

A pause, and then, "Eric?"

He relaxed a little. She didn't sound freaked out. "Hey, sweet pea, how are you?"

"I'm fine. Well, sort of fine. I haven't gone nuts again and shaved anybody bald, so that's a plus. I get worried about the kids, though, Sophie keeps saying they're being good, but that can't be true. I know my boys. So I thought I'd get the straight goods out of you."

"I haven't talked to Soph for a couple days, but I'd have heard if anything was wrong." Come to think of it, he should have heard, because the last time he'd talked to her, Soph was frantic. Maybe she had the kids on tranquilizers. Maybe she was taking them herself.

"Karo, the boys are absolutely fine. Don't worry about them for a second." Eric gave her a detailed rundown on the carnival, skipping the parts about getting stuck on the Ferris wheel and being in a car accident.

"They're going to stay with Bruno and Anna starting next Wednesday. Soph has to go back to work. Bruno's taking time off; they're all going camping."

"Oooohhh, they'll like that." Big sigh of relief. "I've never been away from them before. I really miss them."

"They miss you too, but they're pretty adaptable." They were; they could wreak havoc virtually anywhere. Eric figured nobody else in the family was going to miss them when Karen got back, if their current track record held true.

"So how's it going with you? The parental units trying to borrow money from you yet?"

"Not yet. It's nice here, Eric, I'm turning brown from the sun. The house is open. There's a central courtyard and lots of flowers. Mom has a gardener called Miguel. My room is at the back, and the birds are amazing in the early morning. I can walk to the ocean; I go swimming every day. Mom and Dad spend part of each day at the orphanage. Mom takes care of the babies and Dad entertains the kids with his guitar. I've been trimming everyone's hair."

"Jesus." Eric scowled and shook his head. "That orphanage gig, I just don't believe it." His voice was heavy with sarcasm. "It's not as if they're familiar with kids; they never spent that much time with their own. Have they even asked about Simon and Ian?" He knew his parents were right there; he shouldn't put her on the spot this way.

"I brought a ton of pictures with me."

They were there, but still he had to warn her. "Don't expect anything from them, sweet pea. Don't loan them money; don't let them exploit you with this hair thing. And don't let them get under your skin; they're not worth it."

"I hear you. I don't necessarily agree."

How old did you have to get before you stopped wanting attention from your parents? Older than Karen, that was for sure.

"Don't worry about me, I'm feeling lots better and Mom's cook, Consuela, is teaching me how to make tortillas and something called mole. When I get home I'll cook you guys an authentic Mexican meal." She took a shaky breath. "Have you heard anything from Scissor Happy? Is Junella going to try and get my license lifted? Is Myrna going to sue me?"

"Fletcher's dealing with Junella. He figures she's in violation of several employment laws, so I wouldn't worry about your license. And Myrna can't sue you personally; the salon carries insurance for stuff like that. Don't worry about any of it. Fletch will get it all sorted out. It'll be history by the time you come home."

"Tell Fletcher I'm grateful. Tell him I'll cut his hair free for the rest of his life. Although maybe under the circumstances, he might not think that's the best offer he's ever had."

Good, she could joke about it now. "His hair's thinning anyway. And before I forget, I told the boys you'd send them postcards."

"I already did, tons of them, iguanas and para-sails and big fish. Hopefully they'll get them before I get back, the mail here isn't the best. And oh yeah, how's it going with Synchronicity?"

"They lined me up with this babe called Sylvia, but I flunked out at Dating One-oh-one, so Tessa's got me in her class for losers."

That made her giggle. He smiled. She really was better.

"Learn your lessons, big brother. And tell Tess hi from me when you see her next."

Whenever the bloody rain check kicked in. "Shall do."

"I should go. I love you, Eric. You're the best."

"I love you too, sweet pea. I'll call you again in a couple days. Remember what I said about Georgia and Sonny."

"I will. Bye."

Karen set the phone down, thinking she was going to cry, but she found herself smiling instead at the thought of Tessa and Eric together. So she and her sisters might have pulled it off. And her kids were doing okay. Eric would have told her if they weren't.

She'd been missing them something awful, so she'd brought out pictures of them to show her parents. They'd sort of glanced at them, but then they started talking about famous musicians they'd had *their* picture taken with. And Sonny had dragged out a box of photos, and her kids got buried under her parents' egos.

She'd always thought that if she just had enough time with Sonny and Georgia, she could make them care about her, take an interest, love her the way she wanted to be loved. She knew now that was a pipe dream.

Sonny held up a yellowed photograph. "Look at this one, Karen, this is your mom and I with John Sebastian, from Lovin' Spoonful." He kissed Georgia, full on the lips. "Damn, babe, I used to love that blue dress on you."

Georgia and Sonny bent over the snap, their sun-ravaged faces glowing, their daughter forgotten. Sonny's arm was around Georgia's hips, and she bent and pressed a kiss on his brown-spotted balding head.

They were self-centered, aging, pathetic and sad. Those things were undeniable. But Karen couldn't help but notice that they cared deeply about each other, and that the caring went beyond what might be expected of a couple who'd been together over forty years. Astounding as it was, they were still in love, the way Karen had been in love with Jimmy in the beginning. She even heard them making love at night, their quiet laughter. She saw them touch each other just for the sake of touching.

It made Karen unbearably lonely, but it also gave her something positive. Her brother and sisters referred to Sonny and Georgia as write-offs when it came to parenting, and they were right;

even Karen understood that now. But they loved each other, and they'd made their marriage work, in whatever dysfunctional manner. It was an accomplishment, something in their favor. It comforted Karen.

She even understood a little of their failure at parenting. Kids demanded all you had to give; they drained you—Karen knew that all too well. Most people did a balancing act with their kids, this much for themselves, that much for the kids. Georgia and Sonny simply took a hundred percent for themselves. Somewhere she'd read that the children of lovers were orphans. It was all too true.

The fortunate thing was that she and her sisters had always had Eric to love and care for them. What hurt was that up till now, Eric hadn't had anyone of his own caring for him.

He was so stubborn, so afraid to love anybody in case they didn't love him back, and he needed love so much. If only he'd give in and let himself fall for Tessa.

At noon on Saturday, Eric gave in. He'd told himself he wasn't calling Tessa. She was the one with the rain check; she could damned well call him. There was no way a woman was going to jerk his chain this way, on again, off again, hot, cold, maybe. It was all over with her except for the formalities.

He'd started welding together something he called Woman, because it had dawned on him that ball bearings would make perfect nipples, and a piece of old railway steel was just the right shape for a body. He could leave the center empty where the heart should go. But he couldn't concentrate,

and after he'd come close to blinding himself for
the second time, he snatched up the phone. It was
time to get a few things straightened out between
them. They needed to discuss stuff like was she
okay for money, did she want to come and work
for him just as a stopgap. He'd had women driving
for him before; they were terrific. She could leave
again whenever she liked.

"Tessa, hi." It was a beginning.

"Oh, it's you," she said. Her voice dropped to a
husky whisper. "I'm in bed; I still have a headache.
Why don't you come over and cure it? I'll leave the
back door unlocked."

He'd stuffed some underwear and things in a
sports bag and was out the door before he remembered he still didn't have a car, which was totally
stupid, he owned a flourishing business and four
trucks, for Christ sake. He whistled down a cab,
and at the Volkswagen dealers on Kingsway he
bought a new turbo diesel Jetta. He was going to
get black, but he remembered something Tessa
had said and changed his mind.

Driving it was a dream. It shot ahead at stop
signs, zipped in and out of traffic. It looked classy
parked in front of Tessa's place. No more bitching
about his dump trucks and what the neighbors
would think.

He went in the back door, and down the hall to
her bedroom. She actually was in bed, wearing
something white and see-through; no sheet because it was a really hot day. She sat up against the
soft pillows and he could see her nipples, shad-
owed against the cotton. Her pillowcases were
trimmed with eyelet. He knew eyelet; his sisters
had had dresses out of it long ago. With her wild
curls touching her shoulders and that mouth and

those nipples, she looked like a painting from behind some bar, only better.

She said, "What took you so long?"

"I had to stop at the dealers and pick up a car."
He sat down and pulled off his shoes. "As soon as
your headache's gone, we can go for a ride."

"How old a car?" Her voice was suspicious. "Does
it actually run?"

"New. Right off the showroom floor."

"You bought a new car? I thought you only liked
old ones."

"A guy can change; nothing's written in stone."

"My god, Eric, do you have any idea how sexy
new cars are?"

He took off his shorts and T-shirt. "I'm hoping
maybe you could show me."

"Lie down here." He did, and she slid down his
body, her mouth soft and tickling, teasing and
then urgent, and when he couldn't bear it any
longer he rolled her beneath him.

"Don't close your eyes," she said, so he didn't,
moving in her slow and long, holding back because that way it took longer, looking into her eyes
and sliding, sweat like hot oil between them, hers
and his and then no space, just nerves and heat,
and her eyes, melting, and a long, shuddering
slide, and they broke together, fire and trembling
peace.

26.

Chaste makes waste

Fantastic orgasms just weren't enough, Tessa decided. Probably all the other women who'd fallen for him thought the same as she had in the beginning; they could take him or leave him, no big deal. Wrong, wrong. She loved him; she wanted so much more from him than orgasms. It might not even bother her so much if people didn't keep getting married.

Her father had phoned at eleven last evening.

"We wanted you to know we're in Reno. Your mother and I just tied the knot."

Tessa's heart thumped, and her voice was so quavery she wondered who the heck was talking. "Congratulations." She'd been half expecting it, but it was still an awful shock. What should she say? "I hope you and Mom sell that damned motorcycle and live happily ever after, Dad." That was dumb, but she didn't exactly have a script prepared.

"Thanks, honey. Your mom's here, she wants to talk to you."

"Tessa?" Maria sounded breathless and fluttery.

"Oh, Tessa, it was the nicest wedding. I wish you could have been here. They have the cutest little chapel, and they supply flowers and everything. You're not upset with us, are you, honey? I know you had some misgivings, but we're older now, we know what we want. And Tessa?"

She hadn't meant to cry, but she was. "Yeah, Mom?"

"Tessa, we're so much in love." Maria was crying, too.

"I'm really happy for you, Mom. For both of you." And just like that, she knew it was true. She knew that this time, she wanted her folks to make it. She wanted it so much she'd been afraid to admit there was a possibility, but what the heck had there been to hang her hopes on? Certainly not their past performance, or her own marital track record. But somebody deserved a happy ever after, and it might as well be her parents.

Eric mumbled, "You okay, Tess?" Her head was on his shoulder, his leg across her thighs. "Your headache better? Is there anything you want? Something to drink, maybe?"

Just a little glass of commitment, big guy.

"My mom and dad got married last night. They say they've fallen back in love again. You ever been in love, Eric?"

Time passed and he didn't answer, so after awhile she gave up, slid away and sat up. She kept expecting more; she had to stop that.

"My headache's totally gone; you should patent this cure of yours. Let's go out and celebrate your new car and my new parents. I've got this summer dress I've never had a chance to wear yet."

"You sure you're okay with that?"

"The dress? Absolutely, you'll like it; it's almost

sheer. The car? I'm boondoggled and hornswoggled that you'd break with tradition and buy a new vehicle. What color is it?" *As for commitment, if you think you're riding out of Dodge in a new car without a gunfight, you've got a news flash coming.*

"Red. And I didn't mean the car, I was talking about your parents."

"You bought a red car? But I love red cars."

"I know, you told me once. What about your parents?"

"I love them, too. They're over eighteen and Mom's not pregnant this time, so I'm pretty optimistic about it. C'mon and have a shower with me."

It took a long, long time to get clean, and when they finally made it to the car, Tessa took one look and fell in lust.

"You can drive if you want." Eric tossed her the keys, and when she climbed in, the new leather smelled so good she wanted to bottle the scent.

A guy can change, he'd said. *Nothing's written in stone.*

Maybe there was an opening here. Maybe all she needed was a foolproof plan.

Wednesday morning, Anna sat at her kitchen table with her laptop, charted her horoscope, and tried to plan her life for the rest of the week.

Sudden and unexpected change, thanks to Uranus. That was obvious; Sophie was due to arrive in a couple minutes with the boys. Jupiter in retrograde, so spiritual progress would be limited. How could anybody be expected to make progress with two small boys around? And Pluto aspecting heavily, indicating massive upheaval.

That was happening already. She'd just had yet

another blowup with Bruno; her stomach hurt and she couldn't even finish her yogurt because of it. And all she'd done was point out the things she didn't want the boys to touch while they were here.

"It cost a lot to have the house and yard feng shui'd. The aquarium and the jade plant and the pond in the garden are guaranteed to bring harmony to our relationship, so please tell the boys they're to stay away from all of them."

He'd looked at her as if she was some loonie he'd happened to stumble across sitting at his kitchen table. "Anna, you taught kids for eleven years, for cripes' sake. What's the big deal with your own nephews spending a couple weeks here?"

"You really need to get a handle on your emotions, Bruno, I've told you a zillion times you should learn to meditate. And teaching teenagers art and social studies isn't the same as having a five-year-old and a three-year-old living with us. My pupils went home at the end of the day."

And it had taken her eleven years to figure out teaching wasn't what she was cut out to do; she wasn't that good with kids. Astrology was her mission in this life.

"It's good practice for when our own kids come," he said in that exasperated tone he was using on her these days. "A person would think you didn't even like kids, the way you go on about Simon and Ian."

"I love them. I just don't want to live with them." He was mentioning their own kids more and more lately, and each time she'd get this same sick feeling in the pit of her stomach. Sure, she wanted kids; she'd told him that before they were married. She just hadn't added *maybe, someday, later.* It was too bad, but Bruno just wasn't keeping up with her spiritual growth, and it was causing problems between them. She told him so, and he shoved his breakfast aside and stomped out into the yard.

She went to the window. He was putting up a basketball hoop on the side of the garage, dangerously close to her lilies. She tried to see cleansing light around him, but she couldn't get it past the tension in her gut.

Two weeks. Two whole weeks with Simon and Ian.

Sophie's car had just pulled into the driveway. She heard Bruno call to the boys, and then Sophie opened the back door and came in.

"Anna? How's it going? Got any coffee?"

Coffee wasn't good for the central nervous system, Anna knew that, but she'd just brewed a second pot. She'd have to do a deep tissue cleanse when this was finally over, to get rid of the negative emotional residue in her cells.

"Isn't it a glorious morning?" Sophie was practically singing. "There's nothing like Vancouver when the sun shines." She sat down, looking as if she was bursting with well-being, blue eyes shining, skin creamy and glowing, lips—were Sophie's lips always that swollen?

"What's up with you, Soph? You look—enlightened."

Which was hard to fathom, because the last time Anna talked to her, sometime last week, Sophie had almost lost her famous cool. The boys had knocked over a display of spaghetti sauce in the supermarket—not cans, eighteen glass jars, which had sprayed over Sophie, the boys, three customers and a clerk. Apparently the manager had asked if Sophie would please not patronize his store again.

Maybe Sophie was so happy because it was a huge relief to be getting rid of the kids? *Two weeks.* Apprehension gripped Anna by the throat.

"I'm over the moon, Anna. You'll never guess what's happened." Sophie's voice was lyrical. "Rocky finally caved."

It took a moment to process that. "Rocky? He finally took you out?"

"Not exactly. Apart from taking the kids places, we've been staying home and going to bed early. Thank heavens little kids sleep a lot." Sophie leaped to her feet and threw her arms around Anna. "Oh, God, Anna, last night he *proposed.*"

"In bed?"

"Of course in bed, it's the only place we've been alone."

"You think he meant it?"

Sophie gave her a withering look. "Of course he meant it. He's finally come to his senses. We've known each other forever; it's stupid to waste any more time." She did a whirling dance around the kitchen table. "I'm so happy I can't stand it."

"Well, it's just that men will say anything after sex; it opens all their chakras—" She and Bruno used to open their chakras that way. They used to be good at it, until Anna decided too much sex wasn't good for spiritual development.

"I'm telling you he *meant* it, Anna. We're getting married. A week from Saturday, civil ceremony, down at City Hall. That's the earliest I can get time off work."

"So fast?"

"Like Rocky says, why wait? Once he gets with the program, the man's a mover."

"Soph, that's fantastic." For a moment, happiness for her sister overcame everything. Anna got up and wrapped her arms around Sophie.

"But don't you want a wedding? City Hall, it's so impersonal." Sophie was her sister; there were things sisters did, no matter what. "Why not have it here, in the living room?" With the jade plant and the aquarium and all that harmony. "I met this neat woman at yoga class. She's a justice of the peace; I'll bet we could get her to do the ceremony. Nothing fancy, just family. I also know a caterer; she's the one who gives me shiatsu massage. She'll give us a good price on food for the lunch."

Lordie, how could she handle the kids *and* a wedding? She couldn't handle the kids; she knew that already. The wedding, she could do as long as Bruno was here, every minute. He'd promised.

Sophie shook her head. "But you've got the kids; you're taking them camping."

"We could put it off." That didn't exactly break her heart, tenting wasn't her favorite spiritual practice.

"Well—only if you're sure," Sophie said. Then she clapped her hands like a kid herself. "Oh, wow, it would be so fantastic, getting married here. But shouldn't you talk it over with Bruno first?"

"Bruno will be upset if you *don't* do it here; you know how he is about family." It was one of the reasons she'd fallen in love with him, that magnanimous generosity when it came to those he cared for. Funny how she forgot that when he'd offered to keep the boys.

"It's settled. I'll call everybody, get it lined up."

"Anna, thank you!" Sophie leaped to her feet and grabbed Anna in a hug that almost cracked her ribs. "I'm going shopping right after work

today for something exquisite. I'll look for a dress
for you, too; I know what you like and what looks
good. It'll be my gift to you, for doing this for me."

"Don't forget I've gained about ten pounds in
the last year." Bruno loved her plump. He swore
she was sexier this way. When had he last said that,
anyhow?

Sophie was flicking things off on her fingers.
"Rocky wants Eric to be his best man. I want you to
stand up for me. Oh, I *wish* Karen were here; you
could both stand up for me. I'm calling her tonight.
Flowers, what should we do about flowers?"

"The backyard is full of lilies and roses, we'll use
them."

"And I'm really glad the boys will be at my wedding—"

Pure terror nipped at Anna's heart. She had a
week to arrange a wedding; she could *not* take care
of Simon and Ian as well. Bruno would understand
that. He'd volunteered to have them; he'd just have
to do all the child care—this cinched it.

Sophie left, almost skipping down the walk, and
Bruno came in with Simon and Ian.

"Uncle Bruno's taking us to the store; we're
gonna get a basketball," Simon announced.

"And Auntie Sophereeno is gonna marry Rocky,"
Ian announced in a disgusted tone. "Why can't he
marry our mommy and live with us?"

Bruno was as thrilled over Sophie's news as
Anna had been. He'd forgotten about their quar-
rel, and he came over and kissed her, full on the
lips. "Of course the wedding has to be here. What
should we get them for a gift?"

Anna remembered again why she'd fallen in
love with him. He was the most generous man
she'd ever met, and he never held a grudge. She

was feeling better, making them tomato soup and tuna sandwiches when the phone rang.

Bruno answered, and she knew right away by the conversation and the expression on his face when he hung up.

"You promised," she said as panic started to set in. "You said you'd be here every minute, that we'd do this together, you promised."

He couldn't meet her eyes. "I have to go, Anna. It's one of my best customers over on the island, a surprise audit by the tax department; they want the last four years' records. I've got to see him through this. I'll be back by Friday. Saturday morning at the latest."

Two entire days alone with Simon and Ian.

She knew that only by setting your partner free were you ever free yourself. She knew all the spiritual rules about relationships.

She did hysteria, heavy guilt, tears, and she finally ended up begging. But by one in the afternoon Bruno had packed up his laptop, thrown a clean shirt and underwear in a bag, and driven off to catch the ferry.

"You are not allowed to touch the aquarium or the jade plant in the living room," she told Simon and Ian, her voice trembling. "Don't go near the pond in the backyard or touch the flowers. Go in your bedroom and put away your things in the dresser. If you're good boys for the next couple of days, I'll take you out for ice cream."

"I don't like ice cream. I got sick from it at the fair," Simon declared, lip thrust out. "I want to go fix toilets with Rocky; he gives us salami and pickles on buns."

Ian whined, "When is my mommy coming for us?"

Shaking, Anna sent them to their room and went to hers to meditate for twenty minutes. When she came out, they'd poured orange juice from the fridge into the fish tank and three of her fish were dead.

Trembling, she called Bruno on his cell, but he must have turned it off, the coward. She sent the boys outside to keep from screaming at them and when she glanced out the window they were knocking the heads off the lilies with a stick.

"They had bugs eating on them, they were rotten anyway," Simon told her when she rushed outside. "And Ian peed in the pond."

They both fell on the lawn laughing.

Anna snatched the stick and did deep breathing to keep from using it. She repeated her mantra—*Allllll Is Wellllll*—but it didn't do a thing. She'd lost her center, and it infuriated her. *What good is all this spiritual practice if it deserts you in a time of need?*

She thought of calling Karen in Mexico and telling her to come and get her kids, but she remembered just in time that the reason Karen was in Mexico was she'd flipped out and shaved somebody's head. She probably couldn't be trusted with kids right now. This must be how Karen had felt just before she stepped over the edge.

Finally she called Sophie at the hospital, insisting it was a family emergency. Sophie was apparently dealing with a motorcycle accident or something inconsequential, and it took awhile before she came on the line.

"I hear you," she said cheerfully when Anna stopped gibbering. "They can be real little beggars when they want; don't let them get you down. I've gotta go; we've got an MVA arriving. Why don't you phone Rocky for some tips? Here's his cell number; he's a genius with kids." She rattled it off and hung up.

Rocky. Yeah, right. Anna figured Sophie was in that euphoric sexual state where she believed Rocky could settle the Middle East crisis if somebody just asked him. She'd been that way with Bruno in the beginning.

But maybe Rocky would come and take them. He'd done that for Sophie, and Anna *was* doing his wedding. Wasn't it only fair?

She called him, explaining that there was only the jade plant left and the wedding was *seven and a half days away* and *someone* had to understand that she *didn't know what to do with small children;* she had no experience, what if something happened to them—*besides her beating them half to death with their own stick?*

"Gosh, Anna, I'd gladly take them with me, but I've got this big job on a union site, and they won't allow kids," Rocky said, and Anna's heart hit rock bottom. "They're basically good, but they're boys," he said, grunting as he finished tightening something. "Okay, now let's turn the water on here and see what we've got," he muttered. Anna felt like screaming. He wasn't paying attention. "Just be straight with them. Don't make threats you don't intend to carry out or promises you can't keep. Talk to them; use bribery if you absolutely have to. Watch them every minute. Oh yeah, and remember, you're the boss, you're older and bigger than they are. Ooops, gotta go, Anna, I've got a leak."

So did she. Her sanity was leaking out of her crown chakra; she could practically hear the hiss. She slammed the phone down just in time to catch Simon putting jade leaves in a bowl and pouring milk on them for a snack for Ian. She was going to have to divorce Bruno; that's all there was to it. When a man didn't keep his promises; that was the end.

"Why can't we eat leaves off of plants, Auntie? Food is plants, right?"

Be straight with them. "Because that jade plant is in that corner to bring prosperity and peace to this house," she managed to say through clenched teeth. First opportunity, she was phoning that feng shui woman and telling her it was all a crock. "And it's poisonous; if you eat it you'll get really sick and Auntie Sophie will have to give you something to make you throw up, and you won't like it at all."

"We already did that, after we went to the fair. Ian throwed up on Tessa and on Auntie Sophie's new rug, and it went on the wall, too. We don't like barfing."

What a consolation. "What did Auntie Sophie do?"

"She cried."

That was comforting. Enlightening as well. Even Saint Sophie had broken beneath the strain. Anna felt a tiny bit better. And if she kept them talking, there wasn't much they could get into. "Tell me more about the fair," she coaxed.

Simon was in the middle of some far-fetched tale about the Ferris wheel breaking down when Ian interrupted. He said in a plaintive voice, "Auntie Anna, when is our mommy coming for us?"

She remembered he'd said it before. And like a flash of light, Anna got it; she'd always had powerful psychic abilities. Besides, she'd taken psych at university.

If they were bad enough, if nobody wanted them around, their mommy would have to come and get them.

They were missing Karen, with the same aching

longing Anna remembered feeling when she was a little girl. She'd wanted her mommy, and more often than not, Georgia wasn't there.

Another revelation hit her like an asteroid. Was she afraid to *be* a mommy, because she didn't have a pattern? Was she scared because she knew she'd get it wrong, like she had with teaching? Sometimes it seemed as if the only really perfect thing she'd ever managed was to marry Bruno, and look what these kids were doing to her marriage.

Except it wasn't Simon and Ian. It was her. Admitting it shocked her so profoundly, she forgot how mad she was at Bruno. It also made her heart ache for her nephews. They were stuck with her the same way she was with them.

"Why don't we draw your mommy pictures and color them, and then we'll walk up to the post office and mail them?" She'd write Karen a note, lie through her teeth, tell her how good her kids were, say how much fun she and Bruno were having with the boys. What was the old saying? *Fake it till you make it.* She was going to fake for all she was worth, and when Bruno turned his damn cell on again, she was going to talk really dirty to him the way she used to do, before she took up spiritual abstinence.

Simon said, "Is Uncle Bruno coming back soon to get us a basketball?"

Anna said, "You better believe it, kid."

27.

Trust in God, but tie up your camel

"I can't believe this, Fletch." It was a good thing he was sitting down, because Eric figured his legs wouldn't have supported him. With the wedding only two days away, he'd stopped by to find out what Rocky needed him to do, exactly, as best man. But Rocky had gone for a haircut, so Eric was having a coffee with Fletch.

"I was pleasantly surprised myself," Fletcher said in that mild way of his. "I knew Karen would get some money from Canada Pension, and Nicols was a member of the dockworker's union. They pay survivor benefits. But that shoe box of stuff you brought showed Nicols had been paying extra premiums, pretty hefty ones, too. All together, she'll get about three hundred fifty thousand, not a fortune by any means, but it'll be a nest egg. There was mortgage insurance on the condo as well, and because they weren't divorced, that'll be paid off, too." Fletcher smiled. "Guess the guy had some residual sense of responsibility after all, huh?"

It galled Eric to have to nod. It pissed him off to

admit that Nicols had provided for Karen. Eric preferred to think of him the way he always had, as a man with no principles, no conscience, no saving graces. "Karen's gonna be surprised." Big understatement. "I'll call her and tell her the good news." This was a windfall for her, and that at least made him feel good.

Not much else was doing that these days. He was having some sort of emotional crisis. He missed Tessa when he was away from her; that hadn't happened with anyone before, and it bugged the hell out of him.

Fletcher said, "You guys have always been good friends. It's sorta nice that now you'll all be related."

"Yeah, it is." Although Eric had always thought of Rocky as his brother anyway. Not that he had any problems with Rocky marrying Sophie, everybody had been waiting for it to happen for years now. It just made Eric feel a little abandoned, which was plain old stupid. "So what do I do, on Saturday, at this wedding, Fletch?"

"The usual best man stuff: keep track of the ring and the groom, make certain he's sane and sober and on time, sign as a witness, say a few words at the reception, all that good stuff. It's really kind of Anna and Bruno to have the wedding at their place."

Eric had been pleasantly surprised at that, after the performance Anna had pulled about the boys staying there. He'd half expected there'd be a divorce instead of a wedding, but the other night when Eric stopped by Bruno looked happier than he had in months. Anna too. She'd even invited Gladys and Henry on Saturday.

"They were at my wedding. I feel as if they're

family," Anna had said, which Eric figured was true, if a person happened to be related to the Munsters.

Fletcher leaned back in his chair. "Rocky's moving most of his stuff out tonight, over to Sophie's condo. You could give us a hand with that if you're free. My back's not as good as it once was."

"Sure thing. Gonna be different for you, Fletch, living here alone."

"Maybe it's time for me to sell this place and get myself a bachelor pad."

They both looked around at the clutter, papers and books scattered on tables and chairs, the computer table in the middle of the living room, the bicycle in the corner, ten pairs of shoes by the door. Funny, Eric thought, how different houses looked when women lived in them.

Tessa's house, for instance, was full of big fat soft cushions and armchairs that sort of wrapped around you, and old, faded rugs and healthy green plants. Women's houses smelled different, fresher, not so much like sweat gear and trainers and take-out pizza. He was beginning to think maybe he oughta scrap that couch he'd made and buy one with some springs, whenever he went back to living at his own place again.

"Rocky tell you Tessa's buying Synchronicity?" Clara had caved. She and Tessa's lawyer had hammered out an agreement. Tessa was at her lawyer's office right now, going over the fine points and signing it.

Fletcher said, "I heard that. Tell her congratulations, and I'm thinking of joining Synchronicity myself once the legalities are settled. I want to find a nice lady who'd like to go traveling."

"Give it some thought," Eric advised. "Now that

Tessa's buying the business, you'll have less chance than ever at a refund." He hadn't managed to get the girls their money back, and now it didn't look as if he ever would. The agreement had been with Clara, as Tessa was quick to point out. Funny how the money didn't really bother him anymore.

"I wouldn't be looking for a refund. I'd see it more as an investment. So how are things going with Tessa, Eric? Is she the one you've been waiting for?"

That brought a flash of irritation. What made Fletcher think he'd been waiting for anybody?

"We're just good friends, Fletch." Too good, he'd started thinking. He hadn't been home yet this week except to pick up fresh clothes and his mail. He hadn't touched his blowtorch in so long he hardly remembered how it worked. "Nothing serious, with Tessa and me; we're buddies." Although he'd never used that massage oil stuff with his buddies before. "I'm just not the marrying type. I like being alone." He did, too. He was spending lots of time alone with Tessa. "Freedom, that's where it's at for me. I'm surprised you'd give that up yourself, Fletch."

"Marriage *is* freedom. I was married for twenty-seven years. I felt healthier and happier then than I've felt since Hannah died. I'd certainly marry again if I found the right lady. Men live longer married than they do single."

No hesitation, Eric noted. Rocky, Tessa's father, now Fletch, damn, guys were dropping left and right with this marriage stuff.

"I still miss Hannah," Fletcher added, "but now that Rocky's settled it's time to move on."

Eric figured you couldn't get more settled than Rocky had been, living here in the same house he'd grown up in, with a father who was always there for him. Always there for Eric, too: Fletcher had bailed him out of teenage scrapes, lectured him about birth control, cosigned for him at the bank. He'd sorted out legal tangles, given advice on business matters, listened when Eric was having problems with his sisters. It had never dawned on him until right now that Fletcher had been a father figure to him all along.

"We all know what's best for ourselves," Fletcher was saying. "Marriage isn't for everyone. It takes a lot of work to make a relationship succeed; not everybody wants to put that amount of effort into being happy. It's easier to just say next."

"Isn't that the truth?" For a second, Eric wondered if maybe Fletch was hinting at something, but that was nuts. Guys didn't hint; that was a female trait. He drained his coffee mug and suppressed a shudder. Instant didn't taste as good after you had the stuff Tessa made in that Bodum thing.

He glanced at his watch. It was almost time to pick her up from the lawyers; he'd better get a move on. "Gotta go, tell Rocky I'll come over about six to help him move. He can get me on my cell, or I'll be at Tessa's later on."

They were going out for lunch, to celebrate her buying Synchronicity. And she wanted to get a dress for the wedding, and he needed some shoes. Usually he hated shopping, but Tess had a way of making it almost fun.

Fletch walked him to the door. "See you Saturday."

"Yeah." Eric would never tell Fletch or Rocky either, but for some reason he just wasn't looking forward one bit to this damned wedding.

* * *

When Anna called an hour later, he and Tessa were sitting at a sidewalk café, and it became very clear to Eric why the wedding was bothering him. He must have had a premonition.

She said, "Guess what?"

Eric and Tessa were eating burgers and having a discussion, and the way that was going, he wasn't in any mood for guessing games. He wasn't in the mood for burgers, either.

"Just tell me, okay, Anna?"

"Mom and Dad are here. They brought Karen for the wedding. They drove through; they just got here a half hour ago."

Shit. That explained why Eric hadn't been able to reach Karen for a couple of days. "Did you tell the parental units they weren't exactly invited?"

They must have been nearby, because Anna said in a chipper voice, "The kids are going bananas, they're so glad to see Karen. And she looks wonderful; she's so *brown.*"

"Tell me you haven't invited them to stay with you, Anna?"

"Yeah, Bruno did, but they're staying with Karen, she wants them to get to know the boys."

"Give me a break. Those two losers can't even remember how many kids they had themselves." He was already in a bad mood, thanks to Tessa, and this made it worse.

She'd stopped dipping fries in ketchup was staring at him with her eyebrows raised. He turned away so he wasn't looking into her eyes. "Does Soph know they're here?"

"Yeah, I already called her. She really wanted Karen to be at her wedding; she's glad Mom and Dad made it, too."

"Well, it's nice you girls are so ready to forgive

and forget, but leave me out of the picture," he snarled. "I don't want anything to do with Sonny or Georgia. I'll tell them that myself when I see them."

"Eric, it's Sophie's *wedding.*"

Which was exactly what Tessa said the moment he was off the phone.

"It's Sophie's *wedding,* Eric. No matter what they've done, they're your parents; they naturally want to be there."

"When it's Georgia and Sonny, don't use the words *natural* and *parents* in the same sentence, okay?"

"Okay, okay. They're *your* parents; God knows I have enough issues with my own. But it *is* Sophie's wedding."

He knew that. It wasn't Sophie's wedding he was having trouble processing; it was the conversation he'd been having with Tessa before the phone rang. He took it one more time, from the top.

"So this lawyer from Calgary is here, and you're going out to dinner with him tomorrow night?" She'd tossed it off so casually, while the waiter was standing right there taking their order.

"Sheldon Winesapp, yes. I promised I'd show him around when he came to town; he's here for a trial. And you and the guys are taking Rocky out tomorrow night anyway, so I didn't think you'd mind."

"You didn't exactly ask if I minded."

"I didn't see any need to run it by you. We both agreed this was a temporary thing with us, and you were so clear from the beginning about not wanting commitment or anything permanent, and we certainly never made any agreements about not seeing other people, right?"

"Right." Then why did it feel so goddamned wrong? "I guess I just somehow assumed that while we were together, you wouldn't be dating other guys." Or that it would make him feel like ramming his fist down the bastard's throat, or tying Tessa up. They'd done that, but not the way he was envisioning.

"Oh, Eric, Sheldon and I are old friends; it's not really a date."

Just dinner, at some fancy restaurant, with piano music and lots of wine. He knew the effect wine had on her, and he didn't want her drinking it with some idiot named Sheldon who wouldn't take care of her when she got tipsy. And, as for the friends part, he and Tessa were friends, and they kept landing in bed together naked. And there was the talking. The thought of her in bed naked talking with this Winesapp made him a little crazy. Or maybe it brought him to his senses.

"Tessa, remember when you asked me whether I'd ever been in love?"

She nodded, unfazed at the sudden change of subject. "You didn't answer."

"I was trying to figure it out; it took me awhile. I'm kinda slow about this stuff. I've got it now, though. I'm in love with you, Tessa."

28.

Words are a virus from outer space

He thought she'd be happy, maybe say the same thing back to him and then *they* could live happily ever after, but instead she was scowling at him.

"Eric, is this just an underhanded effort to keep me from going out with Sheldon? Because it won't work."

And all of a sudden he got scared. He could really lose her; she might just care for this guy. Fletcher had been right; she was the one he'd been waiting for, and he'd blown it. There was only one more thing to say, and although he'd never said it before, it came out easy.

"Tessa, will you marry me?"

The people at the surrounding tables all turned and smiled at them. They were all listening, and he didn't care, because he was dying, waiting for her answer.

"I can't, Eric." She shook her head, and her curls bounced and resettled. "I want kids, and you don't, and that's a big thing with me. I was in one marriage like that; I can't get into another. I love you, too. But no."

He saw the pain on her face. He wanted to say, *Okay, so we'll have kids,* but he couldn't, no matter how hard he tried. Instead, he said, "Let's get out of here." He put some money down, walked to the car like a wooden soldier, opened the door for her.

She wasn't crying, but her voice sounded like she might. "Just take me home, okay? And maybe it would be best it you went home, too, until we go to the wedding. If you still want to take me, that is."

That one blindsided him. Hadn't this usually played the other way around, him suggesting the woman go home? The hell with her, he had his pride. "Of course I do. I'll see you Saturday, then; I'll pick you up about eleven."

The wedding was at one. He wished there was some way to get out of going, but he was the best man, it was his sister getting married to his best friend, his entire family would be there, and he'd never felt this lousy in his whole entire life, not even when he thought he'd murdered Nicols.

"I can't wait," Tessa said in a miserable voice. "I just love weddings."

29.

If a guitar ain't never been in a pawnshop, it can't play the blues
          —Frank Edwards, blues artist

Tessa cried through the entire ceremony. She started out small and ended up sobbing out loud, eyes swollen and nose dripping. She'd brought a small package of tissues, but she'd run out by the time the justice of the peace declared Sophie and Rocky legally joined. Rocky's legal name, it turned out, was Richard. And her new sea green silk suit was stained down the front, and it was all Eric's fault.

"Here, honey." Georgia handed over a fistful of tissues, retaining one to wipe her own streaming eyes. On Tessa's other side, Gladys was blowing her nose with a vengeance. She was wearing a startling purple suit and the most incredible hat Tessa had ever seen. It seemed to be made entirely of costume jewelry and it blazed every time a sunbeam from the window touched it. Beside her, Henry wore a perfectly tailored navy pinstriped suit. If he lost seventy pounds or so, he'd be a handsome, heavy man. Tessa was going to introduce him to

Mary Jo Louie. Maybe they'd be a match. Tears welled up again.

From behind her, Simon said in a loud voice, "Is it over now, can we eat, *please*? I'm hungry."

Ian said, "Me too, and then can Rocky marry you too, Mommy?"

Karen shushed them and Georgia nudged Tessa in the ribs and shook her head. "Kids," she said in a fond, soggy voice. "Aren't they something?"

Tessa hadn't expected to like Georgia, but she did. Eric's mother and father seemed to her harmless old hippies, vague and slightly dazed, patently in awe of their grown, competent children. Tessa had caught them in the bathroom, just before the ceremony, furtively sharing a joint.

"Want some?" Georgia had held it out. "It's good stuff; we brought it with us; it'll calm your nerves. Don't tell Eric; he flushed the last one down the toilet."

She badly needed calming, so Tessa took a puff and almost burned her lungs out. She was totally out of practice when it came to smoking anything, which was Eric's fault. If he hadn't taken up temporary residence in her house and her heart and her life, she'd still be sneaking butts once in a while.

And then instead of calming her, the stuff made her even more miserable, which should be illegal. Why did Eric have to be such a jackass? And why had she ever let herself fall for him? He'd come to pick her up today and acted like a polite stranger. So she'd said no to marriage; surely he'd want to go on sleeping with her? Because they really had that going for them.

"Hi, Tessa." No kiss, no nothing. "You look nice." Nice? A three-hundred-dollar suit and a thong and bra underneath that had cost another hundred, and all he could come up with was *nice?*

And he hadn't said a single word about Sheldon, so that hadn't worked the way she thought it might. Something to remember for future reference: If a man didn't want to have babies with you, he didn't get jealous.

"Joy, peace, and love," Anna was saying, hugging the newlyweds. "It's great to have a new brother-in-law. Welcome to the family, Richard." She handed out glasses, and Bruno poured wine, and everyone toasted the bride and groom.

"Long life and happiness," Henry said.

Feeling bereft, Tessa raised her glass. If only Eric didn't look so damned good in a suit. There should be a pill a person could take against his kind of animal magnetism. He wasn't even smiling; he hadn't smiled all day that she'd noticed. And it was like she'd become invisible, because he sure as hell wasn't noticing her.

Now Sonny had a guitar under his arm, and he and Georgia went to stand by the fireplace, which was heaped top and bottom with roses. Sonny said over the voices, "We'd like to do something in your honor, Mr. and Mrs. Hutton," and everyone quieted.

Sonny strummed the guitar, and Georgia sang, "You Are My Sunshine," in a sweet, slightly scratchy soprano. Everyone applauded. They did "Safe in the Arms of Love," and "This Guy's In Love With You" and then "Don't Worry, Be Happy," and every single lousy sentimental lyric reminded Tessa that she was in love with a bozo who didn't do babies.

Everywhere she looked, romance was in full bloom. Georgia and Sonny sang "Have I Told You Lately That I Love You," gazing into each other's

eyes. Fletcher was deep in meaningful conversation
with the justice of the peace, Barbara Thormand.
She was in her mid fifties, with wild white curly
hair halfway down her back, an infectious giggle
and a body that would have looked fine on a
woman half her age. She wore a short red sheath
with a long matching jacket over it, and her legs
were stunning. Tessa had seen all the men checking them out. Except Eric, he just went on scowling into the middle distance. Anna and Bruno
were holding hands and she saw Anna slide her
hand under Bruno's jacket and run a hand over
his buns. And of course Sophie and Rocky were so
much in love and lust, it made Tessa's stomach
ache.

"Let's shake it up a little, babe," Sonny said to
Georgia, and went into "Great Balls of Fire." Rocky
swung his bride into a jive, and then everyone was
dancing.

Tessa looked for Eric, willing him to remember
the afternoon in his office when they'd made love,
and he'd turned the radio on. But he wasn't in the
room any longer.

Karen saw Eric go out to the patio, and she followed him, giving the boys a kiss on the cheek as
she passed them. Anna had set them up at the
kitchen table with a platter of sandwiches and
some bubbly juice.

Eric had a glass of wine balanced on the deck
railing. He was staring out at the pond and the garden, his handsome profile stern, arms crossed on
his chest.

"Hey, big brother, how you doing?" Karen slipped

an arm around his waist and gave him a hug. She noticed he didn't really answer her question.

"Hi, sweet pea. You're looking really pretty. You gain a little weight while you were gone?"

"Five pounds, all any woman will ever admit to gaining."

"It looks good on you. How you feeling? I was hoping you'd stay down south lots longer."

"It was just the right amount of time. I was starting to really miss the boys. I feel strong again, and the desperation's gone. Part of it's the insurance money, knowing I can take my time finding a job, that the kids and I aren't going to be lead weights around your neck."

"I've never once felt that."

"I have. It's past time your sisters grew up and set you free." She reached over and took a sip of his wine. "So what you doing out here all on your lonesome when the party's just getting going?"

"I guess I have a hard time being around Sonny and Georgia."

She needed words here, for him and herself. "This trip was such a gift, Eric. I learned a lot. I'd been holding onto the past, and I found out in Mexico that you've just got to let it go. Otherwise there's no room for the future."

Eric nodded. "I can see that, all that stuff with Nicols, that was tough for you."

Karen shook her head. "Not just Jimmy, although he was a big slice of it. But the biggest thing was Mom and Dad." She struggled for words. "I figured out that all my life, I'd given them way too much power. I wanted things from them they weren't capable of giving, like unconditional love and time and attention and approval." She gave a shaky laugh. "Which is why I got married. I thought having a husband would fill that hole, and then when it didn't, I blamed him. See, it was easier to blame him than to take any responsibility myself."

"Yeah, well, I don't see it like that. I don't know about Jimmy; he was a mixed bag. But Sonny and Georgia chose. They could have done things differently if they'd wanted to."

Karen nodded. "But they didn't. And we can't change that. We can let it stop us from being happy, but it won't alter the past one tiny bit. And the weird thing is, *they're* happy. I think they really believe they did their best for us; they just didn't know how to do things any other way. But we do."

"What do you mean, we do?"

"With our kids. We know exactly how not to raise them, don't we? How many people are that smart about raising kids?"

"You're getting to sound a lot like Anna; it must be a virus or something."

She laughed and took his hand in one of hers. "It's Sophie's wedding day, come and dance."

Sonny was playing the "Tennessee Waltz." Eric walked over to Tessa and took her in his arms. He held her close, and for a moment she resisted him, but then her body relaxed and flowed naturally into his. She belonged in his arms. She belonged in his life.

"Tessa." Her ear was close to his mouth, and under the sound of the music, he said, "Tessa, I can't live without you. You can have the red car if you'll marry me and have my babies."

30.

The most dangerous food is wedding cake

She missed a step and looked up, straight into his eyes, her sexy mouth half open in astonishment.

Elation filled him, because he knew she was going to say yes this time, but at that moment, Simon came running up and grabbed Eric, shaking his pant leg and screaming, "Ian fell in the pond."

Eric didn't remember racing out the door, leaping down the deck stairs, running across the lawn. He saw only the small body floating in the water, eyes closed, arms outstretched, fragile body limp. He plunged in, snatched Ian up, handed him off to Sonny, who somehow had been right behind him, and scrambled out, desperately trying to remember the pattern of mouth-to-mouth resuscitation.

Ian, water trickling from his face and hair, opened his eyes and struggled upright in his grandfather's arms. "We fooled you, Grandpa," he said with a wide grin. "I fell in, but Auntie Sophie taught me how to float."

The entire wedding party was now gathered around the pond.

Ian spotted his brother in the crowd, ran over to him and the two of them threw themselves to the ground, rolling around and giggling at the joke.

Sonny slowly sank to the grass like a deflated balloon.

Eric was shaking, and his knees, too, gave way. He was soaked to the armpits, and he flopped down beside his father, who was almost as wet as he was.

"You okay?" He had no idea how the old man's heart was. His own was pounding its way almost out of his chest.

Sonny looked at him and nodded, blowing out a long breath.

Eric couldn't remember when he'd ever looked fully and at length into his father's eyes. He realized they were the same color as his own, but faded. Sonny smiled at him, and then he shook his head and spread his hands wide. "What can you do?" He started to laugh.

After a moment, Eric laughed, too, and Tessa lowered herself to the ground beside him. He wrapped a dripping arm tight around her.

"About those babies, Tess. How many did you say you wanted?"

"I think we'll start with one," she said. And then she kissed him.

ACKNOWLEDGMENTS

Enormous thanks to:

Eric Chan, for faces and flash cards and
quirky things.
Rob Jackart, for explaining the connection
between cars and personality.
Dan Jackart, for setting me straight on the fine art
of fisticuffs in pubs.
Laine and Ian, for being my grandsons and
reminding me how small boys think.
Trudy Hopman, for sorting out my characters'
legal nightmares.
Lisa Jackart, for her knowledge and use of Newfie
aphorisms.
Vicky Stefopoulou, astrologer extraordinaire.
Tammy Blumhagen, who coined the phrase,
"Catch and Release"—(the brat!).
Peter Pan and the Lost Boys, who gave me insight
into (gasp) the complex minds of men.
And last but not least, the matchmaking service
that provided inspiration and laughter.